Prai

"Susan Coll has written a hilarious, raucous, ride of a novel full of intrigue and insight. *The Literati* is a delightful satire of too many of my favorite things: the literary world, non-profits, fundraising and of course celebrity. But through it all, Coll has infused the book with a warm, earnest pulsing heart that refuses cynicism in our protagonist Clemi: someone no reader whose ever started a new and strange job will not relate to and root for. Smart, funny and deliriously charming!"

—XOCHITL GONZALEZ, AUTHOR OF
OLGA DIES DREAMING AND
ANITA DE MONTE LAUGHS LAST

"This delightful, Dawn-Powell-like screwball comedy was exactly what I needed."

—JOANNA RAKOFF, BESTSELLING AUTHOR
OF *MY SALINGER YEAR* ON *THE LITERATI*

"I have learned to relish every minute I spend in Susan Coll's comic universes, and *The Literati* is no exception. Featuring a glittering array of characters—from cats to clowns, from divas to embezzlers to Malcolm Gladwell lookalikes—this satire of nonprofit dysfunction is up to the minute, intricately plotted and wickedly funny. Above all, it's delicious."

—LOUIS BAYARD, AUTHOR OF
THE WILDES AND JACKIE & ME

"With a poet's flair for language, a comedian's knack for timing, and a satirist's gift for skewering the absurd, Susan Coll sends the reader on a riotous adventure with heroine Clemi, who faces numerous crises over the course of a week—including the sudden disappearance of her boss and the equally sudden appearance of the FBI. *The Literati* is a wickedly smart and funny gem of a novel that I devoured in one sitting. Don't miss it!"

—ABBOTT KAHLER, *NEW YORK TIMES* BESTSELLING AUTHOR OF *EDEN UNDONE*

"Coll's deadpan narrative voice, once it hits you, is like when a stand-up comic finds your funny bone and you just can't stop laughing. And yet the laughter never fails to somehow encompass the obduracy of loss and other woes of this mortal coil. A kooky treasure, rooted in the deeply literary, slightly askew interior world that makes this author's work so fine."

—*KIRKUS* FOR *REAL LIFE AND OTHER FICTIONS*

"Quirky without being saccharine . . . A big blend of genres that is not just effective but delightful."

—*THE WASHINGTON POST* FOR *REAL LIFE AND OTHER FICTIONS*

"If you're fascinated by unexplained phenomena, hop in a beat-up Audi with the kooky and supersmart Cassie Klein and her dog Luna for a voyage of discovery involving a giant moth, a West Virginia bridge collapse, and a hot cryptozoologist. The droll Ms. Coll strikes again!"

—*PEOPLE* FOR *REAL LIFE AND OTHER FICTIONS*

"A heart-forward and perfectly comic starting-over novel, *Real Life and Other Fictions* shows that when you stop searching so hard for certain answers to explain your life, different questions can emerge that reveal the past, present, and future in new and slightly surreal ways. Susan Coll's Cassie is almost every dog-loving woman of a certain age: deeply annoyed, intensely curious, slightly impulsive, and forever hopeful. What an absolute delight."

—LAURA ZIGMAN, AUTHOR OF *SEPARATION ANXIETY* AND *SMALL WORLD*

"Susan Coll is a master of comic fiction, delivering the perfect balance of humor and heart in this deliciously funny book about grief, secrets, and the stories we tell each other and ourselves to survive. *Real Life and Other Fictions* is the charming, warmhearted novel you're looking for!"

—JENNIFER CLOSE, AUTHOR OF *MARRYING THE KETCHUPS* AND *GIRLS IN WHITE DRESSES*

"Don't be fooled by Susan Coll's delightful new novel. You may think you're reading a snappy rom-com with a wacky heroine and an adorable puppy stranded in a town depicted with Nabokovian humor, but *Real Life and Other Fictions* slyly leads us to ponder essential questions: How do we make sense of the inexplicable? What damage is wrought by silence? Can we change our lives?"

—LISA GORNICK, AUTHOR OF *ANA TURNS*

"A crumbling marriage, stalled writing ambitions, and a lifetime of questions suppressed by her family about the tragedy that shaped her childhood lead Cassie on an impromptu journey to solve the mystery that has always plagued her regarding her unusual past. With an unruly puppy as her travel companion, bad weather, broken eyeglasses, and spotty GPS coverage, Cassie has no choice but to let instinct guide her on this chaotic, quirky, and heartwarming quest. *Real Life and Other Fictions* is that rare jewel of a story: one that both entertains and enlightens, one that makes pandemonium profound. Susan Coll is a literary alchemist—a writer who combines comedy and calamity and turns it into storytelling gold."

—LYNDA COHEN LOIGMAN, BESTSELLING AUTHOR OF *THE MATCHMAKER'S GIFT*

"Coll ably juggles chaotic details, turning them into hilarious running gags while making it completely clear why Sophie wants to bury herself in the nook—though she can't, because the power went out. While this is full of nods to the publishing world that those in the know will appreciate, every reader who loves books will relish Coll's comedy of errors."

—*BOOKLIST* FOR *BOOKISH PEOPLE*

"As much fun as Coll has with vacuum cleaners—a truly surprising amount—it's literary humor where she slays."

—*KIRKUS* FOR *BOOKISH PEOPLE*

"Susan Coll's *Bookish People* is a delightful, hilarious, and utterly charming novel about a quirky bookstore and its motley crew—ridiculously lovable people who think way too much about words, writing, dead authors, customers' dogs, cats who torment birds, canceled author events, British ovens, readers, vacuum cleaners, and Russian tortoises. The perfect read for bookish people everywhere!"

—ANGIE KIM, INTERNATIONALLY BESTSELLING AUTHOR OF *MIRACLE CREEK*

"Queen of literary comedy."

—*NEWSDAY* FOR *BOOKISH PEOPLE*

"A smart, original, laugh-out-loud novel that fans of Tom Perrotta will adore. If you sell, buy, or simply love books, *Bookish People* is for you. I wholeheartedly recommend this quirky gem."

—SARAH PEKKANEN, *NEW YORK TIMES* BESTSELLING COAUTHOR OF *THE GOLDEN COUPLE*

"There's not a wittier, zanier, smarter book about books and the people who love them than *Bookish People*. After reading about this single screwball week in the book biz, you'll want to hug your closest bookseller (and maybe apply for a job)."

—LESLIE PIETRZYK, AUTHOR OF *ADMIT THIS TO NO ONE*

"An insightful and entertaining look behind the shelves and into the lives of the people who stock them . . . Coll's novel captures the fragmented overload of modern life so successfully . . . it's satisfying as a trip to your local indie bookstore."

—*THE WASHINGTON POST* FOR *BOOKISH PEOPLE*

"Take a bookstore owner who is sick of books, a pompous poet who has managed to get himself canceled, and a crew of overqualified millennial employees, then add a week of political upheaval and a rare celestial event. The result is *Bookish People*, a sharp yet tender comedy of bookstore manners. Susan Coll has written a love letter to bibliophiles everywhere with too many hilarious parts to list—though the tortoise named Kurt Vonnegut Jr. may be my all-time favorite literary pet."

—LISA ZEIDNER, AUTHOR OF *LOVE BOMB*

The Literati

Also by Susan Coll

Real Life and Other Fictions

Bookish People

The Stager

Beach Week

Acceptance

Rockville Pike

Karlmarx.com

THE Literati

A Novel

SUSAN COLL

The Literati

Copyright © 2025 Susan Keselenko Coll

All rights reserved. No portion of this book may be reproduced, stored in a retrieval system, or transmitted in any form or by any means—electronic, mechanical, photocopy, recording, scanning, or other—except for brief quotations in critical reviews or articles, without the prior written permission of the publisher.

Published by Harper Muse, an imprint of HarperCollins Focus LLC.

Published in association with the literary agency of HG Literary.

This book is a work of fiction. The characters, incidents, and dialogue are drawn from the author's imagination and are not to be construed as real. Any resemblance to actual events or persons, living or dead, is entirely coincidental.

Any internet addresses (websites, blogs, etc.) in this book are offered as a resource. They are not intended in any way to be or imply an endorsement by HarperCollins Focus LLC, nor does HarperCollins Focus LLC vouch for the content of these sites for the life of this book.

Library of Congress Cataloging-in-Publication Data

Names: Coll, Susan author
Title: The literati : a novel / Susan Coll.
Description: Nashville : Harper Muse, 2025. | Summary: "An unexpected catastrophe of
 literary proportions . . ."—Provided by publisher.
Identifiers: LCCN 2025007882 (print) | LCCN 2025007883 (ebook) |
 ISBN 9781400346653 trade paperback | ISBN 9781400346677 | ISBN 9781400346660 epub
Subjects: LCGFT: Humorous fiction | Novels
Classification: LCC PS3553.O474622 L58 2025 (print) | LCC PS3553.O474622 (ebook) |
 DDC 813/.54—dc23/eng/20250505
LC record available at https://lccn.loc.gov/2025007882
LC ebook record available at https://lccn.loc.gov/2025007883

Printed in the United States of America

25 26 27 28 29 LBC 5 4 3 2 1

Give them bread and circuses, and they will never revolt.
—Juvenal

For Charlie, who tells the best stories

Tuesday

Chapter 1

PROUDLY, FIERCELY PUNCTUAL, Clemi arrives at 10:00 a.m. and finds a very large cat sitting on Howard's desk. It is greyish and brownish, this cat, with a long tail and piercing green eyes. Clemi does not know cat varieties especially well and has never thought much about them, but this seems like your basic cat, a run-of-the-mill *Felis catus*, albeit one that has been overfed. It looks to her like a cat's cat. A Volkswagen of cats, more bus than bug, which is not meant as disparaging since at this point in her life Clemi cannot imagine having the funds to care for either a cat or a vehicle, whether run-of-the-mill or extremely posh.

The only especially notable thing about this cat, apart from its size, is that it happens to be here, planted atop the papers strewn across the executive director's massive banker's desk.

The cat stares at Clemi. Clemi stares back at the cat, holding its gaze. If she looks at it long enough, perhaps the creature will explain itself.

Something is off, clearly. Or maybe not. This is the beginning of what will be Clemi's second week on this job, so she doesn't have enough history at WLNP to say what is normal and what is abnormal. Perhaps an occasional cat visitation is a regular thing, like Bring Your Kid to Work Day, except with cats. Or maybe the cat has been here all along, curled up discreetly in a corner, although that seems less likely, given that this is a one-room office and Clemi is allergic to cats.

It is the Tuesday after a three-day weekend, so perhaps she is just bleary-eyed, hungover, hallucinating this cat. She is not much of a drinker, but she did meet River—her sort-of-ex-boyfriend turned sort-of-friend—at a taquería last night, where she downed a margarita and chased it with a bean burrito, several fistfuls of tortilla chips, and a spicy shroom taco. The regrettable smorgasbord has left her simultaneously bloated and dehydrated. On top of which, the fire alarm had gone off in her apartment building at 3:14 a.m., and she was forced to evacuate, descend six flights of stairs in flip-flops and her unflattering nightshirt, too groggy to think to grab a robe, and then stand on the sidewalk for some forty minutes while the fire department conducted a thorough inspection and then declared a false alarm.

Perhaps Clemi's sleep deprivation is causing everything to look askew.

Yet everything *is* askew—and it's not just the anomalous presence of this cat or the mess of paperwork on this desk. As she looks around the office, Clemi sees that the drawers of the three filing cabinets that line the wall to the left of Howard's desk are open, and the contents have been disgorged onto the floor. Stepping closer to inspect, she finds empty folders, papers and more papers, expired wall calendars, a decapitated bobblehead of Washington Capitals captain Alex Ovechkin, and several boxes of obsolete business cards imprinted with the former, now-verboten name of this organization, which presently goes by WLNP:

Washington Literary Nonprofit. Some of the business cards bear names of employees whom Clemi presumes to be long gone.

She wonders whether she ought to be on guard, or whether she should flee the premises. Clearly something strange has happened here, but the cat looks calm, utterly unperturbed. She doesn't know all that much about feline behavior, but she imagines that if she were in imminent danger—if a heavily armed perpetrator were hiding under the desk, for example—the cat would give her some sort of clue.

That said, this desk, which is either an antique or a thrift store special, is large enough to be housing an entire gang of modest-size perps. She pauses a moment to imagine, irrelevantly, how they even got this ancient, bulky thing up the stairs and through the doorway of this small room. Perhaps the answer is simple: Maybe the legs come off, ditto for the slab of wood on top. Or maybe the desk was native to this spot, and the rest of this Georgetown brownstone was built around it to accommodate its splendor and girth, like a heritage tree of the sort one is not allowed to chop down.

Yet for all she knows of cats, this creature might be staring at her peaceably even as Howard is being held at gunpoint or chained to the radiator with duct tape across his mouth in the bathroom, a thought that propels her to boldly turn the corner to inspect. Maybe she ought to be more cautious, to perhaps call the police, but then that seems an overreaction; she can't help but wonder how deranged a hypothetical brigand or band of brigands must be to hold up the offices of a not particularly well-endowed literary nonprofit.

Nudging the door open with her hip, Clemi peeks inside and looks around. The bathroom—with its original, now-crumbling basket weave floor tile and slim, rectangular pedestal sink—is empty. The trash can is overflowing. Someone has left the toilet seat up. In the corner is a bowl full of fishy-smelling cat food that appears to be untouched.

Her contemplation of the bathroom is interrupted by the trill of a phone. She returns to the office and looks around for the source of this overly loud, theatrical—make that *vaudevillian*—noise. The sound is emanating from an old fashioned black landline phone sitting on the credenza behind Howard's desk. Like much else in this office, the phone is of another era, complete with a rotary dial and one of those long stretchy rubbery cords that knot up and tangle. Clemi stares at it for a moment, not entirely sure of the appropriate etiquette, then picks up the receiver and presses it to her ear.

"Hello?" she says into the strange gizmo. It is so heavy that it momentarily disorients her, as does the rush of loud static. "Washington Literary Nonprofit," she announces. "This is Clementine speaking."

More static. She wonders whether this crackling electric noise is part of a thing that occurs with these old-fashioned phones—a prelude to the conversation, perhaps, like an orchestra warming up. She waits a beat, then repeats her greeting, again to no avail.

She is about to replace the speaking device when she hears what might be the sound of a person coughing, then a possible crashing noise, and then, an unmistakable human wail. Might this phone call be related to the disarray in the office? Maybe Howard *has* been kidnapped. Maybe someone is calling to demand a ransom. Or maybe someone is calling looking for the cat.

At last, a melodic, female voice breaks through the cacophony.

The Literati

"Clementine, my darling! Oh, my darling Clementine," the woman sings. Although Clemi is used to this joke, any reference to an old folk song circa the late nineteenth century and a black-and-white shoot-'em-up Western that features her name, Clemi could do without. She once looked up the origin of the song and learned that the titular Clementine is either presumed dead or has been reimagined as a 299-pound woman who is mistaken for a whale, depending on the version invoked.

"This is Zveta," she says. "Zveta Attais."

Sveta Attais!

Clemi tries to remain calm. To be professional. To not act like a fangirl, to not scream out Sveta's name. (It's spelled with an *S*, yes, but pronounced with a *Z*—Zveta. Clemi knows that.) To not let on that Clemi mainly took this job because Sveta Attais has won this year's WLNP Chestnut Prize for Prescient Fiction (an honor that has been discussed internally at WLNP, but has not yet been publicly announced) and will be coming to the ceremony on Friday, where Clemi will get to meet her literary hero in real life.

Clemi is not unfamiliar with famous writers, and she is not easily impressed. Famous writers are, to her, a dime a dozen. She means no disrespect in saying she could go the rest of her life without encountering another famous writer, or in thinking they are—with exceptions, of course—generally a bunch of narcissistic head cases.

She is not without the standing to say this. Clemi's mother is a big-deal literary agent, and her semi-estranged father is, himself, a famous poet. She grew up in a household with famous writers coming and going, sometimes spending the night in the attic guest room when they were in from out of town or if they'd had too much to drink, or in more than one instance, crashing upstairs for months at a time while waiting for book advances or grant money or royalty checks to come through so they could afford to sign a lease on an apartment and pay rent once again. For two years, one acclaimed narrative journalist, who had been living rough as part of his immersion reporting for his book on the unhoused population of the Pacific Northwest, lived with them after his wife kicked him out and he became unhoused himself. Another prize-winning memoirist lived with them for months while detoxing from a double addiction—pills and liquor. Sometimes Clemi would wake to find famous authors sitting at her kitchen table in their pajamas, emptying into their bowls the dregs of her favorite breakfast cereals. Another author of note, a Booker Prize winner, once borrowed—and totaled—her mother's car.

Then, in a career move an uninitiated observer might deem masochistic, Clemi went on to work at a bookstore. In reality, alas, this was one of the few jobs for which she was innately qualified. Her knowledge was practically encyclopedic; she knew books the way some people knew baseball stats. Like some savant of publishing, she could recite the backlist of most well-known (and even little-known) authors, including the publisher and pub date, and she was one of few people at the store who arrived with an understanding of how book distribution works and which imprint belongs to which monopolistic house.

On the one hand, this knowledge significantly lowered the learning curve at work. On the other hand, her job put her in daily contact with an endless stream of authors wishing to speak at the store, where she was then asked to cater to their fussy greenroom needs, order their obscure backlist titles, and procure their specified-to-the-precise-millimeter Sharpie pens. She has unambiguously had enough of authors, yet here she is, repeating history by accepting the position as the programs director for WLNP because—Sveta Attais!

She is as giddy as a Taylor Swift fan who has just scored front row tickets for a concert or, better yet, backstage passes.

Sveta's new novel, *The Marrakesh Social Club*, received glowing reviews from all the major media outlets, is both an Oprah and a Jenna pick, and was optioned by the Obamas' production company before she even finished writing the thing. Although Clemi usually bristles at such hype, she was deeply affected by the book about an introverted Bulgarian-born, Moroccan-raised, biracial college student transplanted to 1990s Los Angeles. Clemi found herself highlighting sentences to do with teenage alienation, difficult mothers, and having a foot in two different cultures. (Okay, maybe London, where Clemi relocated with her mother for a few years, is not as exotic as Sofia or Marrakesh. Nonetheless, she found it surprisingly different from the East Coast of the US, so she could completely relate to Sveta's descriptions of feeling displaced.) She dog-eared pages and stuck Post-it Notes on passages that spoke to her or made her cry. The novel so moved and inspired her that it reignited her desire to write, so she'd pulled her mess of a work-in-progress out of the drawer and signed up for a writing workshop last winter.

And now, Sveta Attais is on the other end of the line!

"Clementine," the intoxicating voice repeats, "I wonder if you can help me. I have a bit of a problem. I cannot seem to reach Howard. We had been texting about my travel arrangements, but suddenly the messages stopped going through. And when I tried to call him, I was told the number has been disconnected."

"That's odd," Clemi says. Although maybe not so odd, given the chaotic condition of the office.

"At any rate, darling, I noticed this phone number in the signature line of one of his emails, so I figured it was worth a try."

"Yes, good thinking," Clemi says. "Howard is just running late." She is not entirely sure why she is being protective of a man she has known for all of one week. Why not tell Sveta that she, too, has no idea where Howard is? That she is new to the job and doesn't know what she is meant to do without his guidance, that it looks like the office has been ransacked? Also, there is this cat.

Because, she supposes, she is inclined to give everyone the benefit of the doubt. Because she is an instinctively loyal employee to a fault. Because, as her mother would be quick to add, she is naïve.

"Well, at least I have you now," Sveta continues. "My travel arrangements are not yet complete, you see."

"Ah, I can help you with that," Clemi says enthusiastically. She has not yet helped anyone with travel arrangements, but this was described to her as part of her job. She'd presumed Sveta's travel had already been organized by Clemi's predecessor, someone named Didi Feldman. Who this Didi is, or was, or where she went, Clemi has no idea, but it doesn't particularly matter. Clemi was told that in the short term, all she needs to do is show up at the awards gala on Friday to help Howard execute what has already been set in motion.

"Fantastic," Sveta says. "I need to upgrade my ticket, if you wouldn't mind taking care of that. And of course, I'll need to upgrade Vlad's ticket too. Well, I misspoke really. Vlad didn't have a ticket before, but he needs one now, and it will need the upgrade."

The cat yawns, then rolls or, really, collapses onto its side and stretches out its big paws, sending a thick wad of paper and Howard's jar of pens onto the floor.

"Vlad?"

"My son."

"Oh, yes, of course." Clemi now remembers the effusive dedication of her book:

To Vladislav, my moon and my sun.

Clemi had assumed this Vladislav person was her husband. Or lover. Or maybe her dog. Sveta is a famously private woman who discloses little of her personal life, so understandably, Clemi was not aware she had a child.

"If you don't mind saying, upgrade to . . . what?" Clemi asks. "I'm new here, and as you know, Howard isn't in yet today. I'm sure he'll be here any minute, but just in case, can you give me the details?"

"I need to upgrade to first class. I have a note from my doctor, if that's helpful for whatever. I did something to my back. I foolishly tried to pick Vlad up. He's really too big for that now, I can barely lift him, but you know how that is, he wanted to cuddle. I must have pinched a nerve. The pain is indescribable. The only way I can make that long flight is if I'm able to fully recline."

"Oh, how awful! I'm so sorry! It's good of you to come all this way, given the situation. If you can give me the details, I'll call the airline right away."

"Dodi has all of that information."

"Didi no longer works here. But I'm here now and happy to help."

"Thank you, love. So I think you might have to cancel my original ticket from Los Angeles to DC. What happened was that I came here to my cousin's wedding last weekend, and then this thing happened with my back, so I'm sort of stranded. I was hoping it would have resolved by now, but I'm still in tremendous pain."

"Oof. Okay. So we are not upgrading—well, we *are* upgrading—but more accurately, we are changing the ticket entirely?" She hopes this doesn't sound hostile; she is just trying to get it right. "I'm really sorry to hear this, that you are in pain," she says. "It's good of you to come," she repeats, "and I'm happy to take care of all of this. So, you are where?"

"Casablanca."

"Oh. Wow. Like *the* Casablanca, in Morocco?"

"Yes, that's the one. And originally, I was flying out of LAX," she repeats.

"Got it."

Clemi has no idea what two last-minute, first-class tickets from Morocco to DC might cost, but this can't be good.

"If you wouldn't mind," Clemi asks, "can you email me your current ticket information, so I can have something to work with? I'll probably need other info, too, like your birthday, passport number, plus Vlad's info, of course."

"Your Dodi has all of that, darling. Listen, I have to run."

"Okay, but—"

The line is cut before Clemi can finish the sentence. Even the static has ceased. There is nothing but silence. No information to work with. This old-fashioned phone line is now as useless as it looks.

Clemi sneezes.

The cat begins to snore.

Chapter 2

AS CLEMI SETS the receiver back onto the strange rotary dial–equipped contraption, pressing it neatly atop the two white knobs that retract, she feels a sudden spasm in her back. Granted, she is a cerebral, bookish sort who could benefit from a healthier diet and a more active lifestyle, but even in her current groggy, hungover, bloated state, she is surely not so unfit as to have pinched a nerve simply by lifting a telephone receiver. Probably this twinge is psychosomatic, the power of suggestion, or even some subliminal attempt to be one with Sveta Attais—a sister in back pain. Or more likely, it might be the effect of her first-ever yoga class over the weekend.

Her current apartment-sitting gig has landed her in a brand-new complex that compensates bougie amenities for what it lacks in soul. Situated just two blocks from the Metro, it features a lovely if overpriced café that sells $12.50 bags of addictive granola and a taquería with a menu full of entrées with amusing names like El Gringo and Chicken Cesar Chavez. Clemi wants to eat them all, and sometimes nearly does. There is also a gleaming, overly air-conditioned grocery store with wide aisles full of prepared gourmet food and a boutique gym, which smells like eucalyptus and is stocked with fancy shampoo.

One of the perks of apartment-sitting is that she has been gifted a six-month membership to the gym, which she is determined to use.

The apartment belongs to the writer Fiona Ceras, one of her mother's clients. Fiona needs someone to take care of her plants while she is at a long-term writing residency in Upstate New York. In addition to the gym and the grocery store and the eating establishments she can barely afford, there is also free parking for the car Clemi does not own, as well as dozens of EV charging stations that apparently mostly do not work and are a frequent cause for griping overheard in the elevators. She has also been told to make use of Fiona's fancy coffee machine and the automatically replenishing special brew pods—the ristrettos and gran lungos and espressos—some of them, according to the labels, crafted from exquisite beans not found anywhere else in the world. As amazing as these perks are, Clemi didn't need any additional enticements. Fiona had secured Clemi's apartment-sitting services with the words *free rent*.

This is the most beautiful apartment she has ever lived in, and the most beautiful gym she has ever awkwardly performed yoga in. The entire apartment/gym/restaurant/grocery complex has been open for only a year, erected on the grounds of what had once been a sprawling senior living facility run by the Methodist Church. Setting aside the matter of the displaced seniors, several of whom were depicted on the front page of *The Washington Post* sitting in wheelchairs with their possessions piled high beside them, this new development encapsulates the things urban planners talk about when they trumpet smart growth, which Clemi knows a little bit about, having listened to an author, Helmut Erickson, opine on this subject at the bookstore. She remembers his book, *Perfect Cities*, and the discussion of compact design, walkable urban centers, and outdoor community spaces. She seems to recall that part of the smart-growth plan is meant to include affordable housing. The rents here are anything but affordable, but at least, for six free months, it is affordable to her.

Sometimes Clemi thinks that most of what she knows in this world can be traced to her time spent absorbing author talks at the bookstore. Her favorite English professor, the one who instilled in her a love of Iris Murdoch, once quipped that the purpose of a liberal arts education was to enable one to engage in cocktail party banter, and Clemi cannot deny this is somewhat true. Between her English degree and her bookstore job, she knows a little about a lot, but not much about anything except, perhaps, the business of books, and while this may not be much, it is at least more than River, her ex-whatever, knows from his consumption of TikTok, which does not prevent him from opining confidently on subjects he has learned about in thirty-second video clips.

At the yoga class on Saturday, she had situated herself on the only available mat, which was very unfortunately in the front row of the studio. Not only was she in the front, but she was directly across from the instructor, who practically radiated well-being with her lithe, elastic limbs and charismatic smile.

Clemi knew that the woman, who introduced herself as Nisha, had nothing but good intentions, but she wished Nisha might have left Clemi in peace to perform her postures imperfectly—falling out of tree pose or doing sun salutations with all the grace of a lumberjack—rather than constantly using Clemi as an example of what not to do.

Worse, on the mat next to her had been a man who looked familiar. She knew him from somewhere; she just couldn't say where. Was he a friend of her mother's? She is lousy at guessing ages but estimated that he is in his forties. Maybe a little younger. Possibly a little older. Everyone in that general age range looks more or less the same to her eye. Perhaps he was one of the customers at the bookstore where she had worked until two weeks ago.

She wished there was an app for this—a sort of Shazam, where instead of uploading a snippet of a song you want to identify, you snap a photo. Probably such a thing exists, but even as a twenty-six-year-old passably tech-savvy person, she sometimes finds it difficult to keep up. She had looked again—thick bushy hair, delicate features, serious gaze, wire-rimmed glasses placed neatly on a towel at the foot of the mat. Definitely familiar, but why, how?

Whoever he was, and whatever his age, he had no trouble keeping up with the instructor's punishing, endless demands, flipping his dog, standing on his head, going into crow pose without breaking an elbow or even a sweat. He was in much better shape than Clemi was, even if she was younger by ten, or twenty, or even thirty years.

As if this foray into yoga had not been humiliating enough, she bumped into him while exiting the class, literally knocking into him and causing him to drop his water bottle, which clanged loudly on the floor. She mumbled an apology and had been tempted to say something more but did not. She didn't want to give the wrong impression, to have him think she was flirting. And she was definitely not flirting. In the wake of the River breakup, she is on hiatus from dating, taking a sort of boyfriend cleanse. Plus, for all she knows, this man is old enough to be too old.

She needn't have worried; he picked up his water bottle and reached into the cubby to retrieve his shoes, giving no indication that he had even noticed her.

Now, as Clemi stands inert, massaging the back of her neck and contemplating the problem of Sveta's air travel, she sees that the cat, after its micronap, is again upright and staring at her with a bemused expression that seems to say, *Congratulations on your new position here at WLNP . . . and lots of luck!*

No big deal, cat! Clemi's a team player; no job is beneath her. She's happy to rebook travel, anything for Sveta Attais.

Clemi pulls out her cell phone and tries to reach Howard. Again, she wonders what might explain the chaotic state of the office. In addition to telling Clemi she is naïve, her mother has also accused her of having an overactive imagination, which she knows is not wholly untrue. Surely there is some rational explanation for the mess—maybe Howard dropped by over the weekend and was in a rush as he riffled through his desk drawers and filing cabinet looking for some very important document. After which, he accidently forgot to retrieve his cat.

And this morning he is simply late to work, probably. She now remembers that he's been complaining of a toothache, so perhaps he was able to schedule a morning dental appointment and forgot to let her know.

His number rings and rings and then goes to voicemail. She sends a text but receives no reply.

She logs onto her computer, pulls up Orbitz, and inputs what little bit of data she currently has available. Eventually she will need the details of the original flight, but for now she can at least get a sense of the options. Casablanca to Washington, DC on Thursday, arriving no later than Friday morning. Nonstop. First class. Done. Easy as pie.

She waits a moment for the options to load. When they do at last, only one flight listed still has availability in first class. Air France. La Première. This could not possibly be correct. The website must be broken. Surely there are more flights than this. Further, no airplane ticket could possibly cost $14,098.78.

She then considers that they are likely on the hook to ferry her home to Los Angeles. She does a little more research, and the number inflates to $15,754.93.

At this juncture, Clemi remembers that she needs not one ticket but two. How old is this Vlad child? Large enough for Sveta to throw her back out lifting him, so presumably he is not an infant, which is too bad, because if he were, he would not need an outrageously expensive seat. Might she be able to send Sveta first-class, and Vlad coach? He could wear one of those signs identifying him as an unaccompanied minor, so he would be taken care of by the crew. That's probably not cool under any circumstances, but especially not cool given that Sveta is a literary rock star whose child, too, deserves the very best—not to mention that Sveta is this year's winner of the WLNP Chestnut Prize for Prescient Fiction.

And who knows? Perhaps this is not even the problem Clemi thinks it is. It's not her money, after all. Perhaps first-class tickets are routine for the winners of this prize, and Didi Feldman erred in booking her coach.

As Clemi contemplates the matter, plotting the path forward, her phone dings with a text. It is Howard, thank goodness. She takes a deep breath. More accurately, she *intends* to take a deep breath and even attempts to take one, but her clogged sinuses make a mockery of this effort.

EmeRgency. Soiree. PLS take care of Immanuel.

*Sorry not soiree.

Thank God he is okay, is her first thought. Although maybe he is not okay given his EmeRgency and his screwy typing. Again she remembers his toothache. He had suspected he might need a root canal or even an extraction. Perhaps he is about to be anesthetized. Before she can reply, another text arrives.

BLUE BUFfalo Adult Flaked Salmon & Adult Flaked Fish & Shrimp. Two cans x xx day.

Presumably this is for the cat. Whose name is presumably Immanuel. Who names a cat Immanuel?

Two cans once, twice, or three times a day? Also, adult flaked salmon *and* adult flaked fish *and* shrimp? Or either, or, or?

Where are you? she types.

Three dots appear, but she waits a full minute and receives no reply.

We need to rebook Sveta's flight.

More dots.

Howard? R U okay?

Howard's reply-in-progress dots go cold. Then, all four of her texts are marked undeliverable. She hits resend to no avail.

This is very weird. Perhaps logging into her email will be somehow illuminating. At the top of her inbox is a message from the board president that appears to have been sent just moments ago. It is addressed to Howard, with Clemi cc'd.

The subject reads: URGENT MAJOR PI PROBLEM.

Clemi is momentarily confused. At first she assumes "PI" has to do with the dreaded mathematical constant that is the ratio of a circle's circumference or relationship to diameter or something she once understood, sort of, but can't possibly begin to remember now. If she is being asked to do anything with math, this is indeed an URGENT MAJOR PROBLEM. But then, it's much more likely that "PI" refers to a private investigator, which would make sense given the state of the office, Howard's possible disappearance, and the mysterious presence of this cat. Now she feels a tremor of excitement. This is all very Raymond Chandleresque! Or at least, very Nancy Drew. Perhaps it will give her fodder for her novel. She begins to read the email:

As you know, per the advice of our crisis consultant, we invited our pal Javier Jiménez-Jiménez to be the public intellectual this year. Although he graciously accepted, sadly he passed away following a choking incident at Sfoglina last night. (I've also heard it was a heart attack, so not sure which is true, although possibly both, as in theory, nothing prevents one from choking while in the process of having a heart attack, nor should it matter.) This means we need a new public intellectual ASAP.

This is an unspeakable tragedy—this goes without saying!!!—but let's try to look at this as an opportunity to score someone even better known. I was thinking someone like Orhan Pamuk or Umberto Eco, but I know neither is local. Perhaps we could go in another direction entirely, maybe someone along the lines of Barack Obama. Any of these will be fine, but it's short notice, I know, so do your best.

BTW I'm about to head into a conference in Nairobi where I'll be offline most of the day. I'll try to make it on Friday but I have a close connection in Frankfurt, and even if that works, I don't get into Dulles until six and you know luggage and customs... plus traffic. I'll do my best but I can't promise, so if someone could be prepared to make the opening remarks just in case, that would be much appreciated.

Cheers,
Eric Jolly, MD

Crisis consultant?
And *Dr. Jolly*! She has heard about this Eric Jolly, MD. Howard said something indiscreet about the board president

not being particularly helpful and had even worse things to say about his book.

"*A lightweight*," he had said, or rather whispered. This had been on Clemi's first day at the job, as he was giving her an orientation that included walking her through a who's who on the board. The comment had made Clemi wince on poor Dr. Jolly's behalf. Sure, she has her own complicated—and not always generous—feelings about writers sui generis, but on an individual level, she tries to be supportive of every person's work.

At the time Clemi had wondered whether Howard was whispering because the office was bugged—which, who knows? In light of today's events, perhaps something odd really is going on here. Maybe the nonprofit is a cover for a spy ring! Howard had, after all, made a point of letting her know that the office is less than a mile from the Russian embassy. Had he been trying to tell her something? But even Clemi, with her overactive imagination, cannot convert that into a viable narrative.

Later on her first day, when they were sitting at an outside table at a nearby deli, Howard had elaborated on the Dr. Jolly situation. He'd said he was basically checked out, busy promoting his book, *Liquid Beauty*, which has occupied the hardcover bestseller list for more than five years.

This level of success for the board president would generally be a good thing for the foundation, he'd said. Under normal circumstances, it would lend some increased visibility and prestige to WLNP, except in this case the attention has arguably had the opposite effect given the "crass commercialism" and "overall ickiness" of the book (his words, not Clemi's).

He had continued trash-talking poor Dr. Jolly as they walked back to the office. He was so worked up that he wasn't watching his steps, then had tripped over the root of a tree and fallen face-first onto the sidewalk.

The subject of Dr. Jolly's book is something called Syntax™, which is an injectable filler. A synthesized version of Botox, he'd explained. The book is not an investigation into the business of Syntax™, or a cultural analysis of the meaning of Syntax™ and beauty culture in general. Rather, it is a love letter to Syntax™, a synthetic version of the botulinum neurotoxin. The book is filled with glossy photographs of Syntax™ successes. Women of a certain age, looking as if they are women of a certain other age, albeit with expressions frozen into place.

Lunch had turned into a very long gossip session, one of what turned out to be many such conversations over the four days they'd had together. Howard had referred to one board member as a tired hack who had only managed to get published because her girlfriend (now wife) was an editor at Scribner. Another board member, he confided, had only been invited to join the board because she was the second cousin of someone who was friends with Mark Zuckerberg at Harvard, which, again, Clemi found puzzling given that the individual in question had written four highly acclaimed novels.

He had also warned Clemi to be wary of one Percy Garfinkle, a board member whose name-dropping was so extreme that he would almost certainly volunteer to connect her, unsolicited, with sundry business tycoons, world leaders, and stars of stage and the silver screen.

The Literati

Clemi is confused by Dr. Jolly's email, but after rereading it, she realizes that the public intellectual must be a reference to the silent auction that will take place during the gala on Friday. The auction is a relatively new fundraising effort, Howard had told her. It had been his brainchild, and last year—the first year of the effort—they had raised an additional $30,000. Howard was proud of the literary luminaries he had wrangled to participate this year, Javier Jiménez-Jiménez in particular. A thick stack of cards advertising the silent auction sits on the far corner of Howard's desk, undisturbed by the cat.

Immanuel stares at Clemi as she scoops up the pile of glossy eight-by-tens. She blows some cat hair off the top of the stack and sneezes, then sneezes again.

WLPN SILENT AUCTION
Promoting Literature That Is Prophetic in Vision

- Private lunch at the Tabard Inn with Ellie Grossman, author of *The Snowbirds*

    STARTING BID: $800

- Dinner for four at Masseria with *The New York Review of Books* editor Renata Chakrabarti

    STARTING BID: $2,000

- Weekend in Vail condo, sleeps five, use of snowshoes included

    STARTING BID: $10,000

- Catered dinner party for ten with Booker Prize–winning author Francis Ruben

    STARTING BID: $10,000

- Private lunch with superagent Lilian Getter; pitch her your ideas for a book

    STARTING BID: $5,000

- Bring five friends to lunch with public intellectual Javier Jiménez-Jiménez, philosopher, historian, and staff writer at *The New Yorker*

    STARTING BID: $12,000

A disclaimer, set in a wispy italic font and tucked discreetly at the bottom of the card, clarifies:

*Auction prices specifically exclude any and all expenses associated with but not limited to food, beverages, accommodations, and travel.

Clemi has a few thoughts about this situation. The first one is especially practical: Thank goodness Javier's name is listed last, because she could take a pair of scissors and remove his name, then salvage each card with a strong transparent adhesive. (Packing-grade Scotch tape might work.)

She flips the card over and realizes there is language on the back, but it is mostly boilerplate about WLNP, including a list of board members, both current and emeritus. Clemi stares at this, considering alternative options. She could take a Sharpie and score through Javier's name. This would be easier, but considerably less sensitive—indeed downright grim—given that the gentleman has, so to speak, departed.

———

Clemi begins to compose a response to Dr. Jolly, explaining that Howard is not in the office today. She considers elaborating, but on the off chance that Howard is having a true emergency and needs the day off, she does not want to get him in trouble.

Still, the problems at hand seem urgent, and she needs guidance. Clemi explains the situation with Sveta Attais's bad back and the need for new travel arrangements that include her child. And she asks for assistance finding a living public intellectual now that JJJ has been relegated to eternal horizontality.

She hits send, then seconds later her email dings. She gets a curt response: Eric Jolly, MD, is OOO.

It is 10:15 a.m. Clemi has been at work all of fifteen minutes, and already she is having a bad day.

Chapter 3

UNDER NORMAL CIRCUMSTANCES, Clemi would not arrive at work at ten and take a break at ten thirty. She is a conscientious employee. A rule follower. Not someone who tacks a few minutes onto the end of her lunch hour or spends time at work attending to personal matters. But already these do not feel like normal circumstances, so when a text arrives from River, saying: Amazing news, you will be super jazzed!
 and when she says: What?!
 and when he says: I'll tell you in person
 she finds herself saying: Right now pls!
 Why does she say this? She doesn't know the answer. She is done with River, or at least trying her best to be. She just saw him last night, and yet here he is again. What news could he possibly have that would make her super jazzed? He has been messing with her mind. Ending whatever it was they had while suggesting he doesn't really want it to end. Nothing short of a personality transplant would convince her to give him another chance, even if at some primal level, she remains more besotted than she should.
 But she agrees to meet him because this day is off to an

inauspicious start, on top of which there is a cat in the office making her sneeze. Perhaps if she leaves and gets some fresh air, then hits the reset button on Tuesday, everything will be okay when she returns. Howard will be at his desk, able to provide leadership, assisting in the reticketing of Sveta Attais, adding Vlad to the itinerary, and procuring the services of a respiring public intellectual. Immanuel, the big fat cat with his imperious stare, will be gone perhaps. Not that Clemi has ill will toward Immanuel; she wishes Immanuel a long happy life full of as much BLUE BUFfalo whatever as he'd like. She would just prefer he not continue his long happy life *here*.

Besides, she is a believer in not overreacting, in remaining calm until such a time when maintaining a calm demeanor ceases to be an option. She finds that half the time, when the computer doesn't start, or the dishwasher breaks, or the car—back when she briefly had a car—starts to make a funny noise, just turning it off or unplugging it or whatever one must do to get a fresh start often solves the problem. At least for a little while. Another word for managing problems this way might be *denial*. Such was the case when she briefly owned a used 2011 Honda Civic, which had more than 150,000 miles and was called to eternal rest while under Clemi's proprietorship—barricading Connecticut Avenue during rush hour, causing glares of condemnation and a symphony of horns and cries from appalled motorists.

River suggests they meet at a coffee shop halfway between the WLNP office in Georgetown and the ten-thousand-square-foot imitation Italianate villa in Bethesda in which he currently resides. She does not point out that the coffee shop is not technically halfway between them. It is in Chevy Chase, a couple of miles from where River lives, and more like four miles from where Clemi works. But in addition to being generally conscientious and—at least per her mother—a naïve person with an overactive imagination, she does not want to be difficult. She dislikes making a fuss.

One of the first assignments in the creative writing workshop she took last winter was to identify characters' telling details. "Melvin puts catsup on his eggs" was one example the instructor gave them. "Melvin stops to talk with everyone who has a dog" was another.

She had enrolled as part of her New Year's resolution, right after reading *The Marrakesh Social Club*. That is where she met River.

"Clemi tends to fall in love with the same boy over and over," she might have written. "Clemi falls in love with cute, bookish boy-men who talk a good game but are ultimately nonstarters."

―――――

She waits for the bus for ten minutes. When it does not arrive, worried she'll be late, she calls an Uber, already throwing off her weekly budget. When she gets to the café, there is no sign of River, so she gets a table in the back of the restaurant, which is surprisingly crowded midmorning, and sends him a text.

Running late, be there in ten, he replies.

She settles in and looks around the room, filled largely with what appear to be retirees with their old-school print newspapers and young moms with strollers.

She looks at the menu, studying the various pictures of eggs. Eggs right side up, their yolks an unappetizing sort of fuchsia-orange. Eggs upside down, a too-bright white. Eggs sitting smugly in little cup holders, presumably poached. There are pictures of a wide variety of pastries as well. All of this looks spectacularly unappealing, largely on account of the sticky menus and the anemic lighting employed by the food photographer.

She texts Howard again. Again undeliverable. She has not activated her work email on her phone, which is probably a good thing, since it enforces some time to decompress. Foolishly, she did not bring any reading material, and she has already completed her various daily puzzles, so instead, she googles "how to find a public intellectual."

Apparently, this is not a thing. But that's okay. She is doing this googling exercise as a diversion, an act of deranged amusement. Directions for how to find a wide variety of other things pop up: How to find a slope. How to find standard deviation. How to find horizontal asymptotes. She wishes she were being asked to find one of those things, because those are apparently things one can find. But those are not the things she needs. She does, however, find information on *becoming* a public intellectual, as well as information on what public intellectualism is and why we should care about it, assuming we should. Personally, Clemi can't think of any reason to care about public intellectualism other than it being a sudden URGENT MAJOR PI PROBLEM, a missing silent auction item at a fundraising event that is going to happen in three days.

"The term *public intellectual* describes the intellectual participating in the public affairs discourse of society, in addition to an academic career," she learns. Or thinks she learns, since this is not a particularly illuminating description.

She scans the room again. Were she to run into a public intellectual, this would be a likely spot. This is an affluent neighborhood in a city with one of the highest concentrations of people with advanced degrees in the country. This is your eggs-and-bacon and coffee-from-a-pot-that-has-been-sitting-around-for-hours kind of joint—not one of those hipster coffee shops with pour-overs and cold brews and white chocolate frozen lattes with vegan scones and avocado toast.

Which is to say, if the likes of Umberto Eco or Orhan Pamuk were hanging out at a coffee shop in Washington, this might well be the one. Maybe this will wind up being one of those serendipitous moments in life where the solution to the problem simply presents itself. She will look up from the menu, glance around the room, and find Umberto Eco sitting at the next table, reading *The Washington Post* Style section unassumingly. She will say to him something along the lines of "Hi! I'm the programs director at WLNP, and this might sound crazy, but our awards ceremony and annual fundraiser is on Friday, and our public intellectual is suddenly unavailable. Might you like to join as our guest? Or . . . actually, you don't even need to be there"—or so Clemi presumes, since she has never been to a WLNP fundraiser—"but might you donate your time, just an hour or two to have lunch on a date of your choosing with a handful of strangers who will pay $12,000—maybe even more!—to absorb your wisdom? It's for a good cause." (Although is it? This is both a practical and an existential question Clemi has been avoiding asking herself. What, exactly, *is* the WLNP cause, apart from celebrating fiction that is *prescient?* What is the point of celebrating fiction that is prescient? Isn't all fiction sort of prescient in one way or another?)

Perhaps this encounter will result in some fantastic story she will later be able to tell her children and grandchildren, about how Umberto Eco happened to be sitting next to her in a coffee shop and she worked up the nerve to invite him to participate in a WLNP fundraising effort, to be an auction item at a gala. He agreed, and they have remained friends ever since, and in fact he also agreed to mentor her, and then blurbed her first novel, which went on to sell many copies and win many prizes.

It occurs to her that one problem with this plan right out of the starting gate is that she has no idea what Umberto Eco looks like, or where he lives, although she is pretty sure he is Italian. She googles Umberto Eco and discovers another problem. Although he looks like he might be friendly and approachable, with a furry beard and a warm smile, he is also, unfortunately, dead. She chastises herself for not knowing this (seriously, how did she *not* know this?), as well as for not having read *The Name of the Rose*. So maybe it is not Umberto Eco she is looking for, but some other public intellectual along those lines.

She checks the time on her phone and once again looks around the room. It's a sleepy crowd this morning, possibly literally. People appear to be inhaling their coffees, flagging down the waiter for refills at three tables simultaneously. Next to her is an elderly man sitting by himself reading a book, and next to him, a middle-aged man wearing a white shirt beneath a rumpled suit jacket. He is leaning in, speaking to a well-appointed woman who is sipping a cappuccino and tapping at the keyboard of a MacBook Air. Perhaps he's a source on an article she is reporting, or she is his financial advisor, or maybe that's his wife, only half listening to him as he talks. Swiveling her head in the other direction to look behind her, Clemi sees what appears to be a pair of young mom friends having coffee. One woman has a sleeping toddler on her lap, the other has a baby conked out in the stroller that is pushed beside the table, blocking the aisle. They do not appear to be much older than Clemi, which is a lot to take in—the idea that she might already have a kid or two. And beside them is a young woman with purple hair, intently pecking at her laptop. She is writing a novel, probably, Clemi thinks. Or maybe a short story or a poem. Something creative and edifying. Committing to the page a shard or two of meaning about this confounding, combustible world. Perhaps even something people will pay thousands of dollars to learn more about over lunch when this purple-haired woman is auctioned off at a fundraiser, someday. Whereas Clemi is sitting here waiting, somewhat inexplicably, for her ex to arrive with news that will make her super jazzed. Or more likely not.

Her phone pings, and it is River, reporting that he is now a block away.

Booth in back on the right, she replies.

She has known River for only a few months, but already they have been through emotional permutations suggestive of a much longer relationship. When they first met in the writing workshop, it had been one of those magical, or perhaps simply inebriated, encounters where a coffee led to a beer which led to a week spent together at his then-apartment, along with proclamations of love and plans to travel to Mexico together to attend his friend's wedding and then, more recently, a sudden cooling off. Longer than usual delays in text replies, a change of plans on the travel, and finally, the dreaded suggestion that They Needed to Talk. That It Was Complicated.

That had been a week ago. It had not been all that complicated. Apparently, what they needed to talk about was how River had become sort of involved with someone. Or really, it seems, already *was* when he and Clemi had first met. A married woman. Significantly older. A novelist. Famous. The disclosures came out in staccato bursts. He had thought it was winding down, maybe even over, which is why he hadn't mentioned it, but now Augusta, the famous married older novelist, has decided to leave her husband and has invited River to move in.

He still wants to be friends. Well, really more than friends. He isn't that into Augusta, he'd explained. He and Clemi are soulmates of sorts. He can't stop thinking about her. That's how she wound up meeting him for tacos the previous evening, when he had suggested that maybe they could go to Mexico after all. Clemi is in no way going to get herself mixed up in this. She is clear about that. And yet there is something about River that she cannot fully let go of, even though she knows she should. She is not an easy mark, not a sucker for physical beauty, and yet there are exceptions, of course. He is, presentation-wise, an enigma of sorts, both sporty and hipster at once. He might be mistaken for a rugby player, or an Olympic rower, or a wrangler of wild horses who wears perfectly broken-in cowboy boots, but one who wears vintage Nirvana t-shirts and is always carrying a novel, usually one that leans pretentious and that he has, if asked, not yet begun to read.

Now here he is, walking through the door of the café, hair adorably mussed, wearing what look like deliberately, artfully torn jeans and—yes, indeed, yet another Nirvana t-shirt. He spots her in the back of the café and nods in her direction, then makes his way toward her, breaking into his jaunty smile as people look up at him as he passes by. And they do look up, because it is impossible not to look.

"Hey, you," he says, giving her a quick, confusing kiss that is not quite on the lips but maybe was intended to land there or maybe not.

"Hey," she says. "Can't wait to hear what's up!"

"You are not going to believe it," he says as he settles into the booth.

"Try me!" She sounds more enthusiastic than she feels. She has begun to detect a pattern: River's news, while good for him, is rarely good for her.

"I found an agent," he says, turning to flag down the waiter, then raising the empty cup on the table and pantomiming the pouring of coffee, which seems a little presumptive and annoys her more than it should.

"An agent?" This is not what she expected.

"A literary agent."

"Yes, of course, a literary agent. Who? Wow! That's amazing!" This *is* amazing. It is very difficult to find a literary agent, Clemi knows, not because she has tried herself—she has not yet worked up the nerve—but because she knows more than is healthy for any person to know about agenting, having grown up with a literary agent mother. But it is doubly amazing because she has read River's work in progress, and it is, to be kind, not amazing. It is navel-gazing, plotless, juvenile, pedestrian. And Clemi is, to a fault, a generous reader, one who was often chided in the writing workshop for being too kind in her critiques of work that others found middling.

"I had an email this morning from Martha Thomas. She has her own agency."

"Sure, I've heard of her. Congrats! I didn't know you even had queries out already. Did you finish the novel?"

"No, I mean it's conditional. She said she'd be happy to read it when I finish, but that she likes it so far and thinks she can sell it when it's done."

"Holy cow. How many agents have you queried?"

"Well, in truth, I haven't really been querying, but Martha represents Augusta, and we had dinner with her a couple of weeks ago, and she offered to take a look."

And there it is, the confirmation of every niggling suspicion Clemi has had about this Augusta/River romance. Not that she really needed confirmation. Although she tried to give River the benefit of the doubt, to applaud his ability to supposedly fall in love with a woman more than thirty years his senior—old enough to be his mother plus change—it had seemed likely to Clemi, and surely to everyone, that some using was going on.

"Amazing news, right?" he repeats.

"Totally," she agrees, although it is certainly not, to her, *amazing news*.

"I knew you'd be jazzed," he says. "See, there's hope for you too!"

Clemi forces a tight smile and tries not to think too hard about the meaning of this remark. Perhaps it was offered in some spirit of generosity. At the moment, her writing is all over the place. A draft of a first novel in the drawer, fragments of other things in progress. But nothing feels quite ready or right.

Whatever River's intention, she would like to leave this coffee shop right now, before she begins to cry. But she sits politely and lets him prattle on for another thirty minutes or so.

Although Martha the agent is super excited, she wants him to consider switching the point of view to include more free indirect discourse, he explains.

Clemi does not know what *free indirect discourse* means. Perhaps that is why River is poised for success, whereas she is not. He then shifts the subject to brainstorming potential blurbers for his novel.

"Ideas welcome," he says.

"Um, Augusta?" she says, trying to tamp down her sarcasm.

"Well, yes, that's a given. But who else? Do you think it's too nervy of me to ask Barbara Kingsolver? I was also thinking about George Saunders. Maybe also Jonathan Franzen. Doesn't your mother know him?"

"She does," Clemi says. She is feeling anxious, jagged, a little nauseous, even. Is he really suggesting that she ask her mother to help him?

One telling detail about River, in addition to his chutzpah, is that he is a self-motivated speaker. He does not need a call-and-response situation to converse. He is capable of sustaining dialogue entirely on his own, so the fact that Clemi is largely quiet does not mess with his ability to continue engaging. He muses about cities he would like to visit on his book tour, including a recitation of his favorite independent bookstores around the country. A few in Europe as well.

He then veers toward the matter of his revision, and the

resolution of a character named Lucas. From what Clemi can remember, Lucas is a twelfth-century monk reincarnated in the body of a frog, who is captured by an eleven-year-old boy and put in a terrarium. Lucas has been sent to this new life in order to better understand the human capacity to destroy, which he is now absorbing by observing the child. Also, he is smoking a lot of weed. Clemi once questioned River about this, wondering how a frog in a terrarium could be smoking weed, but River had chided her for being a literalist, which was perhaps fair. Who knows, maybe a good novel is hiding in there somewhere, but Clemi has not been able to excavate even the germ of what that might be.

On and on he goes. He is not going to look ahead as he rewrites. Like E. L. Doctorow, he will drive the car into the foggy night, able to see only as far as the headlights will allow, but of course they will continue to illuminate the entire way. Or something. Clemi can't take much more of this, which is fine because River, as it happens, needs to dash.

"Augusta is waiting," he says. "I'm sharing my news in person with everyone who is important to me. I wanted you to be the first to know."

Is she meant to be touched by this? Clemi is spared having to react because of a sudden commotion at the table where the two moms are sitting. Coffee is spilled, the baby begins to cry, the waitress rushes over, an older man wearing a beret jumps up from his seat and curses loudly at his companion in what sounds, possibly, like a mix of English and Italian.

Clemi thinks again of Umberto Eco and feels a nearly overwhelming grief about his death. She does not need a therapist to understand that she is experiencing some form of emotional transference, grieving for a writer she has never read because River is a jerk.

"I've got to run too," Clemi says. She needs to get up from this chair and out of this coffee shop this very second. "Immanuel is waiting for me," she says.

"Immanuel?"

"Yes, Immanuel," she says. She doesn't feel like explaining. Nor does she feel like exploring the possibility that she might be pathetic enough to try to make River jealous by dropping an exotic-sounding, or at least intellectual-sounding, male name, failing to disclose that Immanuel is a big fat cat.

"Let's hang tonight?" River asks. "We can celebrate!"

Although this is not entirely without appeal, Clemi is determined not to go down that path again. Plus she has had her fill of him today.

"I can't tonight. I've got yoga."

"Ah, tomorrow then. Namaste," he says and then kisses her, again, in the general vicinity of the lips.

"Oh, young love," says the man who is not Umberto Eco but is possibly Italian, sounding wistful as well as lecherous.

Chapter 4

CLEMI IS NOW officially done with this whole novel-writing endeavor. She has more important things to do with her life. Signing up for that workshop last winter had been nothing but a lark, the sort of thing one resolves to do each New Year, like going on a juice cleanse or embracing Dry January, at least for a week. The intentions are what count; there is zero expectation that a person will follow through on these pronouncements. Besides, the game is rigged. People who sleep with famous writers will evidently find literary agents even if their work is crap. She can write and write and write, but the Rivers of the world, with their charm and their networking acumen, are the ones who will succeed.

It's conceivable that Clemi is overreacting, but on the upside, she is now looking forward to returning to work. At least the problems at WLNP are tangible: things she can fix with a bit of administrative resolve. Plus, oddly, she finds herself thinking about Immanuel with what might be a twinge of affection, notwithstanding that while in his proximity she had been struggling to breathe.

As she waits for the bus back to Georgetown, she watches

clots of well-dressed people emerging from a glassy tower. Some have cell phones pressed to their ears; others are conversing with one another. Eventually they disperse into a variety of eating establishments, and Clemi realizes it is already lunchtime. She looks up and sees Weiner Weiner & Ong LLP emblazoned on the side of the building and recognizes the name of the venerable DC law firm.

A thought occurs, and then another, and the convergence of these two not-inconsistent thoughts feels like the very epitome of an epiphany. Down with these low-paying literary jobs! Enough with trying to write a novel! She will shift gears. She will do something to earn a steady, sizable paycheck. Like all good English majors, she has always harbored the speck of the thought in the back of her mind that she might one day go to law school if the writing thing failed. And she is beginning to feel like it's failed. But it's not just that; practicing law is a reading and writing–adjacent job that, considered in a certain light, is all about storytelling. Even more, the law is full of possible intrigue. And it's also full of paychecks. (Not to mention that lawyers wear tailored suits and pressed shirts, which admittedly has some allure.)

Now planted, the thought blooms. She will embark on a career that will challenge her with real problems that have actual solutions! So much more rewarding than fretting about point of view, and whether to employ free indirect discourse or try the annoying second person party trick of *you, you, you,* or perhaps switch to a more formal omniscient, or mix things up with a talking animal or two. Divorce memoirs are hot these days, her mother says, but Clemi is two steps away from cashing in on that literary bonanza. To hell with writing! It's a fool's game. She will smarten up. She will go to law school.

Not only will she go to law school, but also she will set this plan in motion *right now*. And as luck, or fate, or destiny would have it, the bookstore where she used to work is just a few blocks from here. She will pop in and pick up an LSAT study guide, and then, as soon as she gets back to work, before dealing with Sveta's plane ticket or worrying further about the public intellectual conundrum, she will register for the test.

She has not been in the bookstore since resigning two weeks ago, and she is ambivalent about returning as a customer. She doesn't want to see anyone, to go through the motions of the hellos, the hugs and how-have-you-beens. *How's the new job? The new apartment?* Et cetera. And it's not just her discomfort with this sort of small talk, but also the pang of having left, the bittersweet separation from the bookseller life that felt like a gash to the heart. These are some of the best people she has ever met, or will ever meet, she thinks. Bighearted people, generally. People of the book. She is reluctant to step back inside and stir it all up. But the store is right here, and she needs a book, which is the very point of a bookstore. On top of which, unless there has been a sudden rush on LSAT guides, she knows exactly where they are located and can pop in, grab one, and begin moving on with her life this very moment, which, mental health–wise, feels like the right thing to do.

She hesitates at the door, taking in the new window display that features books with yellow covers and a cheery, campy picture of the sun made from construction paper with the exuberant command: "Spring into spring with a book!"

More like "Spring away from books," Clemi thinks. *"Spring into litigation"* has a better, or at least more sustainable, ring.

Just as she is about to open the door, she hears the chirp of her phone. She glances at the screen. It is her mother calling, which can mean only one thing. Clemi has heard about these mythical mothers who call their daughters just to say hi, to see how they are, to say "I love you." But Elena is all business. She calls when she wants something.

"Darling, sorry to call in the middle of the workday, but can you do me a quick favor?"

"Hi, Mom."

"Hi! Sorry. Hello, hello! I'm in a bit of a rush, in the middle of an auction for Fiona's new book. Would you mind looking something up for me?"

"Sure, I guess?"

"Can you see how many copies your bookstore has sold in both hardcover and paper for *Strife*? And how large her event was? And how many views has the video of her event garnered? If you don't mind, a snapshot of backlist sales would be helpful too. It's just a microcosm, of course, but it's still helpful ammunition to bring to auction."

"I don't work at the bookstore anymore, Mom. I can't get into the inventory system."

"Oh, drat! You did tell me that. I'm so sorry, darling. It's been a week. Remind me . . . you are at some nonprofit now, right?"

"Yes, I've just been there for a few days. It's WLNP."

"What is that? I've never heard of it."

"It used to be called something else. But they changed the name."

The Literati

"*Oh?*" asks Elena in tone that sounds worrisomely portentous. "When you told me you were going to the foundation that gives out the Chestnut Prize, I hadn't put two and two together."

"What do you mean?"

"I just mean there are so many prizes out there, I forget who gives out what. That one used to be called the Arthur Muller Foundation, right? There was some sort of scandal, but honestly, I can't remember what happened. It was so long ago. I think it had something to do with Ezra Pound maybe."

"Ezra Pound? He's been dead for like a hundred years."

"More like fifty, darling."

"Right. But I mean, whatever it is, it's old news." Clemi is pressing the point mostly because she feels foolish. How did she not do more research before accepting the job? Because in all of her time in Washington, which is admittedly only a few years, she has known the foundation by its acronym: WLNP. And obviously it wasn't exactly headline news if her mother, too, is struggling to remember.

"Anyway, Mom, sorry I can't help, but I do know Fiona's books sold well. While I have you on the phone, though, I had kind of a radical thought this morning."

"You're moving to London to be closer to me? Or . . . maybe you want to come work with me? I could really use a junior agent."

"No, Mom." She supposes she should be touched; this is as close to affectionate as Elena gets. This is not the first time she has floated the idea of Clemi working with her, but really, she can't imagine anything worse than having to deal with her mother on a professional as well as personal basis. In her more generous moments, Clemi supposes that her mother, somewhere deep inside, feels all the right maternal things; she just has difficulty sorting the feelings into words. Or gestures, such as hugs.

"I'm thinking about going to law school," she says.

"But how will you pay for it?"

That's her first question? It is, admittedly, a fair question, but still, it would be nice if her initial query had something to do with a consideration of Clemi's life goals.

"I haven't gotten that far yet, Mom. It's still just a thought. But I can take out loans."

"Be careful. You don't want to be in too much debt. It will make it difficult to buy a house someday. Anyway, I thought you wanted to be a writer. Not that I'm encouraging that, trust me. But you should be doing something literary it seems to me."

Buy a house? Right now buying *lunch* is challenging enough.

"I haven't thought all of it through yet."

"I suppose we can always ask your father," Elena says. "I'm sure he would be happy to help pay. Lord knows he owes it to you. Who knows what he does with all of his money. Although I guess he has a bunch of other kids to support. Probably more than either of us knows."

Elena says this sort of thing from time to time about Clemi's estranged father poet, with whom her mother seems to still be involved, both on and off romantically as well as in the capacity of his literary agent. She is so casual about the number of children he has possibly fathered that she might as well be talking about his collection of ties. Clemi met him for the first time a couple of years ago, when he did a reading at the bookstore.

After all these years, he would now like to have "a relationship." Clemi has not entirely shut him out, but she's been keeping him at a distance.

This unexpected conversation with her mother has triggered Clemi on so many different levels that it has counterintuitively been clarifying; running from the messy literary world of her parents, doing something concrete and with a reasonable chance of renumeration, seems the smart thing to do.

They say goodbye, and Clemi is about to disconnect the call when Elena interrupts. "Wait! I just remembered more about WLNP."

"More?"

"Yes, it's coming back to me. Something to do with the executive director. Something bad."

Oh dear God no please, Clemi thinks. "With Howard? Howard Zevin?"

"No, Someone Berkowitz. It was a while ago. Hyman, I think."

"Ah, well, if it was a while ago—"

"About five years ago maybe? That was one part of why they changed the name."

"What's past is past," Clemi says, as if she is suddenly a sage. "I've got to go, Mom. Good luck with your auction." She ends the call and then springs into spring by opening the door to the bookstore, always a reliable haven from the problems at hand.

She feels a twinge of nostalgia as she inhales the smell of new books and takes in the familiar, albeit unusually sleepy tableau of the store. Not many customers. She sees a graduate student who practically lives at a table near the history section tapping at her laptop, and a frazzled young dad pushing a stroller with a wailing child and pulling on the leash of a hyper Havanese. It is early in the day, after a holiday weekend. Would-be customers are probably still away at the beach or wherever it is they have gone.

She makes her way to the back of the store and grabs a random LSAT study guide—surely they are all more or less the same—and is then rung up by Michael, a painfully shy Yale grad whom she remembers as being partial to obscure literary fiction in translation. She hands over her credit card without any verbal exchange, and when he presents her with the receipt, she realizes he has given her the employee discount—40 percent! Apparently he hasn't noticed she no longer works here, which is simultaneously good and sad.

Chapter 5

NEWLY COMMITTED TO building up the foundation of a life plan, Clemi now feels able to get through the rest of this day, whatever it might yet have in store. She is empowered, the way she feels when she puts on a new pair of sturdy boots: Mess with her, and she will kick you in the teeth. Or in this case, clobber you over the head with her heavy LSAT study guide. Not that she would, or could. But still. It's a feeling.

Also, mercifully, not all that much of the day is left to be gotten through. By the time she alights from the bus and begins to walk toward the office, it is nearly two o'clock.

When she reaches the WLNP townhouse, she sees a bearded man in a dark green windbreaker leaning against the heavy wrought iron door that opens into the tiny lobby. Something about his presence seems menacing. Maybe it's that his head is ensconced inside the hood of his jacket on this otherwise warm, clear day. More likely, this is just her overactive imagination, again. Still, something is off; he shows no sign of moving away from the door as she approaches. In fact he appears intent on blocking her entry.

"Do you by any chance work for WLNP?" he asks as she approaches.

She would like to say that she does, but she will be resigning soon because she has resolved to grab life by the horns, take the LSAT, and set her feet on the path toward becoming a reasonably compensated human being. Or, barring that, she would like to say that she does, but she has only worked here for a week and part of one day, and for most of that partial day she has been in work avoidance mode. Or even better, she would like to simply say no, because she senses that whatever this man wants can't be good.

"I guess I do?" she says softly.

"You do or you don't?"

"I do."

"Fantastic! Your name, please?"

What right does this man have to know her name?

"Clemi," she says reluctantly.

"Clemi. Last name, please."

She is not going to give this stranger her last name. Neither does she want to start up with him. "River," she says, surprising herself with this act of clever dishonesty.

"Fantastic. Clemi River," he repeats, handing her an envelope.

This is a relief of sorts. It's just an envelope. An envelope imprinted with the word SUBPOENA.

"You've been served," he says. "Have yourself a nice day, Clemi River."

Well, what are the odds, she wonders, of her having just decided to become a lawyer and being served a subpoena on the same day? Surely this is auspicious. That or the opposite of that.

The Literati

Clemi punches the code into the keypad that opens the door, then makes her way up the stairs toward the WLNP office, walking past the other businesses that occupy the building. There are two think tanks—the Institute of Thought and the American Council on Poultry—as well as a therapist's office and the office of a well-known divorce attorney with a reputation for representing high-powered Washington types of the sort whose names appear in the indexes of books. Howard filled her in on some of this during her job interview. The attorney was currently representing a senior conservative member of the US House of Representatives who had left his wife for a male intern. Clemi had seen something about this on her newsfeed. Howard said he had seen the congressman in the lobby on more than one occasion, waiting for his appointments.

Howard also told her that the divorce attorney sometimes refers her clients to the therapist down the hall, and the therapist sometimes refers his clients to the divorce attorney down the hall, adding that he—Howard, that is—finds this to be a little incestuous. He then made a crude gesture with his fingers, which she found both puzzling and gross, but she was uncertain as to whether it had to do with business ties between therapists and divorce attorneys, congressmen and interns, or more specifically family members engaging in sexual relations with one another, even though the latter was not specific to the situation at hand.

She is not sure what to make of Howard. He has so far been pleasant enough to work with, even if she is a little put off by his gossipy side. Yet something about him doesn't fully compute.

He seems more finance bro than executive director of a literary nonprofit, both with his sometimes crude demeanor and his presentation: Top-Sider shoes, no socks, khaki pants, a rotation of brightly colored Brooks Brothers shirts, blond hair, and sparklingly white teeth. He looks as if he has just stepped off a yacht or emerged from the pages of *The Great Gatsby*. She supposes his sartorial choices make sense given that his job presumably involves hobnobbing with wealthy board members, attending their cocktail parties, meeting their friends, and charming the ladies and gents, all with the aim of getting them to write large checks.

Howard has provided enough detail about his life that she can place him in his late forties. He once mentioned some basketball championship situation at Duke, for example, where he let drop that he had clinched the game by scoring thirty-two points and twelve rebounds. She is not a basketball enthusiast, but she gets that this is impressive, particularly given that he does not appear especially athletic and is of average male height.

One of several curiosities about Howard is why he is even here, in this role, given his success as a writer. He has told Clemi about the bestselling series of detective novels he has penned involving a grizzled yet charming detective in Amsterdam. A Dutch version of the popular Swedish detective Wallander is how he has described it. He was published in the Netherlands, but the books never took off in the US because they were too sophisticated for American audiences, he'd said.

WLNP is situated in a one-room office on the top floor of the townhouse, once a single-family home. The space now occupied by two desks was once the maids' quarters, or so Howard told her, pointing to a narrow stairway that leads directly to what was previously the kitchen two floors down but is now the therapist's office. Via this staircase, he explained, the servants could slip between their quarters and the kitchen unseen.

Clemi reaches the fourth-floor landing, and as she presses the code into the keypad—the same code that opens the front door, which happens, somewhat alarmingly security-wise, to be 1234—she pauses to contemplate the makeshift sign taped to the door, fashioned from what looks like half of a manila folder. In Sharpie are the letters *WLNP*. Prior to the conversation with her mother, this sign had failed to trigger her curiosity. But now that Elena has mentioned something about a scandal, and now that Clemi is possibly a rising member of the legal profession, she is curious. She peels back the sign and looks beneath, but all she sees is the ghost of etched out words.

Inside, she is greeted by the smell of cat. Or maybe of the cat's food. Having never owned a cat, she is not sure which smell is which. Immanuel remains impassive, unaffected by either Clemi's departure or return. He does not appear to have moved in the time she's been gone. She is reminded that she should have stopped at the store to get some allergy meds, and also cat food, which in turn reminds her to check on whether Immanuel has eaten anything today.

She goes into the bathroom and sees that his bowl of mushy, stinky food appears untouched. She wonders where he excretes, should he choose to leave the desk to engage in such activity, and notices a litter box placed discreetly in the bathtub—a still-intact remnant from when the townhouse was an enormous single-family home. Like the food bowl, the litter box does not appear to have been touched. Is something wrong with this cat that neither eats nor excretes? Is there someone she ought to call?

She returns to the main office area and sneezes three times in a row. After which, the next breath she draws goes in and comes out as a wheeze. She needs to get out of here, get some allergy medication, and figure out what to do with this cat. But first she needs to check her inbox lest it shed any light on what is going on.

She settles into her chair, which is too low for the desk. It's one of those ergonomically designed office chairs with a futuristic name, something like Sirius. The Sirius is equipped with a space-age mesh to perform the job of the cushions. Alas, the lever that regulates its verticality is broken off, so the Sirius is now forever frozen on the wrong level of the y-axis. She wonders how tall Didi, her predecessor, had been. Leaning back, she feels the twinge in her back again, but is pretty sure it is yoga-related, given there are roughly a dozen other spots on her body that ache.

She wakes the computer with a click of the mouse, hoping to find something in her email that will help illuminate the various challenges of the day. She opens the first email, which proves to be spam, then looks up and sees Immanuel staring at her.

"What do you want, cat?"

She may be projecting again, but his intent gaze feels judgmental, like maybe he has thoughts on her sloppy application of eyeliner, or thinks her hemline is too long, or maybe too short, for someone her age.

Then again, perhaps Immanuel is trying to communicate something more urgent: *Open the effing subpoena!*

Clemi has almost forgotten about the subpoena, so distracted is she by concerns about the cat's bodily functions as well as the height of her Space-the-Final-Frontier chair. She finds a letter opener on Howard's desk, which seems the sort of quaint instrument one ought to employ when opening a subpoena, then stares at the thing for a moment, wondering if she really ought to open the envelope. She is, after all, a brand-new employee, and a relatively junior one at that. And yet the unfriendly subpoena server did say that working for WLNP was good enough to be served, so presumably she must be qualified to open the thing too. She carefully inserts the blade beneath the sticky seal and pries the envelope open, moving slowly as if defusing a bomb. She then removes the piece of paper inside.

It is, unsurprisingly, a legal document. And it is written on letterhead from the law firm of Weiner Weiner & Ong.

Okay, seriously, what are the odds of that? Talk about your fate, your serendipity, your karma, whatever. This is, clearly, the sound of the universe talking to her! The same law firm she stood in front of just a couple of hours ago, the very totem that sparked a life-changing epiphany, has now served her employer with a subpoena? Perhaps this fate, serendipity, karma, whatever, will continue, and she will go to law school and secure herself a respectfully compensated associate's position at said Weiner Weiner & Ong.

The letter is addressed to Eric Jolly, MD, the board president, which is somewhat concerning—perhaps she should not have opened this after all. She reads on, holding the letter away from her face as if she is farsighted, which she is not, but she feels it's probably better to have some physical distance from whatever is contained on the page.

RE: *ZHANG V. ZEVIN*, IN THE MATTER OF THE COMPLAINT FOR ABSOLUTE DIVORCE.

She reads this again. Perhaps this is a mistake. Howard's last name is indeed Zevin, but he has not mentioned anything about a wife, never mind a divorce, not that this is the sort of thing that should have come up in the workplace, or at least not on day four of training a new employee, notwithstanding the fact that he spent half that time gossiping about everyone else. But more to the point, why would Dr. Jolly, and WLNP, be involved in litigation pertaining to a divorce?

This has been quite the day! Prior to this morning, Clemi didn't know Howard had a cat, and prior to opening this letter, she didn't know he had a wife. A soon-to-be ex-wife, apparently.

She soldiers on: The subpoena is for WLNP's bank accounts.

YOU ARE HEREBY COMMANDED to turn over the following records and provide access to the following accounts...

The letter lists two brokerage accounts, one at Fidelity and one at Charles Schwab, as well as a checking account at TD Bank. Whatever is going on here, it is none of her business. This is a private matter involving the presumably tragic dissolution of a marriage.

Or is it? The subpoena was sent to WLNP, Clemi reminds herself. Putting her legal mind to work, she pulls the subpoena closer, studies it again, and metaphorically slaps herself on the head. The accounts in question belong to the nonprofit of which Howard is a fiduciary, not to Howard the individual.

Clearly, his wife must think something nefarious is going on with the Z family finances.

This is out of Clemi's pay range, so to speak, although *above her station* would be more accurate, since *out of her pay range* would apply to just about any job she might qualify for at the moment, given the cost of living in DC.

What she needs is help. But who can help? She hasn't yet met anyone on the board, but on day two of her employment, she was told that WLNP has an intern and that the intern's name is Skylar.

This Skylar handles WLNP's social media accounts and comes in on occasion to help with administrative tasks. Alas, Clemi doesn't have Skylar's contact information; why would she? She doesn't even know Skylar's last name.

Probably the thing to do is to find a member of the board who is not currently delivering a keynote address in Nairobi.

She pauses to self-flagellate for having accepted this job without doing due diligence. Also, really, her labored breathing, which had until now been more of an annoyance, is beginning to transform into an unceasing bronchial growl.

She glares at the cat, walks over to the window, pulls it open, and takes a deep breath of the famously pollen-infused DC air. She should have spoken to this Didi Feldman person to ask her why she left, or she should have asked Howard more insightful questions, possibly inquiring, even, about his marital status and whether his wife might someday have reason to subpoena the WLNP bank accounts. But instead, she had been seduced by the prestige of this job, by the idea of meeting Sveta Attais, by the higher salary than the one she was making at the bookstore. What's an extra sixty-four dollars per week, you might ask? It's not nothing. And the job offer had coincided with the opportunity to plant-sit in the fancy new apartment with the free gym and the free parking for the car she does not own.

She clicks on to the WLNP website and finds the list of board members under the "About" tab. It's true that Howard had trash-talked a number of them, but with a few exceptions Clemi had not really focused on their names. In the due diligence department, this, too, is something she clearly should have done before accepting the job. As it turns out, the board vice president is a writer whom her mother stopped representing on not entirely amicable terms. Not that this ought to have anything to do with Clemi, but still, it is awkward. She remembers her mother talking about this author, Ellen Lapidus, complaining about how demanding she was, always wanting to get her on the phone, pushing for higher advances, practically blaming Elena for her poor sales and unfair reviews. Elena is reasonably loyal to the clients she takes on, but with Ellen she had finally had enough and had even said disparaging things about her pretentious novel in verse about a cardinal at a kitchen window, and how it was no wonder it had tanked. (*"This is America, Ellen,"* Clemi overheard her mother saying on the phone. *"In America, novels in verse always tank!"*)

Clemi would prefer not to reach out to Ellen if she can help it, but then, she is here to do her job, and she decides she will remain professional. Also, Ellen might not even notice the name or remember that she'd met Clemi at the Miami Book Fair back when she was a kid, tagging along because Elena couldn't find a babysitter. She clicks the link on the website that takes her to Ellen's email address and carefully composes a message introducing herself as the new programs director of WLNP, explaining that Howard is not in today, that she is unable to reach the board president, and that she has a couple of extremely urgent questions.

She gets an immediate reply: "I am away at a writing residency with limited access to email. Please be patient. If your matter pertains to WLNP business and is urgent, please contact Didi Feldman at dfeldman@WNLP.org."

Is everyone away at a writing residency? Why is Clemi not away at a writing residency? How quickly can she get herself admitted to a writing residency so that she, too, can write an away message relieving her of all responsibility? Of course, that's moot, she reminds herself, a distant echo of pre-epiphany resentments.

Okay then. She skips ahead to see who is next in line in the power structure of WLNP. This would be the treasurer, who in the photo appears to be a very thin, distinguished-looking man named Samuel Samaraweera. Clad in a suit and tie, he stares resolutely ahead, into the very soul of the camera. About Samuel Samaraweera, Howard has said only that he is "a good guy."

She copies the initial message, changes the email address and salutation, and flips the thing to Samuel. The landline rings just as she is hitting send. Perhaps it's Ellen, who has seen the email and understands the urgency. But it is someone named Penelope, looking for Howard.

"He's not in today," Clemi says, trying to sound normal and not like the house is on fire.

"*Oh . . . kay*," comes the tentative voice of Penelope. "We were supposed to meet this afternoon at the hotel. He was going to bring me a check. I've been waiting for twenty minutes. I've been texting him, but my messages aren't going through."

"Oh, how odd," Clemi bluffs.

"And you are?"

"I'm Clemi. The new programs director."

"Well, Clemi. Might you be able to meet me here? With a check?"

What the what? Surely this is a bad dream. An especially bad movie. A video game in which she is dipping into different possible versions of her life, and in this life she is being punished for leaving a perfectly good job in pursuit of a somewhat higher salary.

"So sorry. I'm pretty new here, and as mentioned, Howard is not available today. So could you tell me where you were meant to meet, and what is the nature of the check?"

"The *nature of the check*," she says, her annoyance clearly on the verge of rage, "is to cover the balance of the catering bill for Friday. Which would be exactly $40,542.53. That's the balance after the deposit, which I might add took some wrangling to get from him as well. And we were meant to do the walk through today."

"I'm so sorry. Howard is out sick. But if you can give me until tomorrow, I'm sure we can sort this out." Why she continues to cover for Howard she has no idea, other than her truest hope that this is all some sort of misunderstanding—that his possible dental surgery is just taking a very long time. That, plus she is a natural people pleaser.

"I cannot give you until tomorrow. In fact, I'm going to pull the plug on this right now. And sue WLNP for breach of contract."

Clemi is not a lawyer yet. She has not so much as turned the page of the LSAT study guide, which is still nestled in her tote bag, but she suspects this does not constitute breach of contract. Isn't that what deposits are for? Nevertheless, she does not particularly wish to find out, especially given that one subpoena is already sitting on Howard's desk.

"Please? I promise I'll meet you tomorrow with a check," she bluffs again.

"Tomorrow is hellish for me. I have two weddings this weekend, plus a gala for the National Association of Insurance Professionals. I was already doing you a favor, taking this on late in the game after your other caterer fell through."

The other caterer fell through? Yet another thing to add to the growing list of red flags: bad juju with caterers.

"But I have a brief window tomorrow at three. Be prompt. You'll find me in the lobby of the hotel."

"Either Howard or I will be there at three sharp. Thank you!" Clemi says.

"Don't forget to bring a check—seriously. More bad publicity is the last thing you all need."

Chapter 6

CLEMI HANGS UP and, for a moment, sits very still. Why has she just made a false promise to the caterer? Unless Howard suddenly appears, she has no idea how to produce a check in just over twenty-four hours. What she ought do is walk out the door. This is not her circus. Not her monkeys. On top of which, she needs to deal with the fact that she can't breathe. So why is she still sitting here, watching Immanuel stare out the window at a bird that has landed on the sill? His expression remains inscrutable, even though presumably he, too, is asking himself the same question. Flee, Immanuel, flee! And she should follow him right out the door.

She tries to rationalize her inertia. For one thing, she needs the paycheck. She is close to broke. That said, she does have a bit of a cushion with free rent for the next five months; if she is frugal, she could hit the pause button, cut down on Ubers, margaritas, and caffeinated drinks, and take some time to think about next steps, even dig in deep on the LSAT studies, perhaps.

Also, for all she knows, there is a reasonable explanation for everything that has transpired thus far. She doesn't want to jump to any conclusions. Is it also possible that she wants her mother to be proud of her? Of her very literary job at a prestigious nonprofit? Yes, it is, admittedly, possibly so.

And let's face it: She very much wants to meet Sveta Attais. She can at the very least hang in here until the end of the week.

This pileup of rationalizations is interrupted by a knock at the door. What fresh hell is this now?

Immanuel swivels his head and arches his back like a cartoon version of a frightened feline.

"It's okay, Immanuel," Clemi says in her most soothing voice. But who knows if it's okay? Maybe Immanuel knows something she does not, having witnessed whatever has led to the current discombobulated state of the office. She looks over to the disemboweled filing cabinet, reflects on Howard's undeliverable texts, the not-so-thinly-veiled threats from the caterer, the freshly served subpoena, the mysteriously abandoned cat. Should she call the police?

The door swings open before she can think the next thought.

"Oh my God, so sorry!" says a tall, thin woman with expensively highlighted hair. "Howard did tell me to always knock, which I did, but I should have waited a beat. Honestly didn't know anyone was here. Who are you?"

"I'm Clemi. I'm the new programs director. Who are *you*?"

"I'm Skylar. Skylar Papadopoulos."

"Oh! *You're* Skylar the intern?" She doesn't mean to be rude, but this woman, who is at least twice Clemi's age and is dressed in sporty shabby-chic designer wear that makes her look like she is running away from a very affluent home, does not look like anyone's idea of an intern.

"I come in every Tuesday. Or I aim to. Sometimes more,

sometimes less. I was at the country house last week, so I guess that's why we haven't met. But now we have met—so, onward!"

Skylar looks around, taking in the disheveled state of the office, then at the cat. "What happened here? And why are you allowed to bring your cat to work? Howard said I wasn't allowed to bring my daughter to work, but he lets you bring your *cat*?"

"This isn't my cat. When I got to work this morning, he was already sitting there on Howard's desk. His name is Immanuel, and I think he belongs to Howard. Or at least, Howard asked me to feed him."

Immanuel's ears prick. He seems to recognize his name.

"How old is your kid?" Clemi is intrigued by this Skylar-the-unlikely-intern person, trying to make sense of her.

"I have three kids. The older two are in school. I asked Howard if I could bring the baby—well, by now she's a toddler—but he said no. Honestly, I like Howard, sort of, as much as one can—he's a little slippery, no?—but I thought that was petty of him. It's not like I'm being paid to work here. Saying yes seemed like the least he could do. I even thought about filing a suit of some sort, but my mother pointed out that the only deep pocket here is . . . well, *me*, ha ha."

Clemi laughs politely but is confused, unsure which part of that statement is funny.

"Where is Howard anyway?" Skylar asks.

"Honestly, I have no idea. He was supposed to meet the caterer this afternoon. She just called and was very upset. She wants a check. She is threatening to sue."

"Was it Penelope?"

"Yes."

"Oh, Penelope! She can be such a drama queen. He's just having scheduling problems, most likely."

"Maybe, but I can't reach him, and there are a lot of things piling up here. Like Sveta Attais called from Morocco this morning and said we need to rebook her tickets. I guess she was originally coming from LA, but now she is in Morocco and has a bad back. She needs two first-class tickets, one for her and one for her son, and—"

"A bad back! *Please*. Oldest trick in the book to get an upgrade. We don't pay for first-class air travel, and we can't pay for the son's travel. The plus-one is on the author."

Clemi is a little crestfallen. She's not an idiot, she knows people lie about such things, but not Sveta Attais! She is determined to give her the benefit of the doubt.

"Okay, well, I kind of wondered about that, but I didn't know who to ask. I tried to reach Dr. Jolly but—"

"Eric is completely useless."

"So I've heard. What should I tell Sveta? Also, what do you think I should do about getting a check to Penelope by tomorrow afternoon?"

"I mean, you're in charge. I'm just an intern. But if I were in your shoes, I suppose I'd just go ahead and buy her the tickets. The board will grumble, but they'll cough up the money in the end. If they don't, my mom will figure something out. And the check part is easy. They're in the top drawer of the filing cabinet. But, like, who even writes checks anymore? Why don't you just wire the money?"

"Good point. That's so helpful. Thank goodness you are here. But why would your mom be able to help? And how do you know so much?" This does not strike Clemi as the kind of information an intern would know, but then, what does Clemi know about the duties of an intern?

"My mother is Frieda. She's on the board?"

"What? Okay, how did I not know this? That's great! Does that mean you know how to get into the bank account?"

"Why would you want to get into the bank account?"

"Well, like you said, maybe to wire money to the caterer?"

"Oh, right! Ha! You had me worried for a moment. I don't think that's something a board member would know how to do, plus my mom is on one of those barge trips through Burgundy with her book group and is impossible to reach, but we can probably figure it out.

"Still, I don't see why Penelope can't wait on this. She is such a pain in the neck, always wanting money, money, money. She was always hounding me for money for my wedding, too, even while I was on my honeymoon. I mean, obviously I was going to pay her. She acts like we are a bunch of scofflaws."

"She catered your wedding?"

"My first wedding."

"Even better," Clemi says for no reason at all. This reminds her that she has nearly forgotten about the subpoena. "Also, just FYI, I should probably mention that we've been served."

"Served what?"

"A subpoena."

"A subpoena for what? Hopefully nothing to do with the whole Nazi thing. I'm so over that already!"

"The whole Nazi thing?"

"Don't worry about it. So, what's it for?"

"Believe it or not, Howard's wife is filing for divorce and wants to see our bank records. So, in addition to figuring out how to wire money, it would probably be a good idea to see what's going on in the account."

"That's so odd. How can WLNP finances figure in Mae and Howard's divorce? Let's take a look. Do you know what bank?"

"The subpoena mentions three accounts. Fidelity, Charles Schwab, and TD Bank."

"Let's do it!"

Clemi sits down at her desk, and Skylar leans over. "Try Schwab first," she says.

Clemi brings up the log-in page for the account, then waits.

"Do you know the username and password?" Skylar asks.

"That's what I was asking you. I was hoping you'd know."

"How would I know? I'm just an intern."

"I guess you wouldn't. But . . . don't you do the WLNP social media stuff?"

"I do. What's your point?"

"Maybe the password is the same?"

"*Ohhhhh*. Right. Brilliant!"

As Skylar leans over Clemi's shoulder and begins to type, they hear shouting from outside the window.

Then a car horn begins to honk.

"I wonder what that's about."

"Probably just my car."

"Your car? What do you mean?"

"It's double-parked. Since I was passing by, I figured I'd just pop in to tell Howard I wasn't coming in today. You know, since he hadn't picked up the phone."

Given that it is nearly four, Clemi supposes Skylar's absence might already have been apparent to Howard were he here to observe.

"I'll go back down in a minute. In the meantime, they can all just chill the eff out." She keeps typing possible passwords, then deleting, then trying again.

"Be careful," Clemi warns. "I hope they don't freeze the account or something."

Skylar ignores her, along with the sound of the horns growing louder. Then a new sound: Someone is leaning on the buzzer in the lobby. Clemi goes over to the ancient intercom system and presses the button to speak.

"Can I help you?"

"Does anyone up there own a Mercedes wagon? Silver?"

"I don't know. Let me check." Clemi takes her hand off the buzzer. "Do you own a Mercedes wagon? Silver?"

"No. Wait . . . let me try one more thing."

Clemi hits the speaking contraption again. "Sorry. We don't know anything about it."

"I didn't say that," Skylar says. "I just said I don't own it. It's my mom's. I'm using it while she's away."

"Oh," Clemi says, confused. "I think maybe that's not what they are asking, really." She walks over to the window and sees a silver Mercedes wagon double-parked, clogging the entire road. People are standing in the middle of the street, shouting.

"Do you want me to move it for you?" Clemi offers ever so politely. She does not want to distract, or worse, alienate this woman with the possible passwords, nor does she want to be responsible for the traffic cataclysm unfolding below.

"I'll move it in a minute. They can back up or use the alley. They'll figure something out."

"Are you making any progress?" Clemi asks. She is a little afraid of, or at least intimidated by, this Skylar.

"I'm just trying a couple more things. And . . . OMG, Bob's your uncle. I'm a genius."

"You're in?"

"I'm in! Almost."

The landline rings and Clemi wonders whether it might be Sveta, calling to check on her ticket, but Skylar grabs the phone. She listens for a moment, then sets the receiver down and taps at the keyboard. "We're in!"

Clemi sneezes, then sneezes again, and then wheezes audibly.

"Are you okay?"

"Not really. I need to get out of here. Who was on the phone?"

"That was the bank with the code. Two-step verification. The landline is attached to the account."

"You *are* a genius."

"And the balance is . . . $23.76."

"Hmm . . . that's weird. But maybe that's why there are three accounts. Probably that's an old account, which makes sense because who uses a landline to verify an account anymore, right? Can you get into Fidelity? Maybe try the same password?"

Skylar pulls up the Fidelity site, types in a string of characters, and the account information appears. "Yup. Same password. Not the greatest security hygiene here. I mean, half the world seems to have the passcode for the office doors. They probably have the log-in for the bank accounts too. Someone must have hacked the accounts and wiped us out."

"Seriously, there's no money in the account?"

"Well, not *no* money. There's fifty-six cents."

"What the hell? Can you try the TD account? Maybe he moved everything over there since it's an actual bank. Right?"

Clemi doesn't know much about finance, but she does at least know the difference between a brokerage account and a bank account.

Skylar taps at the keyboard for a few minutes, then gives up. "I can't get into TD. Different password."

A police siren joins the cacophony of multiple civilian car horns.

"I think you might want to move your car before something happens," Clemi suggests. "Like, before you get towed."

"For the love of God! Okay, I've got to pick the kids up anyway."

"Wait, before you go, can you give me the password? The one that worked on the other accounts? Or maybe, do you have ideas about variations?"

"Sure. I don't want to get too personal, Carmi, but it sounds like you're struggling to breathe."

"Clemi. Short for Clementine. And yes, you're right. I need to get some allergy meds."

"Oh, sorry, Clemi. I see now. Orange hair. Like a clementine. So cute. I'll remember that next time. Try 'herring' with a capital *H* question mark. Or maybe an ampersand. Or the 'at' sign. Also try a number. Four, I think? Maybe five? All one word."

"Hair ring? All one word?"

"No, *herring*. H-E-R-R-I-N-G."

"Oh, gotcha. My grandmother loved herring."

"The man or the fish?"

"What do you mean?"

"Let's just focus on the password. Keep trying various variations on herring."

"Um, sure. Okay. But one more question: If there's no money in that account either, what should I do about Penelope?"

"Just write her a check. Tell her not to cash it until Friday."

"That feels possibly illegal, no?"

"You are such a worrywart. I'm telling you, the board will take care of it. You have my word."

"I have never written such a large check. I'm not sure I even know how to do it. Makes me a little uncomfortable, honestly."

"Oh, good grief. I'll walk you through it. Grab the checkbook." She points toward the mess by the filing cabinet, and Clemi walks over and locates a checkbook in the top drawer.

"Great," Skylar says. "Make it out to Penelope, Inc." Clemi takes a pen from the cupholder next to Immanuel's front paws and looks at him imploringly, as if doing so will get her out of this mess. She fills in the name.

"Okay, now write out the words *forty thousand and*—"

"I know how to do it. There, it's done. I'm just saying it's a lot of money. And it doesn't feel right."

"Good girl," Skylar says. "Now just sign it."

"Sign my name?"

"Your name is fine. Or Howard's name. That's probably better."

"Either way, this is fraud."

"Oh, for the love of God, just give it to me," Skylar says. She takes the pen from Clemi, scrawls something on the signature line, then hands back the check.

Clemi holds the check hesitantly between her thumb and forefinger like it's radioactive.

"Also, I should have suggested that you call Mr. Samaraweera.

He might know what's going on. And maybe he'll be able to take care of this somehow."

"Oh, the treasurer? Funny, I emailed him just before you got here. Let me see if he's replied."

She checks her messages, and indeed, he has: "I'm out of town until tomorrow, but stop by my place Thursday and we can discuss."

"He says he'll see me Thursday."

"That's great. But take care of yourself first. There's an urgent care on the corner of Porter and Connecticut. Do you want me to drop you off on my way to pick up my kids?"

This is tempting, given how awful she is beginning to feel, but Clemi does not want to be a burden, nor does she want to be associated with the double-parked Mercedes that has paralyzed the street for nearly thirty minutes. People might throw rocks at them as they exit the building.

"No, I'm fine, really. I can go later, after I sort this out."

"I'm a mom, and I'm telling you that you sound pretty bad. I'm basically ordering you to come with me right now. Don't worry so much about WLNP. We've survived far worse problems than whatever is happening right now."

Chapter 7

SKYLAR WAS NOT wrong to insist on taking Clemi to urgent care. Until the cool, soothing nebulizer treatment begins to filter through her system, she had not realized the extent to which she'd been struggling to take in air. Like a frog being slowly boiled alive, she had begun to acclimate to the diminished oxygen flow.

"Asthma," the doctor says.

"I do not have asthma," Clemi says.

"You do now."

"Maybe just a little bit then."

"No such thing," he says. "That's like being a little bit pregnant."

Clemi is somewhat puzzled by this equivalency, which strikes her as wrong on both counts, but then, she hasn't gone to medical school.

"Does this mean I'm allergic to *all* cats? Or just this one? What about dogs? Or rabbits? Or guinea pigs? I once had a friend who only learned she was allergic to camels when she took a camel ride on a trip to India and couldn't stop sneezing!"

The doctor does not want to engage in this conversation, evidently. He is not a good-bedside-manner kind of guy, but who can blame him, given the accumulation of patients in the waiting room? Instead, he sends prescriptions for two different asthma inhalers plus two allergy meds to the pharmacy and gives her a referral to an allergist before heading out the door with the forceful suggestion to stay away from cats.

Eventually someone else pops into the room to check on the amount of liquid left in the canister from which she is drawing puffs of air. He then takes her pulse and presses a stethoscope to her chest.

"Just another ten minutes or so," he says. "Then we'll test your oxygen levels again."

Clemi nods, then gives a thumbs-up.

"What are you reading?"

She almost forgot that on her lap is the LSAT study guide. She keeps lugging this thing around but has yet to open it, which may or may not be a sign. She has the nebulizer mask on, so rather than remove it, she hoists the *LSAT Logic Games Primer*—"Higher Score Guaranteed!"—and presses the book toward him like she is presenting him with a plaque.

"Oh, the LSAT. My sister took that last year. She says it's easy once you crack the code. She's now a first-year at Harvard."

One benefit, perhaps the only benefit, of having a mask clamped to her face is that she is not expected to answer, to say, "Hooray for your sister who cracked the code and is now a first-year at Harvard!" Instead, she gives him another thumbs-up.

After he leaves the room and the door clicks behind him, she decides to finally open this thing, oddly embarrassed for reasons she can't articulate, other than law school feeling like a cliché of a thing for a frustrated wannabe writer to do.

The Literati

She brushes past a few pages of what read like the same inspirational aphorisms employed by the yoga teacher last weekend—embrace your intrinsic worth, drown out the negative voices in your brain, you do you, et cetera—except in this case, the pep talk is geared toward a person's ability to master this test by simply following the tips that will be shared in the following pages, "Higher Score Guaranteed or Your Money Back!"

She opens the book to the first sample question:

In a single day, exactly seven clowns—Sam, Tom, Ursula, Wendy, Xochitl, Yann, and Zeke—are the only clowns to arrive at the circus. No clown arrives at the same time as any other clown, and no clown arrives more than once that day. Each clown wears either green or red (but not both). The following conditions apply:

Seriously? What does this have to do with practicing law? Perhaps she has misread the prompt. She looks back at the page and continues.

No two consecutive clowns wear red.

Yann arrives at some time before both Tom and Wendy.

Exactly two of the clowns that arrive before Yann wear red.

Sam is the sixth clown to arrive.

Zeke arrives at some time before Ursula.

Her head hurts from simply imagining the sorts of questions that are likely to ensue, as well as the alphabet soup of multiple-choice answers.

Which one of the following could be the order, from first to last, in which the clowns arrive?

X, Z, U, Y, W, S, T

X, Y, Z, U, W, S, T

Z, W, U, T, Y, S, X

Z, U, T, Y, W, S, X

U, Y, T, S, W, X, Z

W, T, F.
This seems the only logical answer, but it is not one of the options.

She places seven short lines at the bottom of the page as if she is playing hangman, then stares at her piece of paper. She has some questions that the prompt fails to address.

- Are any of the clowns related, and might this impact their desire to arrive together and/or avoid one another? (e.g., perhaps Xochitl and Ursula are cousins, and one of them has been left out of their grandmother's will.)

The Literati

- Are any of the clowns involved in romantic relationships, either with another clown in this particular arrival scenario, or with some unnamed clown, that might impact their desire to arrive together and/or avoid one another? (e.g., perhaps Xochitl and Ursula are at this time lovers, or they are former lovers who can no longer abide seeing one another.)

- Does any clown owe money to another clown (or clowns)? (e.g., perhaps Xochitl paid the down payment on the condo she and Ursula once occupied together, but now that they have split up and Ursula has kept the condo, she owes Xochitl more than $25,000, and in fact Xochitl is considering hiring Tom, a disbarred attorney, to try to get the money back, and therefore would like to arrive at work around the same time as he does so they can discuss.)

This is only the beginning. She could go on and on. And on. Still, she forces herself to stay inside this sadly limited, unimaginative box. She rereads the prompt and sees at least one clue: Clearly, the answer is not E, because Sam is the sixth clown.

This is an extremely exciting development. Perhaps she can become a lawyer and function as one after all. It provides her the encouragement she needs to press on.

If Yann arrives before Tom and Wendy, she can knock option D off the list of options. As well as C.

But whether the order might be Xochitl, Zeke, Ursula, Yann, Wendy, Sam, Tom, or Xochitl, Yann, Zeke, Ursula, Wendy, Sam, Tom . . . she doesn't even know how to begin figuring this out.

All of this mental exertion, plus the soothing white noise of the nebulizer machine, is making her sleepy, and the next thing she knows she is asleep, and she is dreaming about clowns. Red clowns and green clowns. Blue clowns and yellow clowns. Big clowns and small clowns. Clowns embracing. Clowns fighting. Clowns in cars! Clowns in trees! Go, clowns, go!

She is awakened by the nurse, who has returned to remove the mask. He listens to her breath again, then takes her vitals and declares her much improved, reminding her that the doctor has sent prescriptions to the pharmacy.

"Good luck on the LSAT!" he says. "Really, once you figure it out, it will be a piece of cake."

Wednesday

Chapter 8

AT LEAST THIS time, when the fire alarm goes off in the fancy new building where she is plant-sitting, Clemi is prepared. It is only 5:38 a.m., but she is already dressed. She has heeded the 5:00 a.m. alarm on her phone, put on yoga pants and a t-shirt, pulled her hair into a ponytail, and slipped into her pink and grey training shoes, purchased when she first moved into Fiona's apartment and vowed to go to the gym every day.

Maybe she hasn't gone every day, but she is doing her best. She needs to stay balanced and focused, and nothing balances and focuses a person more than yoga, or so she has heard, although this has not been her experience. Her experience has been the opposite. It has been destabilizing and humiliating. At that first yoga class she'd gone to, she had kicked the person next to her in the face when she flipped her dog in the wrong direction. As if she had not already attracted enough unwanted attention with her clumsiness, she had forgotten to put her cell phone on silent, and River had begun to aggressively text her midclass.

After class she had tried to work in some aerobic exercise but was thrown off the treadmill when she set it to interval training and ramped it up accidentally to quadruple speed. Had she not fallen into the arms of a trainer who was serendipitously standing nearby, she might have made headlines: "Freak Treadmill Accident at Upscale Washington Gym Fells Scandal-Plagued Nonprofit Employee."

Nevertheless, she has not given up on the idea of becoming fit and finding inner peace, if only because the gym is right here, and it is free.

Although the fire alarm has been wailing loudly for more than five minutes, Clemi takes her time. She is feeling great now that she can breathe. Her thinking might be a little muddled from the meds, but she slept well, is strangely energized, and is ready to tackle the various WLNP problems at hand. Ready, even, to persevere with the red- and green-clad clowns. She has *LSAT Logic Games* tucked under her arm.

Her neighbors seem equally unbothered by the alarm. As she exits her apartment, she sees the couple in the unit next to hers emerge in matching pajama sets adorned with moose. One of them even has his pillow. Clemi then bumps into another set of neighbors, two women being pulled toward the elevator by an exuberant terrier. Together, they all shuffle down the stairs and spill out onto the sidewalk.

She is the first to arrive in the studio, ten minutes before the six o'clock class is set to begin. As an early bird, she has her choice of mats—no need to humiliate herself in the front row. And yet she finds herself drawn to a place by the window, the same spot as last time. She sees the evacuees spread out on the curb, including one person wrapped in a blanket like a burrito, who appears to have gone back to sleep. Others are pacing. Most everyone is staring at a phone. She can also see into the apartments across the way, including her own, awash in the green tint of the many plants that have been left in her charge.

She settles into lotus mode and decides to use the next ten minutes to consider the clowns, to attempt to determine whether Yann is wearing red or green and whether Xochitl arrived before or after Yann or before Tom and Wendy.

She flips open the book and lands on a page with the following suggestion:

"Keep your focus on the 'need to know,' and don't get caught up in the 'nice to know.'"

She underlines this. She gets that this pertains to the stupid clowns and whatever stupid prompts are forthcoming in this book, but it sounds prophetic too, like something the Wizard of Oz might say. Also, it seems weirdly applicable to her life.

What does she actually *need* to know to get through the next three days? She is a person who likes to keep lists, often in brand-new notebooks using brand-new pens and sometimes employing colorful highlighters and stickers, as if by spending money on items to help her organize and then creating visually pleasing notations, her various problems will more easily resolve. Since she has no such notebook in front of her, she flips to a blank page at the back of the study guide and makes a to-do list:

Find a public intellectual.

Figure out WLNP finances (e.g., pay caterer, purchase first-class air travel).

Sort out personal finances. (How long can I exist at this job? Should I quit? How will I pay for law school? etc.)

Do something about the subpoena (but what?).

Buy cat food.

She could keep going—the pileup is massive—but she is distracted by the arrival of two fire trucks outside the window, sirens wailing, kaleidoscopic colors flashing, uniformed fire people spilling out and beginning again with the charade of inspecting the building and giving the *all clear*.

A few people trickle into the yoga studio, then a few more. The instructor appears and fidgets with the lights and music. Fleetwood Mac's "Landslide" is sung, or rather mangled, by an unidentifiable cover band who washes through the speaker. Clemi returns her attention to the LSAT guide for a few more minutes, and when she next looks up, the room is nearly full. Next to her is the same vaguely familiar man as last time.

She studies him in his very put-together yoga outfit. He looks techy in some hard to pinpoint way; she makes assumptions about his paycheck based on what appears to be his ability to (a) belong to this gym and (b) purchase a new yoga ensemble from the shop downstairs, where even a water bottle costs upward of forty bucks. How does she know this about his outfit? Because it is emblazoned with the name of the gym.

She studies him out of the corner of her eye. This morning he has tamped his hair down with some expensive-smelling product that is wafting in the direction of her mat, but he is otherwise the same: same delicate features, same serious gaze, same wire-rimmed glasses placed neatly on a towel at the foot of the mat. How does this person manage to be such an enigma age-wise? This analysis of her fellow yogi is interrupted by the instructor, who tells them to assume a child's pose.

An hour later she is on her way back to the locker room when she hears someone calling to her.

"Miss, I think you left your book."

She turns and sees the familiar-looking man.

He presses *LSAT Logic Games* toward her, and she feels a wash of embarrassment.

"Oh, that!" she says, flustered. "Funny, I don't even think of that as a book."

"It looks like a book," he says.

"Yes, it's definitely a book!"

She wishes she had left behind a different book, something more literary, so they might be engaging in a more interesting conversation, if only because she likes to talk about books.

"Oh. Okay. Well, goodbye!" he says.

"Wait! Sorry, I'm sure you're in a hurry and this is really awkward, but you look familiar. Do you live around here? Or do you maybe know my mom?"

"I am living here temporarily. And I don't think I know your mom," he says. "But I suppose that depends on who you are."

"Are you a writer?" she asks, evading the implicit question.

"Yes."

"Seriously? It is such a small world. Everyone is a writer. Even people who can't write are writers. They especially."

What is she even saying? She recalibrates. She means no disrespect to aspiring writers—she is well aware that she, too, might fit into this category. It is almost certainly River who inspires this snarky remark.

"I didn't mean you, of course! I'm sure you're a great writer! What do you write? Fiction?"

"Content."

"Ah! Content! That's great!"

What is wrong with her? What is she even saying? Why does she feel the need to punctuate everything with an exclamation point?

"Content . . . for what? If that's okay to ask."

"Content for a new travel start-up. I'm in the area for another week, gathering material. Local restaurants, hotels, gyms, that sort of thing. In fact, I'm going to include this gym, which is why I'm here."

"Ah. Sounds like a fun job. With fun perks! Anyway, sorry to have kept you. You just look familiar, not sure why."

"It's okay. I get that a lot, really."

"You get what?"

"I get people confusing me with Malcolm."

"Strange. I must know this Malcolm too."

She runs through the various Malcolms she has known, which are not many. *Malcolm in the Middle*. Malcolm X. Janet Malcolm, but that's the wrong order of name. Malcolm Johnson, who was in Clemi's first-grade class and who used to entertain people by singing the alphabet backward. Malcolm Gladwell. She looks back at the writer of content and blurts out: "Malcolm Gladwell! Yes! That's it!"

"Yes, apparently," he says, unimpressed by her conclusion. "The first time it happened, the barista at Starbucks didn't even ask me my name, just wrote *Malcolm* on my cup. I stood there for, like, fifteen minutes waiting for my order until he came over and handed it to me. I mean, I was the only one there, so I guess I should have realized . . . and then he started to ask me questions about the book *Blink*, so I googled Malcolm and *Blink* and voilà!"

"Yes. *Blink: The Power of Thinking Without Thinking*. But really he's better known for *The Tipping Point*."

He is still stuck on *Blink*, evidently. "What does 'thinking without thinking' even mean?"

"It must mean being intuitive. Making snap decisions. Going with your gut. Kind of like how everyone assumes you are him even though you appear to be younger."

"I'm thirty-seven. Next week I'll be thirty-eight."

"Oh, happy almost birthday!"

"Thank you."

She stares at not-Malcolm for a moment, taking him in. It is uncanny, the resemblance. She remembers reading something recently about doppelgängers, about how we likely all have them, and that we may share DNA even if we are not related.

She is working on formulating a sentence to this effect, but not-Malcolm looks at his phone and says, "Well, I need to get going. I have a private tour of the Library of Congress this morning. Enjoy your book."

Chapter 9

AS CLEMI APPROACHES the WLNP office, she sees a figure heading toward the building's front door. She tenses, remembering yesterday's subpoena-server. But this doesn't look like a subpoena-server, not that she means to put all subpoena-servers in a box.

As she draws closer, she sees it is a very pretty Asian woman in a floral summer dress. She is wearing tortoiseshell cat-eye sunglasses and has skin that glows, possibly from one of those moisturizers with special properties available exclusively on Instagram but usually out of stock. On her feet are strappy sandals that nicely complement the dress. Clemi considers asking questions about her outfit and her skincare regimen but is aware that might seem weird. Her restraint is definitely a good thing, because now that they are face-to-face, Clemi sees that the woman looks angry. Then she remembers the divorce attorney on the third floor. Perhaps this is where she is headed.

Whatever she is doing here, she is blocking the door and staring hard at Clemi.

"Excuse me," Clemi says, shifting the heavy bag of cat food into her left arm.

The woman does not move. Clemi tries again.

"Sorry to be a pest, but if you could just scoot over an inch or so, I need to open the door."

"Is he up there?" the woman asks.

"Is who up where?"

"The thief."

"I'm sorry. I don't know what you are talking about," Clemi says, inputting the code to unlock the door.

The woman squeezes in behind her and follows her up the steps.

This is more than a little creepy. She is following Clemi so closely that it feels threatening. They continue past the second-floor landing. Evidently, she is not planning to patronize the Institute of Thought. They pass the therapist's office and now, rather concerningly, they move beyond the attorney's office without stopping. She continues to follow Clemi toward the fourth floor, where WLNP is the sole occupant.

Clemi stops mid-flight and turns to the woman. "Can I help you?"

"*Can you* help *me?*" she echoes, as if this question is absurd. "I don't know. You tell me."

"Um, the only thing on the top floor is a literary nonprofit, so maybe I can redirect you?"

"Is he there?" she repeats.

"Like I already asked, is who where?"

Clemi hopes the woman does not have a weapon concealed inside her pretty summer dress. A knife strapped to a thigh or such, the kind of thing one sees in action movies.

"Let me rephrase the question. Is my husband up there?"

"Your husband? Oh! Are you Howard's wife?" Clemi says,

extending her hand. "Mae, right? I've heard so much about you!" She doesn't know why she says this, other than her knee-jerk reflex to be polite. She has heard nothing about her. She was not aware that Howard even had a wife until she received the subpoena yesterday. Looking at Mae Zhang in this light, they certainly seem—on a superficial level, at least—like a charmed couple. She, so beautiful and composed, even in anger; Howard, with his pressed shirts and prep-school good looks.

"Well, I haven't heard a thing about *you*," she says.

Does this woman think Clemi is . . . the other woman? A home-wrecker? Is *that* what's going on? Gross! She wants to tell her that she does not find Howard attractive in the least, even if she supposes that in a classical sense, he is a good-looking man. Not only is he too old for her, but also she is put off by his constant boasting and gossiping.

"That's probably because I'm new. I started last week. And I don't know where Howard is. I'd really like to find him though."

Clemi unlocks the door, lets her into the office, and waves her arms to indicate the absence of Howard.

"See? I don't know where he is. But he's left this cat."

"Stupid cat," Mae says. "He knows I'm not a cat person. But did that stop him from bringing one home?"

Clemi assumes the answer to that question is no.

"He loves that stupid cat more than he loves his family. Never have you seen a grown man more attached to a useless pet."

Immanuel remains very still, apparently choosing to rise above these slights.

"Then again, the cat is the only one who's not on to him and his lies."

"His *lies*?"

"*Please*. I don't know the last true thing he might have told me. He's nothing but smoke and mirrors. I bet he told you he is a bestselling author in the Netherlands."

"Yes, the books sound intriguing. I'm a big Wallander fan."

Mae Zhang lets out an amused huff as Clemi silently runs through what she knows about Howard, wondering what might be true and not. "I don't want to disillusion you, but he's not a bestselling author. He published one book, and it sold approximately eighty-three copies."

"Oh," Clemi says. She's not sure how she has wound up in the middle of this, whatever *this* even is.

Mae Zhang scans the room as if Howard might be crouching in the corner. She walks over to the bathroom and opens the door, then looks in the closet. "He has the car keys. I'm going to assume this part was a mistake, give him the benefit of the doubt since he didn't take the car. I scoured the house, then came here and looked around yesterday but couldn't find them anywhere. Any chance you've seen them?"

"Oh! Was that *you*? Did you make this mess?" Clemi asks, waving toward the filing cabinet.

Mae ignores this question. "The kids had a soccer game in Virginia. And I had no car."

"How did you even get in?" Clemi asks absurdly.

"Please," Mae says. "I told him he ought to change the code. But he never listens to me. Anyway, I figured I'd check one more time in case he'd been here, had maybe left the keys."

"No, sorry, I don't know where he is, and I know nothing about the keys. When I got to work yesterday, the place looked like this," she says, indicating the general disarray. "And like I said, this cat was sitting on his desk."

"That's such a Howard move. I told him to take his effing cat, and what does he do? He dumps it in the office. On you."

"Well, it is a problem, I must say. I'm allergic. I was at urgent care yesterday. I'm pumped up on so many meds right now that I could probably go to work at a vet, but obviously that's not sustainable long-term. Is there any chance you could take the cat back until you and Howard sort out whatever is going on?"

"No effing way. I'm sorry about your allergies, but even if hell froze over and my you-know-whats fell off, I wouldn't take this cat."

Immanuel stares hard at Mae Zhang. He seems to understand the depths of her dislike.

Clemi realizes she is still holding the heavy sack of cat food, clutching it to her chest like a shield. She now sets it down in front of Immanuel as a show of allegiance.

"I suppose I can hang on to him for another day or two, but we have to figure something out soon because . . . well, because I don't want to keep taking these meds, plus I don't know what is happening here, how long I'm going to stick around. There are a lot of little—well, really not so little—problems piling up."

"No doubt. But if Howard isn't here, and you don't know where he is, how did you know what kind of food to get?"

"He texted about the cat food, but that was it. I responded, but my message wouldn't go through. His phone seems to have either gone dead or been disconnected."

Mae looks skeptical.

"I wish I could reach him, truly. I'm kind of worried about the cat. He doesn't seem to be eating anything. Unless maybe he finally did," Clemi says, walking over to the bathroom to check the bowl. "Nope, he still hasn't eaten a thing."

"He's fussy. Just dump out the old food and fill it with new. And don't worry about him. I mean, look at him—he's obviously got plenty of fat reserves. He's not going to starve."

They stare at the very large cat, appraising. It's true. Immanuel is in no danger of wasting away anytime soon. Not only is he well upholstered, but he also appears to have been sitting in this same spot for at least twenty-four hours, as if he's powered down, conserving calories.

"I don't mean to pry, but I saw the subpoena. Does that have anything to do with Howard being missing?"

"Why don't you tell me?"

"Tell you what?"

"Where Howard is? Where my car keys are? Where the money has gone?"

"Honestly, I have no idea what's happening here. All I know is the award ceremony is on Friday, and I have a lot of problems piling up and no one to help me."

"Have you tried to reach Eric?" Mae asks.

"Yes, I tried. He's in Kenya delivering a keynote."

"No big surprise there." Mae is now rummaging through the papers on Howard's desk. "Are you absolutely certain you haven't seen my keys lying around? Maybe under the cat?" She reaches her hand underneath Immanuel, to no avail. "The asswipe has cleaned out our bank accounts, including the children's college funds and our two retirement accounts. Our personal checking? Less than zero. I learned just this morning that he even refinanced the house and took out a home equity loan, which I don't know how he managed since the house is in both of our names. And I guess now I'll have to get new car keys made. Do you have any idea what that will cost?"

"Wait, seriously?" Clemi reflects on what she has seen so far of WLNP's accounts. Clearly, something extremely bad is going on.

"Yes, seriously. When I realized what had happened, I called a lawyer and filed for divorce. The lawyer suggested we subpoena the WLNP accounts first thing, since we're guessing he parked the money there.

"So, while I hate to make this your problem, whoever you are," Mae Zhang says, looking at Clemi, "you might want to run for your life if you are not already a part of this."

"Well, it might be too late for that. I opened the subpoena yesterday—which was a funny coincidence, since I had just made the decision to go to law school, and then I was served my first subpoena!"

Mae Zhang looks at her blankly, evidently failing to see the humor.

"Anyway, Skylar helped me get into a couple of the WLNP accounts yesterday afternoon, and it looks like they've also been drained."

"*Skylar Rockefeller?* What was she doing here?"

"I think it was Skylar Papadopoulos. The intern?"

"Oh, that's right. She remarried again. Howard and I went to her second wedding. It was spectacular. That one was in New York. At the Guggenheim. They cleared out the entire museum for her. I guess that didn't last long. Wait . . . Skylar is an *intern*? And what do you mean by *drained*?"

"I mean I checked two of the three bank accounts, and they are basically empty."

"There must be some other accounts. Maybe he opened a new one?"

"I guess anything is possible. Do you have any sense of how much was supposed to be in the WLNP accounts?" Clemi is not sure whether this is the sort of thing that might constitute pillow talk in a marriage. Further, who could say if Howard and Mae Zhang talked, period, given how it was clearly not an especially transparent marriage, at least not when it came to finances.

"I don't know the balances, if that's what you are asking me. But my understanding was that WLPN had about half a million in cash reserves. He mentioned that most recently, when we talked about his plan to ask Eric whether the board might approve a raise. He felt underappreciated as well as underpaid, so he'd say stuff like, 'With half a million dollars just sitting there gathering dust, you'd think they could at least give me a cost-of-living increase.' And I'd urge him to ask for more. I don't think Eric is cheap. I think he's just living in his own head most of the time."

"I don't know anything about all that, but I can tell you he's left me with a lot to figure out," Clemi says. "I have to buy airline tickets, or rather new airline tickets, for this year's winner—I mean, it's Wednesday and she needs to fly tomorrow—and we have to pay the caterer this afternoon."

"That's easy," says Mae. "Just write the caterer a check. The event is Friday. Stall. Say you'll give it to her today, then come up with some last-minute emergency. But make it sound plausible. Then say you'll meet her tomorrow but make it as late in the day as you can, like after the banks have closed. By the time she figures out there's no money on Friday, it will be too late. Just get through the event so you can figure out the rest later. The board will come up with the funds. They're all rolling in money."

"Funny, Skylar told me to do something similar. I mean, I have the check ready. But it makes me really nervous. I don't like lying to people. Plus, I'm a little afraid of Penelope. She sounded kind of threatening yesterday."

"Don't worry about it. You're just doing your job."

Is Clemi just doing her job? Maybe she didn't sign the thing, but still, she is not entirely innocent here. She doesn't want to get disbarred before she's even become a lawyer.

"I'll leave you to it. But let me know immediately if you hear from my future former husband."

"Sure, but I don't know how to reach you."

"Give me your phone. I'll type in my contact info."

"Please let me know if you hear from him too," Clemi says, handing over her phone. "I'm not sure what I'm meant to do."

"You look like a smart girl," Mae says, opening the door and turning to leave. "You will figure it out."

Chapter 10

CLEMI WILL FIGURE it out!

But what, exactly, is she trying to figure out? She has already gone over the list of accumulating problems ad nauseum. Perhaps the thing she ought to figure out is why she is still here, presiding over this mess, but she has gone over that question ad nauseum, too, although perhaps it needs a little recalibration given that she has now glimpsed the bank accounts and the mess has grown exponentially worse.

That, plus her mother's comment nags. She really ought to better understand the scandal she referred to. Where does Ezra Pound fit into the picture? Ditto for Skylar's comment about "the whole Nazi thing." Add to this equation the reference to a "crisis consultant" in the email from Eric Jolly, MD.

Perhaps now is the time to run for her life. Or at least do a bit of belated sleuthing.

She had, of course, looked up WLNP before accepting the job, but she had stupidly—*naïvely!*—failed to look beyond WLNP's own website, a functional if architecturally outdated compendium of facts that included the nonprofit's mission statement and a catalog of all award winners for the past sixty years, since it was founded in 1965.

She types into the search bar on the hulking desktop computer the words *WLNP* and *Nazis* and *Ezra Pound*, and bingo: Up pops an article from *The New Yorker*, circa three years ago, with the title "Arthur Muller Visits the Bughouse." The article was written by Javier Jiménez-Jiménez.

What the what? The very same dearly departed Jiménez-Jiménez who was meant to be the public intellectual on Friday? Presumably, yes. How many Javier Jiménez-Jiménezes can there be, especially with a connection to WLNP?

She begins to read and learns that Arthur Muller, who was born in 1925, had been a novelist—a minor novelist, as her mother might say, possibly even a failed one, depending on which of her several harsh metrics she used. Clemi recalls taking a special order for his one and only novel while working at the bookstore, but it turned out to be out of print.

She reads on. She was already aware, thanks to her mother, that WLNP had once been called the Arthur Muller Foundation. But apart from a vague familiarity with him as a (minor, possibly failed) novelist, she knows very little about him.

Young Arthur was raised in New York, attended Harvard, and had been a conscientious objector during World War II, she learns. Interesting, but it seems to be the usual biographical stuff until she sees that in 1943 he did a stint in the Danbury, Connecticut, federal prison for objecting. While in prison he met the poet Robert Lowell, who was doing time for the same.

Robert Lowell *and* Ezra Pound have something to do with WLNP?

Clemi pauses, bracing herself. *Please, dear God, let this not be about poets, please.* She knows more than she would like to know about famous poets and their messy lives—her estranged, famous, alcoholic poet-father being exhibit A. And she is pretty sure that Robert Lowell was no exception to the messy, complicated poet situation based on what she recalls of his tumultuous marriages and multiple hospitalizations for bipolar disorder.

She presses on: Evidently young Arthur became enamored with Robert. They stayed in touch postprison, and at some point Arthur decided that he, too, wanted to be a poet.

Short version: Arthur was not a natural-born poet. Robert Lowell, in turn, was. They stayed in touch, but after a few years, Arthur began to get on Robert's nerves with his unrelenting letters and his pleas for Robert to help him publish his lousy poetry. Robert tried to cut off the correspondence. He was subtle at first. Then, over time, less so:

"Please do not ever write to me again," Robert wrote to Arthur.

"If you continue to pester me with letters, I shall be forced to retain legal counsel and have them issue a cease and desist."

Clemi stops to recap: Arthur Muller, the founder of WLNP, was a stalker.

Nice.

She reads on. It gets juicier, more complex.

At the time of the cease-and-desist threat, Robert Lowell was living in Washington, DC, serving as Consultant in Poetry to the Library of Congress. Arthur, too, was living in Washington! (Whether he was already a resident of DC or moved there to be closer to Robert is unclear, Jiménez-Jiménez explains, but evidence leans toward the latter.)

Lowell had long been enamored of the famous Modernist poet Ezra Pound, who at that point had been committed to

St. Elizabeths Hospital, also in Washington, DC. Pound had been charged with treason but pronounced insane, thereby evading the death penalty. The treason charges stemmed from his radio broadcasts critical of then-president Franklin Roosevelt, and his support of Hitler and Mussolini. He thought Jews were responsible for World War II.

Clemi is somewhat puzzled—Ezra Pound was considered psychotic because he was a fascist? This is intriguing, but it seems a deep dive for another day.

Ezra Pound received many visitors in Chestnut Ward, where he was interned while at St. E's. These turned into regular gatherings. Literary salons. On Tuesdays, Thursdays, Saturdays, and Sundays, various literary luminaries would make their way along Asylum Road, sign the visitors' log, and share mayonnaise sandwiches, chocolate brownies, peach candy, and jasmine tea. Robert Lowell visited, as did T. S. Eliot, Elizabeth Bishop, and William Carlos Williams, along with a conspiracy theorist or two or ten.

Arthur Muller was not invited.

He tried to network his way into one of these gatherings, to no avail. Even the publication of his novel failed to open any avenues to tea with the bughouse literati.

However! Arthur learned from a friend of a friend that Ezra was a tennis player, and in need of partners. So he finagled his way in, masquerading as a tennis coach who could help him improve his backhand.

Arthur's journals, discovered by his daughter after his 2014 death, describe Ezra on the court: "He was by then a man in his early sixties, but he hopped around the court like a manic bunny rabbit."

When Arthur's daughter discovered his papers and made the

connection between the name of the prize and Ezra Pound (the Chestnut Prize for Prescient Fiction evidently drawing from the name of the psychiatric ward, and the "prescient" part quite possibly having to do with . . . well, who knows, but there are many possible applications to do with Pound's vision and the modern political landscape), she contacted Jiménez-Jiménez, whom she knew because their kids had gone to the same preschool.

The very long Jiménez-Jiménez article includes several excerpts from Muller's journals describing multiple courtside conversations about Hitler as a martyr. About *Mein Kampf* as a work of art. About Jews controlling the media and the Federal Reserve.

His journals record more than twelve visits with Ezra—all confirmed by the hospital's visitors' log.

Clemi is . . . confused. Very. So many questions, but in the need-to-know category: How did Arthur Muller have the money to begin this foundation? How did the foundation, for all these years, manage to be separate from its founder's fascist roots? Also, what's up with Jiménez-Jiménez? From what Clemi can tell, he was responsible for digging up some pretty unflattering dirt on the founder of this nonprofit. So why was he invited to be the public intellectual at the gala?

She reads on: Family money is unsurprisingly the answer. Also, no one paid a lot of attention to Arthur given that he suffered a stroke in 1966, the year after the foundation was established in his name, and never fully regained his health. But he had left enough money in his trust to keep the trains running for fifty years, by which point the nonprofit was sort of sustainable without his monthly cash infusions.

Just when Clemi thinks this opus is nearly done, she finds a whole new section of the essay describing the near implosion of the Arthur Muller Foundation after these discoveries were made.

Ah! Here it is, the Berkowitz situation to which her mother referred. According to Jiménez-Jiménez, a young man named Hyman Berkowitz was brought in as the new executive director after someone named Mary Lewis was fired for botching her response to the press when the Muller journals were revealed. (She was evidently quoted in *The Washington Post*, saying, "While we do not endorse the views attributed to Arthur Muller, our founder was a generous philanthropist, and we will continue to honor his legacy. Also, we are not now, nor have we ever been, racist. We once gave an award to Toni Morrison. And we love Jews, and do not believe they control either the media or the Federal Reserve.")

After a series of emergency board meetings, Mary was relieved of her position, and it was determined that the best way to combat charges of racism and antisemitism was to hire a Black Jew.

Enter the next executive director, Hyman Berkowitz, who claimed his mother was Jewish and his father Nigerian. (When questioned about his Nigerian father being named Berkowitz, Hyman explained that he had taken his mother's maiden name.)

Seriously, is this Jiménez-Jiménez article ever going to end? It goes on, and on, and on, and on, and Clemi does not have time to absorb every exquisite detail—she will read it properly later—but skimming through now it she sees . . . ah . . . more scandal! Berkowitz was not really Berkowitz. His real name was Jamie Sánchez, and he was born in Havana. His Catholic family had fled Castro's Cuba.

Evidently, the board imploded all over again upon this discovery. Nearly all members quit, and Eric Jolly, MD, stepped in as president. The crisis consultant was hired. The board, such as it was, decided to take a page out of the NFL playbook, following the Washington Redskins' decision to—after decades of complaint—finally shed its racist name and become the Washington Football Team before eventually becoming the Commanders.

"'Keep your focus on the need-to-know, and don't get caught up in the nice-to-know,'" she reminds herself. None of this is her immediate concern. She is going down a rabbit hole when all she wanted to learn was . . . well, what was it she even wanted to know?

———

She stops reading the Jiménez-Jiménez opus and returns to the open tab of the log-in page for TD Bank. She then tries two combinations of *herring*, ampersand, question mark, the at sign, and the numbers four and five, and is about to give up for fear of locking the account when she randomly tries a different order: herring&?@5. Miraculously, the account opens with the greeting: "Good afternoon, Hyman Berkowitz!"

Um, okay. So no one has bothered to update the bank account since all of this happened some four years ago. But she is so excited by her success at hacking her way in that she says aloud, "Good afternoon, TD Bank!"

As she begins to study the account, she quickly grows less cheery. It is not a very good afternoon after all. Someone made a withdrawal of $2,000 this morning, and the account balance now stands at $39.21.

Chapter 11

REALLY WHAT SHE should have done was to follow Mae Zhang out the door. It wouldn't have taken much. She hasn't brought many personal items to work yet; all she has here is a cache of Moleskines and a cupholder full of colorful pens. All she'd need to do to permanently exit this place is grab those few items along with her LSAT prep guide and walk down the stairs.

So why on earth do I continue to stand here? she wonders yet again.

She looks at Immanuel as if he might have the answer. And maybe he does, transmitted kinetically—no, *catnitically!*—because she begins to process a semiproductive thought:

She has a job, even if she is employed by a nonprofit with a shady crypto-fascist past. WLNP might or might not be imploding, but at least the organization is making an effort to relegate its past to the dustbin of history—leaning into the problem, even, by inviting the late Javier Jiménez-Jiménez, the man who aired their dirty laundry in the national media, to be a guest of honor at the gala. (She assumes this was on the advice of said "crisis consultant.")

Moreover, common wisdom holds that it's better to apply for a new job when you are employed. So what she ought to do is stay put, do her job, and begin to look for alternate employment. That said, she is aware that looking for a job when she has been employed for all of five days does not make her an especially attractive candidate.

It's rough out there, from all she's heard; she has at least three friends who have recently been laid off. Rana, a childhood friend with whom she is still in touch, at least in a social media kind of way (they fill each other's Instagram feeds with heart emojis, and sometimes make plans, which they then let drift), had a very cool marketing job working for an emerging makeup brand. She earned more than double what Clemi was making at the bookstore and got to travel to trade shows all over the country. Plus she got free product, which she bartered with colleagues working for other luxury brands. (At the bookstore, Clemi got all the free book galleys a person could possibly want, and sometimes she scored free finished books, albeit ones whose pages were printed upside down, or whose book jackets were ripped, or whose bindings were coming unglued. While in the great scheme of things Clemi would prefer free books to free makeup products, on certain days she would have gone with the lip gloss.) But last month Rana was let go, and then, a week later, an announcement was made that the entire company had gone bust.

Clemi's other good friend, someone she worked with at the bookstore, had also taken what seemed like a dream job, working as an assistant editor on the book section of *The Washington Post*. But shortly after she was hired, there'd been a round of layoffs, and her job—poof!—vanished. Another colleague,

Autumn, had given up all literary aspirations and moved to Ohio to be closer to her family, and last Clemi heard she was working in an optical shop—so Clemi supposes she ought to hang on to this prestigious-sounding, low-paying job and figure out what to do about the most pressing of the many problems it presents, cat included.

Mae Zhang is right: There must be another bank account somewhere. Clemi doesn't know much about Howard, but he doesn't *seem* like a criminal. Then again, the matter of his possibly having wiped out the Zhang-Zevin retirement and college funds argues against the likelihood of his innocence. Putting a positive spin on that will be hard, but surely there is a logical explanation. The money must be *somewhere*. The bank accounts Skylar helped her access must have been abandoned years ago, back in the inglorious era of Hyman Berkowitz, which is why those old passwords still work. The balances she saw were likely just the dregs of what had been left in the forgotten accounts.

This line of thinking has one glaring flaw, however: Someone has withdrawn $2,000 as of this morning.

She sits very still for a moment, thinking. Truly she does not know what to do. Again she contemplates calling the police. But then, what if she is overreacting? She knows absolutely nothing of WLNP's finances, and as the mere programs director, she probably shouldn't be hacking into the nonprofit's bank accounts to begin with.

She briefly pauses to imagine herself in court, explaining to the jury that she was merely following instructions from the intern, acting on advice from the soon-to-be ex-wife of the missing executive director. Then again, said intern's mother is on the board, so that's almost like having authorization. Besides, the gala is already set: The tickets are sold, the caterer is engaged, the talent is largely secured. All she needs to do is pacify the caterer and get the award winner to Washington.

She uses the landline to make the call, as she does not have an international dialing plan on her cell phone. Even though her mother lives in London—or perhaps because her mother lives in London—she doesn't have WhatsApp or Telegram or FaceTime, either. She inputs the long string of numbers using the rotatory dial, which is so incredibly inefficient she wonders how people got anything done back in the day. She then listens to a long string of clicks, followed by white noise, followed by some beeps and static. Just when she is convinced this is going nowhere, that she has dialed her way into some zombified vortex accessible only through outdated telephone technology, she hears the familiar, elegiac voice of Sveta.

"Hi there! It's Clemi from WLNP," she says in as cheerful a tone as she can muster. "I'm ready to book your tickets! I'll just need your passport numbers."

"Oh, lovely, lovely. Just a minute. Let me get my things."

Clemi waits a few minutes, listening to muffled chatter in the background in a language she does not understand. She also hears birds chirping, a dog barking. Sveta returns a few minutes later and relays to Clemi various strings of numbers: birthdays, TSA PreCheck numbers, passport numbers, expiration dates, as well as seat and dietary preferences. Vlad is an enthusiast of chicken nuggets, apparently. And he likes them fried to a crisp.

Clemi jots all of this down dutifully and then braces herself for the $31,509.86 question. "Great. We are nearly done. Now can you read the credit card number to me?"

There is a moment of silence before Sveta replies, which is not unexpected. *"My credit card?"*

"Yes, it's a courtesy. A new thing we are doing for all the winners, per their requests," Clemi bluffs. "This way you get all of the reward points on your credit card. Assuming you have a credit card with rewards. I mean, we're happy to put it on our card . . . A trip like this will earn a lot of points, and we could definitely use them next year, but it's up to you. If you want to put it on your card, I'll write you a check and give it to you, along with the prize, on Friday."

Clemi can practically hear the churning of brain cells, clicking and hesitating and deliberating from halfway across the world.

"No, I see what you mean," Sveta says. "That's great. You're right; it is a lot of points! Hang on, let me just find my wallet." Another few moments pass while Sveta procures her credit card and then provides the numbers, thus concluding the most expensive transaction of Clemi's life thus far, not counting the rubber check she has yet to pass along.

"Done! The tickets and itinerary should be in your email, and if they aren't, let me know—I've already got them here so I can forward everything."

"Fabulous, my darling Clementine. Can't wait to see you on Friday."

This woman, this Sveta, is so lovely that Clemi lets the other problems fade. This is what it's all about, she reminds herself. Sveta is a gorgeous writer and a lovely person and her literary hero, and *please, dear God, do not let her be faking this thing about her back*. She is possibly the only writer in the world Clemi cares to meet. And she will meet her—on Friday!

"I can't wait either! Just grab an Uber or a cab from the airport, and we'll reimburse you!" Clemi would be feeling more guilty about all of this had Skylar not told her to go ahead with the tickets. Besides, she is confident in the existence of other bank accounts, somewhere. And if not, well... as Skylar said, *someone* will pay up.

To reassure herself of this hypothesis, Clemi returns to her desk and logs back into the Fidelity account. She toggles her way to the transaction log, expecting to see that the last time money went in or out of the account was circa 2019. While she also wishes this to be true, she senses in her heart of hearts that it's possibly not. And it's not. Five days ago, a check made out to Howard Zevin cleared for $23,843, nearly cleaning out the balance of the account. She continues to scroll and sees many, many checks written for roughly $10,000 a pop, cashed monthly over the past two years. She finds the feature that lets you view the image of each check, and she sees that they are all made out to Howard as well as signed by Howard.

She is naïve, she knows well, but she longs for a rational and benign explanation anyway. Maybe Howard was simply writing himself paychecks, which might make sense—her guess is he is earning in the ballpark of $120,000 a year, perhaps a bit less.

She opens the Schwab account and finds a similar situation, except the account was drained about a year before the Fidelity withdrawals began. In this case, no checks were involved. Instead, the money was extracted in the form of wire transfers to a bank she has never heard of—in London.

There is no need to bother with the TD account, which she already knows is down to its last $33.29. But since she is doing this forensic accounting, she might as well see it through to completion, and indeed, the account is now down to $3.29. A cash withdrawal was made this morning for thirty dollars. Presumably, wherever Howard is, he has just funded his lunch.

She is startled by the sudden movement of the cat. Immanuel has decided to leap from Howard's desk to Clemi's, landing on the computer keyboard. He is just inches away, staring straight at her.

"Well, hello, Cat-Who-Should-Not-Be-Sitting-This-Close-to-Me. Where is your friend Howard?" There is no reply. "He has left us in quite the pickle!"

Again, Immanuel does not respond, but that's a good thing, Clemi knows. Were Immanuel to respond, she would be in more trouble than she is already in.

"I'm going out, cat. I need to meet the caterer. Wish me luck."

She hesitates. She feels like she's forgetting something. And she is: food!

She goes into the bathroom and dumps the old fishy-smelling kibble into the trash, refills the bowl with the fresh fishy-smelling stuff, and refreshes his water bowl. She peeks into the bathtub and looks at the litter box, which does not appear to have been disturbed. She wonders whether she should be more concerned. At what point does a cat starve to death? Or dehydrate?

"Okay, Immanuel, you're all set in there," she says. He is rather handsome, this cat, in a sort of brooding, intellectual way, as if he is thinking deep thoughts, philosophizing. The notion makes her laugh. Immanuel the philosopher cat! She remembers, from her freshman year colloquium, reading Immanuel Kant. Another dim memory forms: Kantian ethics. The means—and not the end—of an action determines its moral value. Is that right? Or maybe it's the opposite? Also something about the categorical imperative, something like "do unto others."

She thinks for a minute, trying to squeeze some value from her $266,826.85 liberal arts education—a number her mother recently cited to Clemi in response to a well-reasoned request for a microloan.

"Don't think too hard about what I'm about to do, Kant," she says.

Immanuel looks at Clemi and blinks. Maybe she has it all wrong. Maybe this melancholic gaze is not the churning of the brain so much as the churning of the gut. Maybe he is not lost in thought. Maybe he is constipated.

"And for the love of God, get yourself off that desk, use your litter box, and after that, eat some food."

Chapter 12

SHE IS IN no particular hurry. She is moving slowly, possibly too slowly, contemplating the check in her bag for $40,542.53 that's been drawn from an account with a balance of $39.21. Categorical imperatives notwithstanding, she is doing nothing wrong here. Should you be inclined to postulate that the check happens to be bogus right now, also be prepared to accept that in the spirit of Kantian ethics, this minor infraction is being perpetrated in the name of a greater good. Maybe. If you apply a smidgen of John Locke. She feels she ought to stop right here and write a note of apology to her beloved political theory professor, Dr. Boesche, for not remembering this as well as she should. Regardless, any person or persons inclined to challenge this analysis should do so forthwith or forever hold their tongue.

Clemi is sacrificing pedestrian, some might say bourgeois, ethics in the name of supporting Literature That Is Prescient. Helping people enjoy their fancy night out at the gala, eating their $800 plates of overcooked salmon or, alternatively, rubber chicken or dry mushroom risotto, the latter of which (her selection) is being represented as foraged in the forests of New England—all of which will enable the gala attendees to connect with literary heroes, the toilers of quill, the engineers of human souls! Perhaps this is not a justification, but rather Clemi, supernaturally, tapping into the emanations of the brain of the public intellectual she has yet to identify and secure.

Clemi has an hour before she is meant to meet Penelope at the hotel, and she has decided to walk rather than take the bus. She needs to spend the liminal time ambulating—time in which she can do nothing about the problems at the office or the problems ahead.

It's a bright, clear day utterly devoid of humidity. A thing of perfection weather-wise, an anomaly for Washington, DC. Everyone out walking seems to be in a good mood, or so she thinks until she collides with a woman roughly her age who is walking and texting. Upon crashing right into Clemi, the woman glares at her, no doubt rewriting history to suggest this is not her fault but Clemi's.

Clemi sees a miniature Australian shepherd, or maybe it's one of those Australian shepherd doodles, and in a conscious, *id est* intellectually driven effort to force herself to stop philosophizing, squats down to say hi to the cute dog. The latter growls and nips her hand, which she jerks away, blotting a trickle of blood with a tissue in her pocket. The owner looks the other way. Clemi had always thought herself a dog person, but maybe it's time to rethink her loyalties and get some regular allergy shots; it seems unlikely in the extreme that Immanuel would so resolutely reject her entreaties.

So, okay, maybe not everyone is in a good mood. But Clemi is determined to squeeze a few moments of serenity out of this effed-up day, so she sticks her earbuds in and turns on a Spotify DJ mix, which happens to be tonally all wrong, way too gloomy and emo and not at all what she is in the mood for today. Isn't this AI algorithm supposed to be able to read her mind? She is trying to be upbeat. She needs something with energy, something more Taylor Swiftian.

Winding through the cobblestoned streets of Georgetown, she pauses in front of one particularly stunning row house, so tiny it looks like a house for a mouse, with its brick painted yellow, wrought iron pots on either side of the door with geraniums in early bloom. Two little boys are standing in front of the house, watching a garbage truck in a standoff with a very large U-Haul. One of these vehicles is going to have to back up. But which one? Someone opens the door to the house and calls to the boys, who seem reluctant to go back inside until this duel is fought.

The simplicity of this moment stops Clemi cold. She is not pining for domesticity. She doesn't feel ready for that, doesn't want to be put in charge of sustaining the lives of geraniums, or getting children washed, fed, and into clothes. Yet something here is calling to her. It's the poetry, perhaps, of two little boys drinking in the clash of two trucks.

After another block of sweet little row houses, she hits a stretch of mansions. One of them is set back on such an unfathomably large lot that it might be a hospital or an embassy or a school. Howard told her that some of the board members live in houses like these, and that they sometimes host fundraiser luncheons for WLNP. In fact, he told her, one is coming up in a couple of weeks where she will hand out programs and make sure the guests—especially those with mobility issues, of which there are many, given the average age of the wealthier donors—will be able to find their seats. Now she wonders whether that luncheon will be canceled, considering Howard's disappearance plus what she has discovered in the bank accounts.

That said, given all she has just learned about Nazis, executive directors with false identities, and the near collapse of the board, she wonders whether missing funds would qualify as a catastrophic problem or simply business as usual—nothing to get worked up about.

A few blocks later, she checks the time and realizes that if she is to continue at her leisurely pace while indulging in daydreaming, ruminating, and philosophizing, she'll be late. A shorter route has her weaving through the inside-out part of the city, traversing alleys lined by trash and recycling bins, where she can see into people's yards. She cuts through a parking lot and winds up on Connecticut Avenue, just across the street from the Hilton.

She does not know the language of architecture, but this place, which she has walked by dozens of times without really noticing, now appears to be some incongruous juxtaposition of futuristic and very last-century. There's probably a name for that. Brutalist, perhaps. Or maybe just ugly. Or more politely, someone else's cup of tea.

She makes her way to the entrance and into the lobby, where she is startled, almost accosted, by the dizzying black, white, and grey carpet. It looks somehow atomic. Squinting, it is possible to imagine the shapes are martini glasses. Atomic martini glasses at that. Like something out of the television show *Mad Men*. But she is not here to study interior design; she is here to find a caterer. She scans the room for Penelope. One problem with this plan is that she has no idea what Penelope looks like. Neither does she have her number, nor does Clemi have her work email on her phone.

She looks to the left and sees at least a dozen people sitting in chairs, pecking at laptops or screens large and small. Might one of them be a caterer? What does a caterer look like? None of these people appears to be scanning the room, looking for a nonprofit employee bearing a rubber check for a very large sum.

Only one of them, she can't help but notice, is reading a book, and it happens to be a cute guy who is unlikely to be Penelope. Although who knows? She draws nearer, just out of curiosity, to see what book he is reading, but closer inspection reveals (a) he is not that cute up close but rather is scruffy and possibly in need of a shower, and (b) the book is in another language, possibly German, so whoever he is, he is almost certainly in from out of town or on his way out.

She continues to assess the assembled group. Is Penelope the elegant older woman wearing so many silver chains around her neck that Clemi wonders how she will stand up? Or the short-haired, efficient-looking woman in the business suit and heels who looks like she is about to walk into a courtroom, possibly to address the arrival times of seven red and/or green–clad clowns, hailing to us from the universe of LSAT? Or is she the casually dressed, somewhat schlumpy woman who is talking loudly into her phone, shouting "Hinckley!" over and over, as if the person on the other end is hard of hearing?

Clemi feels a hand on her shoulder. As she turns, startled, she sees what is, in fact, the embodiment of every preconceived notion she might have ever had about what a Penelope might look like, which is, admittedly, the legacy of the preppy girls' school she was forced to attend that was populated by more than a few Penelopes. Perfectly coiffed hair pulled into a side ponytail, a wraparound dress that shows off her svelte physique, kitten heel shoes that look elegant and comfortable at once.

"You must be Clemi," she says.

Clemi wonders whether she, in turn, looks exactly like a Clemi, which she supposes she does with her long orange hair. Freckles, too, which she has long wished she could make disappear. Of average height, average weight, she has been described by her mother as "pretty enough." Enough for what, she has no idea. Then again, perhaps she is easy to identify in that she looks like the programs director of a literary nonprofit, what with her simple cotton summer dress and indie bookstore tote bag hanging from her shoulder.

Clemi puts out her hand to shake Penelope's. As they are exchanging forced pleasantries, the schlumpy-looking woman who had been shouting "Hinckley" into the phone yells the word again so loudly that people turn and stare. Clemi knows this word, this name, but she is having trouble thinking why.

Penelope gestures at Clemi to follow her toward the elevators.

"What is she going on about?" Clemi asks.

"People still can't stop gawking. It's appalling."

"Gawking at what?"

"It's ghoulish," Penelope continues. "It doesn't do anyone any good. Surely you remember back in—"

They are interrupted by the arrival of the elevator, which is already full of people who need to exit with their luggage before Clemi and Penelope can get in. At last, they descend to the lower level, then make their way down the hallway and into an enormous ballroom.

"I don't have much time," Penelope says brusquely. "Let's go over the run of show."

"Sure," Clemi bluffs. "The run of show." She does not know anything about the run of show.

Penelope extracts a mini iPad from the mini bag on her shoulder and pulls up a spreadsheet.

"So are we still set for 242 guests? That would be twenty tables of twelve."

"As far as I know," Clemi says. "I'll double-check when I get back to the office and email the final number by end of day." She knows nothing of the final numbers, but this seems like the right thing to say. Hopefully, she can figure out how to reach Skylar, her lifeline to whatever information is currently attainable.

"Perfect. And Howard sent over the seating arrangements, so I'm guessing nothing has changed?"

"Not that I know of. But I'll get you that info, too, by COB today." Again she is just bluffing her way through this, considering the likelihood of changes. For one thing, Howard probably won't show up, and given recent developments, Mae Zhang won't either. And Sveta is now bringing her son. At least that doesn't change the numbers by much.

"Excellent." Penelope taps at her electronic device, pulling up some very important new data point, presumably.

"Next up, the menu, which is finalized. Just to recap: We will begin with drinks and passed appetizers in the lobby outside the ballroom, and the salads will be set out once the guests are ushered inside. Then, while people are eating their salads, we will play the video about the history of WLNP. Well, some of the history, as I understand it. The revised history."

Now clued in on the Arthur Muller and the Hyman Berkowitz situations, et cetera, Clemi understands this not-so-subtle jab, which feels weirdly personal. She supposes it is personal in a way, now that she is in the WLNP employ.

"After the video, we will clear the salad plates and set out the main course, during which your board president will deliver opening remarks."

Trying to remain calm, Clemi remembers the email from Dr. Jolly mentioning that he was not certain he would make it to the event. Now Clemi adds to her list of anxieties the question of who will make the opening remarks if he doesn't show—especially if Ellen Lapidus, ensconced at her writer's retreat, does not respond and if Howard remains AWOL. She realizes with an anxious start that the task might fall to her.

"And then your board president will introduce your winner."

"Right," Clemi says.

"Then it says in my notes that your treasurer will present the winner with the check . . ."

"Right," Clemi says again. "Fantastic."

"And then your treasurer will also present the silent auction results."

"Exactly!" Clemi says enthusiastically, perhaps to mask the little wave of terror reminding her of the public intellectual auction item.

"So, we are mostly set, but I do have a question about the silent auction," Penelope continues. "People need a chance to bid before everyone is seated, of course, so that should take place during the cocktail hour. We'll have tables with displays of each item. In your case, since only *people* are being auctioned off, we can have giant blowup photos of the authors or whatever. Didi already sent over the signage, so I'm just checking that nothing has changed on that front. What happened to Didi, anyway? I really liked her."

"I have no idea. I never met Didi. But yes, one thing has changed, sadly. Javier Jiménez-Jiménez has passed away. We are looking for a new public intellectual. I'm working on that."

Penelope scowls. "That really messes things up. We already have the giant blowup of his photo."

"I'm sorry," Clemi says.

"Will you be able to get me a photo of the new public intellectual soon? We don't have much time."

"I'm working on it," Clemi says. "I have lines out."

Penelope looks disappointed.

"Okay, I think we are set with everything else. Cocktails, dinner, buffet dessert, we've got the audio tech arriving at five . . . I've got the allergies and food restrictions listed, but let me know if anything else comes up."

"Sure" is all Clemi can think to say.

"I think we are good. Everything is under control. All I need is the check."

"Right here!" Clemi says, perhaps too eagerly as she reaches into her tote bag and produces the dodgy financial instrument that might or might not land her in jail. She is a simple soldier, just following orders, albeit the orders of an intern, and of the AWOL executive director's future former wife.

Anyway, not to worry. Skylar's mother, when she is back from her barge trip, or the treasurer Mr. Samaraweera, will sort it all out, injecting funds into the account ASAP.

Penelope takes the check, studies it, and looks skeptically at Clemi.

"Something about this doesn't look quite right," she says. Which is sort of but not entirely untrue. The check is made out to Penelope, and for the right amount. What more does she want?

"Howard's signature looks a little funky."

"He was in a hurry. He was late for the dentist and was in a lot of pain."

Penelope stares at Clemi, taking her in, assessing her scuffed flats, her scruffy tote bag, her sale-rack dress. As if Clemi is, herself, representative of the funds behind the check. Remarkably, she passes some sort of test.

"You look honest enough, I suppose. I'll take you at your word," she says surprisingly. Even foolishly.

Is this a compliment? Clemi wonders. Does she *want* to look honest? Does that imply she is boring? Would it be better to look dishonest? Like someone with an enviable wild streak, perhaps, a joie de vivre, living the life of an artist, rather than a cog?

Whatever the existential meaning of this comment, Clemi needs to add a caution. "Maybe just wait until tomorrow afternoon to deposit it. We need to move some money around. Transfer some funds."

Penelope's expression begins to slow-motion change. Clemi is half inclined to turn and run out the door.

Mercifully, Penelope's phone chirps. She looks at the screen, and her attention quickly shifts.

"Damn it, my ex was supposed to pick our son up at school today. But, well, let's just say he did not," she overshares. "I've got to run."

Clemi backflashes on her own time spent standing on the curb in the pickup area of her elementary school, wondering whether her mom was running late this time or had forgotten about her. She would not wish this terrible feeling of abandonment on another child, ever, except for right now. *Run, Penelope, run! And don't spend another moment thinking about that check!*

Chapter 13

THE CAT THAT was once here is here no more. Clemi stares at the empty spot on the desk, taking in his absence, musing on how strange it is that in only two days she has grown attached to this creature, even though they have had no meaningful interaction and he has made her so sick that she wound up at urgent care.

Where is Immanuel?

Perhaps he's in the bathroom, hydrating or excreting or finally eating his BLUE BUFfalo Adult Flaked whatever. Any—and all!—of these activities would be good. A cat can only sit in one spot for so long without exercising some of its God-given bodily functions. Or so she presumes. Admittedly, she is not fully up to speed on the digestive systems of cats.

Alas, Immanuel is not in the bathroom. The litter box and the food bowl appear to have been untouched.

Is it possible she is somehow failing to see him? Maybe he has fallen asleep and has keeled over sideways onto the floor, or maybe he has burrowed beneath a sheaf of papers. She looks everywhere she can think of, including under both desks, where she sees dust balls and pieces of debris that were presumably lobbed toward the trash can but missed the mark. In the trash can she sees a candy wrapper and a wadded-up Post-it Note, and some junk mail of the usual sort—credit card solicitations and flyers from real estate agents. This reminds her that WLNP must have a mailbox somewhere, perhaps in the lobby, or maybe at the post office in a rented box. Wherever it is, she wonders if the mail key might be on the same chain Howard has taken with him wherever he has gone, the one containing the key to operate Mae Zhang's car. The list of things she does not know is so long, it boggles the mind. Ditto for the list of things that have gone, and will likely continue to go, wrong.

She looks again on top of the desk, pushing the books and papers around absurdly, as if Immanuel might have shrunk himself to the size of a paper clip and accidently slipped inside an envelope, possibly the one that holds the subpoena. She looks inside the desk drawers because you never know. How a cat might have pulled open a drawer, crawled inside, and shut the drawer again is a mystery, but then, Clemi's mother recently adopted a dog that had been rescued by Ukrainian soldiers in the vicinity of Mariupol. In London, the dog, named Oksana, quickly figured out how to depress the handles on the French doors and take herself on unsupervised strolls around Hampstead Heath.

Clemi finds no sign of the cat, but in the bottom of the three drawers sit three pairs of socks, a small pile of neatly folded light-blue boxer shorts, a toothbrush, and a half-empty bottle of some kind of liquor. She picks up the bottle and sees it still has a gift tag hanging around the neck, with a note written in a foreign script that is possibly Cyrillic. She doesn't know what it says, but the author of this note is aware that Howard cannot read it either, because it has been translated. Beneath the Cyrillic it says, *Zel, spasibo. Thank you. You the man.* It is signed, simply, *H.* She wonders whether *H* has anything to do with Hyman Berkowitz. Or with *H-E-R-R-I-N-G*, the man or the fish.

Although she doesn't know her alcohol varieties especially well, this looks to Clemi to be vodka, and the slim elegant bottle suggests it is not the sort of rotgut that her friends drank in college. She is tempted to take a sip, because why not? It has been that sort of day, but drinking vodka from a bottle in the desk drawer seems like a new low, and it makes her think of her father, who is as famous for his alcoholic binges as he is for his dark, concise verse. He has more than once landed on the front page of the British tabloids. He once drove through the front door of a grocery store, plowing into the meat counter when he confused the gas pedal with the brake, and another time he was pulled over for going the wrong way on the M11 in London. Despite multiple stints in rehab, he has failed to give up the bottle. Even before she knew who her father was—she didn't meet him until a few years ago—she sensed that alcohol was not her friend and has been increasingly careful of her habits of consumption.

She replaces the bottle in the drawer, careful to set it down flat, which requires shifting things around. Her hand brushes a tube of toothpaste, which makes sense given the toothbrush, but then she flips the tube over and sees it is not toothpaste but rather K-Y Jelly.

She nearly screams.

She is about to apologize to Immanuel, but of course he is not here, which is a little sad. Locking eyes with another mammalian creature might have been comforting right now. Could it be that Clemi misses Immanuel?

She closes the drawer and steps away from the desk carefully, as if the tube of K-Y Jelly might explode. Perhaps she is overreacting again. Surely there is a practical, completely benign (i.e., not sexual) reason for keeping K-Y Jelly in the office of a literary nonprofit. But she cannot think of one.

She returns to the bathroom to wash her hands.

So the office is home to vodka and clean underwear and a toothbrush and ointment to enhance sexual pleasure, but apparently no longer a cat. There is only one possible explanation: Howard must have dropped by and scooped up Immanuel, which would be a very good thing for all parties involved. This would mean Howard is alive and in the vicinity, and even if he is on the lam, perhaps he can give her a bit of advice. Also, it means she does not need to worry about how she will continue to breathe.

She pulls her phone from her bag to see whether he has tried to get in touch. He has not, but she has a text from River:

More great news!

Oh boy. She is not sure how much more great news from River she can bear.

You are not going to believe this coincidence. Turns out Augusta bought two tickets to the WLNP gala on Friday, but she can't go. Want to come as my date?

Is he for real? She puts the phone face down on the desk, picks it back up, and turns the volume off before setting it back down.

That doesn't work, really, because she needs her phone to text Howard:

Did you pick up Immanuel?

The text is immediately deemed undeliverable.

She sighs, then sits at her desk and thinks. Her eyes seize on the window, which is only cracked an inch at most. She is mortified that she never thought to close it yesterday, after pulling it open for air. But then, how could such a large cat have squeezed through what amounts to a slit? Might Immanuel have flattened himself like a cartoon cat and found his way out? He is a very large cat, but who knows? There are so many things she doesn't know about the animal world. She once read somewhere that rats can stick their pointy snouts through the tiniest of openings, and then collapse their rib cages to squeeze through. And she has seen on TikTok some kind of salamander that can regenerate limbs. And she has heard of the wood frog that freezes itself in the winter. And of reindeer that switch eye color according to seasons. Why can't cats flatten into pancakes as needed, then revert to their previous shapes?

She looks out the window, down to the street below. Mercifully, no cat has splattered on the sidewalk. Nor is there a cat in the small front garden outside the building. She looks out into the middle distance, and up into the trees. There is no cat anywhere in the vicinity, as far as she can see.

Unless Howard slipped in and out, the only other likely possibility is that Mae Zhang came to get him. Perhaps the Zhang-Zevin kids missed their cat. But given her general attitude about Immanuel, this seems highly unlikely too. Clemi's head hurts from all this rapid churning of scenarios. She needs to stop thinking, to simply act.

She picks her phone back up and sees a long string of messages from River, which she ignores while she phones Mae, who does not answer. She walks over to the window again and yanks it open further, then sticks her head out and calls Immanuel's name.

"You okay up there?" asks a man who has just emerged from an Uber and is approaching the front door.

"Have you seen a cat?"

"I've seen a lot of cats. Do you have a particular cat in mind?"

"A tabby, I think."

"I see you. And you look like quite the tabby," he says.

Ew. She slams the window shut and watches him enter the building. He is on his way to the divorce attorney, no doubt.

Her phone continues to vibrate with missives from River.

Oh duh. Almost forgot you work at WLNP. Of course you will be there!

Trying to decide what to wear!

Never mind! Augusta just texted the info.

Even more good news! Augusta offered her ticket to Martha, and she said yes, so I'll go with her.

Clemi is reminded of those puzzles where you are meant to spot the things that are wrong with the picture: the horse with spots, the typo in the street sign, the upside-down bird in the tree. In this case, in no particular order, the wrongs include (a) River forgetting she works at WLNP, (b) River asking her on a date after they have broken up, and (c) River suggesting that bringing his literary agent—or his wannabe literary agent—is news Clemi will somehow think is good.

She looks around the office one more time for Immanuel, checking the closet and looking, again, under both desks before deciding to call it a day.

Thursday

Chapter 14

CLEMI IS NOT sure what she expects Mr. Samaraweera's place to look like, but she is under the impression that most of the board members of WLNP are of means, and not just of normal means. Means of the luxury vehicle in the driveway, of the housekeepers and gardeners and private cooks, of either ostentatiously large houses or, on the flip side, of elegant, impeccably maintained, ivy-covered Georgetown homes that might be much smaller in nature but probably cost just as much.

Between the board chair who flits around the world promoting his bestselling beauty book and the intern in her double-parked Mercedes, Clemi has drawn certain conclusions, made certain assumptions. So, as she exits the Metro and walks half a mile through a decidedly not gentrified neighborhood of Washington, DC that is dominated by shuttered businesses and boarded-up apartment buildings, she can't help but wonder if she has written down the wrong address.

She sees a cat sitting on the doorstep of a townhouse and feels a pang of guilt about poor Immanuel. How could she have failed at such a simple task? All she had to do was feed and water the poor thing. Even if she would like to strangle her boss, she nonetheless hopes he is alive and well and has simply scooped Immanuel up.

Clemi walks another couple of blocks, past a defunct CVS and the husk of a Hecht's department store, until her GPS tells her she has reached the destination. She stops to double-check the address, then presses the buzzer on the door of a modest apartment building. She hears a burst of intercom static and announces her arrival.

"Hi! It's me! Clemi! From WLNP."

She winces at her too-cheerful voice, at the inadvertent sing-song rhyme.

"Come on up!" a male voice replies in a warm, welcoming tone. "Third floor, second door on the right."

As she treks up the stairs, she catches a whiff of something delicious. Toast, perhaps. She is not good at discerning food smells. Not good at anything to do with food, really, apart from being a talented eater. She can't follow a recipe, is bad at chopping things, and is too lazy to acquire niche ingredients.

When she arrives at the next landing, slightly winded, she catches a whiff of a different sort, something sweet this time, like baked goods. She follows her nose to what appears to be the WLNP treasurer's apartment. A tall, skinny, dapper man wearing a white starched shirt and a navy vest opens the door. Perhaps it's the sweet baking smell or the warmth of his greeting, but she is invested heavily in this visit, hopeful that he is a gentle, lovely soul who will solve all her problems.

"The timing of your email was serendipitous," he says. "We have a week of professional days, and they are letting us use them remotely."

Clemi has no idea what he is talking about, which he evidently deduces from her puzzled expression.

"At school. The kids are not in this week."

She is still confused, but a little wary of making some faux pas. Still, she figures asking is better than not asking at all.

"School?" is all she can think to say.

"Prep Academy, of course. I'm Lucy's teacher."

"Lucy?" The name Prep Academy is equally puzzling.

Now it's Mr. Samaraweera's turn to be confused. He looks at her with suspicion, like maybe she has scammed her way into his apartment and is now going to convince him to convert his retirement savings into Bitcoin.

"I'm sorry, perhaps there has been some mix-up. Tell me your name again?"

"I'm Clemi, the new programs director at WLNP."

"*Ah!* Nice to meet you," he says. "You're *new*. That explains it. I thought you were the other young woman I'd been talking to. But I don't think she and I ever met in person, so I thought you were her. Didi, I think was her name."

"Right. She's gone. Somewhere."

"That's a shame. Anyway, I'm Lucy's teacher. She's a good student. Acing advanced calculus."

"And Lucy is . . . ?"

"Lucy is Eric's daughter."

"Oh, Dr. Jolly! Yes, I've heard about him."

"I've also had a couple of other board members' children in my classes over the years."

Clemi lets this sink in. WLNP's treasurer is the math teacher of the board president's daughter. He has had other board members' children in his classes too. Something about this might deviate from best practices. Although what does she know of the nonprofit world? Certainly, less than she thought.

"Oh, I had no idea. That's so nice," Clemi says. "If you don't mind my asking, how long have you been treasurer?"

"About four years. They were having trouble finding anyone on the board who could do math, so Eric suggested I join."

"Wow, that's really generous of you."

"Well, really, it's very generous of *them*. I meet a lot of interesting people at WLNP events, plus all these authors, and am introduced to a lot of books I might not otherwise learn about. And the treasurer gig is ridiculously easy. Howard basically takes care of everything. He manages the money, sets the budget, writes the checks. All I do is sign off on what he does. And fortunately, he is as honest as they come."

Now Clemi recalls something Howard said about this aspect of WLNP governance. He had mentioned that on a board full of literary-minded people, getting anyone to fully engage on money matters was a challenge. He said that once, when he had been running through the proposed budget with him, Eric had actually fallen asleep. Clemi had laughed at this, imagining the board president's head flung back, snoring. But now, with hindsight, this lack of oversight might explain a thing or two.

"Um, actually, that's why I'm here. Have you taken a look at the accounts lately?"

"I don't have access to the accounts, but Howard and I check in quarterly. We are in very solid shape. Our brokerage accounts are well balanced, with a nice blend of ETFs and stock, plenty of cash, a few CDs. And the TD account is, of course, all cash, as it should be. Just last week, Howard and I discussed how we would use those funds to front the expenses of the gala. Next we're planning to meet to balance things out, see how much we brought in . . . Why are we standing here in the doorway?" he asks. "What sort of host am I? Come on into the living room. I need to check on the muffins, then I'll be right in."

Muffins! The source of the delicious baked-goods smell. She hopes one might be on offer because she is suddenly craving muffins and it's almost all she can think about: blueberry muffins, bran muffins, chocolate chip muffins. She needs a muffin, several muffins, stat!

"A few more minutes," he announces. "So where were we? Oh right, the gala expenses. Honestly, if it were up to me, I would kill the gala entirely. Nonprofit math can be goofy, in my opinion. I hope I am not offending you as the person in charge of programs, but it makes no sense. You spend something like $100,000 to throw an event that brings in about $120,000. Last year, we even lost money. There are better ways to fundraise—but no one asked me."

"Oh, I'm not offended in the least. I'm new at all this, but you raise a good point."

"Also I would propose skipping the dinner and focusing on the silent auction. That's where the money is. Did you know that last year, the public intellectual alone brought in $25,000?"

"Seriously?" She keeps forgetting about the PI problem, given all the other problems, such as being an accessory to the writing of a bad check and losing a cat. She is reluctant to disappoint Mr. Samaraweera with news of the dead public intellectual. But she must.

"I don't know if Dr. Jolly told the whole board yet, but he let me and Howard know on Tuesday that Javier Jiménez-Jiménez has passed away."

"This is terrible news!" he says. "Not just for the poor man and for his family, but our crisis consultant was quite insistent that we should celebrate Javier, acknowledge the problems he raised in his *New Yorker* article. His presence was to be part of our rebranding. This is meant to be the year where we finally have a fresh start."

"I'm so sorry," Clemi says. As if this is her fault.

She looks around the tidy apartment and sees diplomas on the wall, family photos on shelves full of books, snow globes, small icons, and other meaningful souvenirs. This helps to steady her. There is more to life than WLNP. There is family! Maybe not so much family for her, at least not right now, but still: The space reminds Clemi that she is merely stuck in a moment. Just look at Mr. Samaraweera at a beach somewhere with his presumed family, two small boys and a very pretty woman, possibly his wife. Surely no one in that photo is fretting about dead public intellectuals. Behind them is an entire universe—the sky, the waves. *The Sea, the Sea!* ("How huge it is, how empty, this great space for which I have been longing all my life." Ah, to be back in English class, reading Iris Murdoch novels.)

"We are from Colombo if you are wondering. That was taken many years ago. My boys are grown. One is at Stanford. The other is a cardiologist in private practice in Memphis."

"Oh, that's great. Very impressive. By the way, given all of your travels and various connections, might you happen to know a public intellectual?"

"Sure. But back in Sri Lanka."

Clemi runs concurrent calculations in her head. How much might this particular public intellectual, whoever they are, fetch at a silent auction? Would it at least offset the price of the flight? She supposes they wouldn't have to come in for the gala, but in order to make lunch or dinner or whatever possible with the winners, they would have to get the public intellectual here, eventually.

"Whom do you know?"

"Well, let me think a moment. We emigrated some twenty years ago. My second son was born here. My wife died of breast cancer five years ago. I went to University of Sri Lanka and later did some graduate work at MIT.

"You are probably wondering why I am teaching high school math. Oh, I almost forgot—the muffins are probably done." He pops up from his chair and returns to the kitchen.

Clemi *is* interested in his family history. And practically salivating for a muffin. But all she really wants to know right now is: Who is the public intellectual?

"I'm sorry to hear about your wife. And I wouldn't presume to wonder why you are teaching high school math. That's a noble occupation. Not to change the subject, but you mentioned you might know a public intellectual?"

Mr. Samaraweera reappears with a tray bearing the muffins, as well as two mugs of tea, and offers both to Clemi.

"Well, sure, my old family friend is the writer Pradeep Jayakody."

The name is familiar. She thinks for a moment and recalls that he has written an award-winning trilogy called Ceylon, a family saga set on a tea plantation that is also a sweeping history of independence. She owns a copy of the first volume but has never read it. This would be a huge win!

"Do you think he might be interested in being auctioned off?"

"Probably not. Sadly, he has been in a vegetative state for several months, following a stroke."

Is this entirely disqualifying? Clemi wonders. They could arrange to bring the auction winners to visit him, bedside. They could throw in a vacation in Sri Lanka as part of the package.

Perhaps she ought not be thinking along these lines. She has only worked at WLNP for just over a week, and already she has begun to lose her soul.

The muffin is indescribably delicious. A blend of spices, nutmeg and cinnamon and ginger, still warm from the oven.

"These are amazing. You're a baker too? A mathematician and a booklover and a baker."

"Funny you should say that, because the recipe is from a *New York Times* article about a writer and her muffins. Besides, baking is simply a math problem. Also chemistry. But it's quite straightforward."

"Well, the various problems at WLNP are not very straightforward, which is why I'm here. You're the only person I can even reach on the board."

"Yes, they are all busy people, so busy writing their books. I am full of admiration for all they do."

"I'm not so sure about that. Teaching math seems the higher calling."

She says this because (a) she is terrible at math and easily impressed by anyone who can do sums without a calculator, but also because (b) she has spent a lifetime observing writers and their ups and downs. She frequently overheard her mother on the phone, for example, talking her writer clients off the ledge. These poor souls were on the brink because (a) their editors were late to weigh in on their latest work, or (b) they had not been nominated for a prize, or (c) they had just received a bad review in *The New York Times*, or (d) *The New York Times* had failed to review their book, or (e) they had won every prize known to humankind and were in a state of profound existential despair just the same. And that's not even adding into the mix the would-be writers in Clemi's workshop. Or River.

She takes a sip of tea, burning her tongue. "The thing is, Mr. Samaraweera—"

"Please, call me Sam."

"Sam," she says, unsure of whether this is short for Samaraweera or for his first name, Samuel. "I took a look at the WLNP accounts yesterday, and they have been emptied out."

He sips from his own teacup and then says calmly, "Surely Howard has just transferred the funds into a different account."

"That's what I thought too. But then... well, I don't know if I'm supposed to be sharing this information, but..."

"If it has to do with WLNP, I'm a trustee. A fiduciary. You can, and should, tell me what is going on. Especially since I am the treasurer."

"Good, well, that's a relief, since I need to tell someone. And I can't reach Dr. Jolly."

"Oh, that Eric Jolly," he says. "Always jetting around. So famous with that book."

"We received a subpoena yesterday."

"A subpoena? For what?"

"For our bank accounts. That's how this all began."

"But why? I mean, for what reason are we being subpoenaed?"

"Howard's wife is filing for divorce, and she has subpoenaed the WLNP accounts as part of the proceedings since he seems to have drained their family bank accounts. Their retirement funds and the children's college funds are gone. I guess her theory is that he moved the money over to the WLNP accounts. Except that when I looked, that money is gone too."

"That's impossible," he says. "This doesn't sound like the Howard I know. And it makes no sense... All was well during our check-in last week, although I suppose I should have asked to see the actual bank accounts. I always take Howard at his word. I have never been a treasurer of a nonprofit before. No one ever told me what I'm supposed to be doing, to be honest. I was told the position was largely honorary."

"I mean, it's not your fault!" Clemi has no idea whether this is true. Maybe it is his fault. Maybe he *should* have been micromanaging Howard and the finances. She knows even less than he does about what a nonprofit treasurer is meant to do. "I don't know Howard very well, but I agree, this is not what I would have expected. Have I mentioned he seems to have gone AWOL? He's left WLNP with a whole lot of problems. Skylar said you would be able to help."

"I'm not sure how I can help, exactly, but let me try to reach Herring."

"Herring! Who, or what, is Herring?"

"The financial advisor," says Sam.

"I thought *you* were the financial advisor."

"No, I'm the treasurer. That's different. I attend the board meetings and sign off on the budget and approve expenditures, but Herring handles the investments and makes the high-level decisions. Then Howard implements his suggestions."

"Okay, interesting. No one explained this to me. This is helpful, I think. I hope. Can I talk to him?"

"Sure. He's in London nowadays, but it's still a reasonable hour to call the UK. I'll try him right now."

Sam reaches for his phone and taps the screen, puts it on speaker, then sets it on the coffee table. The call goes straight to an automated voicemail that announces the mailbox is full.

"Hmm," Sam says, hitting redial, then reaching the same recording. "Let me try Howard."

"Howard's phone has been disconnected."

"Are you certain?" asks Sam. "I spoke to him over the weekend."

"It seems to have happened Tuesday. My texts won't go through either."

Sam tries to call and text to no avail. They sit in silence for a moment, absorbing the possible implications.

"I mean, I have never actually spoken to this Herring person, but I was told that if any problems of significance ever should arise, he's the silver bullet."

"Well, we definitely need some sort of silver bullet right now," Clemi says. "He's in London, you said?"

"I believe so. Do you want me to find the exact address? Are you thinking of going there?"

"I don't know what I'm thinking. I mean, my mother lives in London. Maybe she could . . . never mind. No." No, definitely no, even though she doesn't even know what she's vetoing, other than the idea that her mother might become involved in any way.

Something thumps onto her lap, and she startles. It is, of all the possible things, a cat. This one is small and white and very fluffy, with piercing blue eyes.

"Oh, so sorry!" says Sam. "That's Fluffy—silly name, I know, but my kids named her when she was just a kitten. She's very old. Seems to be deaf and blind, and sometimes she just kind of sneaks up on you like that. She must like you!"

"That's very sweet, but I'm allergic."

"Oh, you should have mentioned. I would have put her away. And vacuumed before you came."

"No, I'm already knee-deep in cats. There's a cat at the office . . . or there was . . . and I'm pumped up on meds anyway, so I'm good for now."

"That's not right," Sam says. "A cat should not be at the office. Especially if you are allergic. You should lodge a complaint. I can bring it up at the next board meeting if you'd like."

Clemi knows very little about WLNP and nonprofit life, but the idea that a board meeting might take place in which the matter of a cat in the office is discussed seems quaint—adorable, even—given that from what she can tell, the entire operation is about to implode.

"Well, the cat was there, but it's gone. I don't know if it will be back, so please don't be concerned about that for now."

"Do let me know if it comes back. And in the short term, please don't worry. I already have the check for Friday night."

Clemi is so happy to hear this that she wants to pop champagne and throw her arms around Mr. Samaraweera.

"Do you mean for Penelope? I gave her a check but will tell her to wait and use yours instead!"

"No, I don't know who Penelope is, but I have a check for Vivian."

"Vivian?"

"Oh, sorry. I think maybe I wasn't supposed to mention this yet," he says. "It's a board thing."

"Oh, okay." Clemi has no idea what he's talking about, but whatever. A check is a check, and if it's for the gala, it's one less thing for her to fret about.

Chapter 15

BY THE TIME Clemi gets to the WLNP office after her visit to Sam's, it is early afternoon, and the place is eerily quiet. Still no Howard. Still no cat. No fresh subpoenas or angry soon-to-be ex-wives. No ringing phones. Not even any meaningful email—just a bunch of spammy messages, including one inviting her to a ninety-minute webinar on executive compensation (why?), and another inviting her to a four-hour live virtual training on Microsoft Excel (no thank you). She checks the bank accounts again. Same. Same. Same. Nothing in, nothing out.

Has the world stopped spinning, or is this simply the calm before the storm? She supposes that rather than fret about what is going on, she might as well leave work early, walk home the long way, maybe stop to browse in a shop or two.

By the time she approaches her apartment building, the city is awash in a beautiful orange glow. The golden hour, she believes this is called—the time of day the characters in an Evelyn Waugh novel might slip on their boat shoes and sip their gin and tonics by the dock. She imagines Howard among the fictional crew, wearing a pressed pink shirt and regaling the others with tales about his charmed career as the brains behind the Dutch Detective Wallander.

Getting out, having a leisurely stroll, is surprisingly cathartic. She is feeling light, even a little euphoric, thinking about how much she loves this city as she walks past a Neapolitan pizzeria she has been meaning to try, which is next door to a new brewery serving only local beer, which is next door to yet another about-to-open indie bookstore. This city! She loves this place! She may have wound up here by accident, tagging along with her college roommate who found a very DC job working on Capitol Hill, but it is beginning to feel like home, even if she is technically a plant-sitting nomad.

She hesitates to burst her own bubble, but it occurs to her that this strange sense of bliss—especially at this moment when things are flat-out falling apart—might be the effect of the allergy meds. Then again, maybe it's the yoga. She has heard of something called a "yoga high," the result of the release of endorphins. Perhaps she ought to self-fortify with another dose, attempt to immunize herself from what lies ahead tomorrow. She pulls out her phone and checks the gym app. If she picks up speed, she can make it to the 4:00 p.m. class.

A few blocks from her apartment, she sees, on the other side of the street, the man who is not Malcolm Gladwell. He is clad in a muted tomato-colored yoga ensemble, his head pointed at an odd angle that is neither looking up nor straight ahead, like he's in his own headspace. Maybe he is listening to some transporting music. Or an engrossing podcast. Or maybe he is just lost in thought.

He is a curious character, this not-Malcolm person. Clemi can't quite get a grip on him, beyond how he is quiet and brainy and somewhat socially inept. She watches him cross the street, his head still cocked at this odd angle of oblivion. He is, unsurprisingly, also headed to the gym.

It's weird. Or maybe it's not weird. Maybe it's just again with the coincidence. But by the time Clemi arrives, the only mat left in the studio is next to not-Malcolm. Now he is staring out the window, into the apartment complex across the street.

"Hi there," Clemi says. "Is it just me, or does it seem a little hot in here?"

"It's supposed to be," he says. "It's hot power vinyasa."

"Oh, how did I not realize that?" Hot power vinyasa sounds kind of terrifying.

He turns and looks at her blankly, as if he has no memory of who she is. Perhaps he is one of those people with face blindness, a subject she knows a little about on account of having scheduled an author to speak at the bookstore for the publication of her memoir about the social and workplace challenges of not being able to decipher one face from another.

Alternatively, perhaps Clemi is so unremarkable that he does not remember talking to her at all.

"I left my LSAT book in the cubby outside this time," she says, hoping to jog his memory. This happens to be true. She has again brought her study guide to the gym just in case . . . well, you never know.

"Oh, right," he says. "The lawyer."

"Soon-to-be, perhaps."

Not-Malcolm does not respond, so she leaves the conversation at that and follows his gaze. He is again staring intently out the window.

"What are you staring at?" she asks.

She is generally a mind-your-own-business sort of person, not at all one to engage someone in mindless chatter, especially not moments before yoga class is set to begin, and yet something about not-Malcolm makes her want to needle him a bit. She is becoming a little desperate to know what is going on inside his mind.

"Clowns," he says.

"Clowns? What do you mean, clowns?" Perhaps the allergy meds are making her not so much euphoric but delusional, or even hard of hearing. Surely he did not just say "clowns." Now she sees a flash of light in one of the apartments across the street, and two figures moving about the room. The figures are oddly shaped, bloated, almost inflated, like Macy's Thanksgiving Day balloons. One of them moves closer to the window, and it is indeed a clown.

The yoga instructor—a large, muscular young man who looks more like a linebacker than a yoga teacher—introduces himself as Gabriel and tells them to lie on their backs, put their left legs in the air, then cross the right legs over the left and into a figure four.

Goodbye, clowns, Clemi thinks, no longer able to see out the window upon assuming the pose.

Some five minutes later, when they are finally instructed to stand upright in mountain pose, she sees that one of the clowns has opened the window and is leaning over the ledge.

No, clown, no! She wants to shout. *Please don't jump!*

The clown is not going to jump. Evidently, the clown is going to smoke. It lights a cigarette, removes its red nose, and takes a long drag. Then the other clown appears behind it. Clown 1 places the cigarette on the window ledge and turns toward Clown 2, and they appear to engage in conversation. After a moment, by which time Clemi is pushing her hips toward the left while arching her arms overhead and to the right, Clown 1 sticks its head back outside and takes another puff. Clemi's not sure if she is projecting or making assumptions because of the smoking, but Clown 1 seems a little anxious to her, even bereft. And why shouldn't it be? Clowns are people too, of course, with real problems like securing affordable health insurance and paying taxes, finding childcare for their kids.

What's bizarre is not that the clown is possibly an anxious smoker, but that the clown is a clown at all. Is this a sign? A voice from above giving her clues about the arrival times at the circus, perhaps? Or telling her to go—or not go—to law school?

Clown 2 again seems to call to Clown 1, who stubs the cigarette out on the window ledge and then flicks it onto the street below. A moment later they are both gone, the lights are switched off, and the apartment is again empty, as far as Clemi can tell.

She looks over at not-Malcolm to see whether he is still watching this, but his eyes are closed. He appears to be deep in the zone.

One very sweaty hour later, Clemi returns her blocks to the shelf at the back of the studio and cleans off her mat. She takes a look at her phone, which has been face down, on silent, and sees that River has sent three more texts.

Can't wait to see u tomorrow!

Tell me what to wear!

You will love Martha!

She tries to not let the River situation penetrate her sweaty yoga high. As she exits the room, still staring at her phone, she collides awkwardly with not-Malcolm—again!—inadvertently exchanging sweat molecules with him.
"Sorry!"
"No, I'm sorry!"
"It's my fault!"
"That was a great class!" she says, ending the blame game by allowing him to claim culpability, although it was, in fact, her fault.
"Oh, so great," he says.
"Totally," Clemi lies. "But is it supposed to be that hot? I've never done hot yoga before."
"It was somewhat hotter than I expected."
"Yes, it was indeed very hot. Actually, it is rather hot out here too."
This conversation is beginning to remind her of high school Spanish class, where they would repeat things over and over, sometimes with minor variations on the theme, so as to drill the words into the brain. *Sí, hace muy calor, todavía.*
She decides to try again, to send the conversation in a new, possibly more productive direction. "It's so weird, the way you can see right into the apartments across the street. I guess they can see us too."

"Yes, it's sort of like *Rear Window*."

"That sounds familiar. Is it a book?"

"It's a Hitchcock film."

"Of course. I know about it because of the book *The Woman in the Window*. Which everyone compared to *Rear Window*, but not entirely favorably."

"Oh, sure. I know that movie."

"It was made into a movie?"

"Yes, but not favorably compared."

"To the book or the movie?"

"To the movie *Rear Window*. I don't know anything about the book. I'm not a big book person."

"I thought you were a travel writer."

"Yes, but online content only."

"Ah, I see. Well, that's too bad."

"Too bad why?"

Good questions. She supposes she just means it's too bad to learn that anyone is not a book person. But she also means they have potentially missed a conversational intersection. Not that there is any reason for them to converse, necessarily. It's more of an experiment, a sociology project of sorts, trying to get this odd man to interact.

Her phone rings. It's River. And while she generally would not pick it up, doing so at least enables her to avoid answering not-Malcom's question—to hit the pause button, and perhaps end entirely, this awkward exchange.

River asks for the name of the hotel where the gala is taking place, which she is pretty sure is just an excuse for calling her since he can easily get this information from Augusta. Or from Martha. Or from the WLNP website.

"It's at the Washington Hilton. The one on Connecticut near Florida Avenue."

"The Hinckley Hilton?" not-Malcom asks, suddenly animated.

"Who are you talking to?" River asks.

"Just my friend at the gym. I'll call you later," she says.

"Immanuel?" River asks.

"No, someone else."

She ends the call, feeling unexpectedly good about having possibly just made River jealous. She has no romantic interest in not-Malcolm—he is too awkward, and he lives in another city, on top of which she now has confirmation that he is too old—but still, this feels like a small, albeit petty, win.

"What were you saying about the Hinckley Hilton?" not-Malcolm asks.

"It's a work thing. We have a big event there tomorrow night."

"Amazing. Can I come? The hotel is on my bucket list. I'm planning to write about it for the guide."

This is indeed awkward. Can she get him in, she wonders? She ought to be able, given how she is calling the shots at this point. Plus, there should be at least one extra, already-paid-for seat.

"I can probably get you a ticket since I don't think my boss or his wife will be able to make it. But it's a whole thing, and you might find it boring if you don't like books."

"I mean, I have no problem with books. I just don't like to read them. Unless they're for work. Other travel guides, for example. But if it's at the Hinckley Hilton, that's another story. Yes, please. I'm something of an aficionado of political assassinations. And assassination attempts, of course."

"That sounds kind of... niche," she says. It also sounds like a red flag.

Then it clicks. How had she not realized that the Hinckley in question is John Hinckley Jr., the person who shot Ronald Reagan and his press secretary, James Brady, along with two others? She now dimly recalls learning about this in high school.

"It's a fancy sort of thing," she says, now backpedaling on the invitation. Why did she blurt this out so impulsively? What sort of person is obsessed with political assassinations?

"You will probably need to wear a suit." *And not a muted tomato-colored yoga ensemble*, she does not say.

"I own a suit."

"Oh, great. I didn't mean to imply that you might not own a suit."

"I always bring a suit when I'm traveling, just in case someone dies and I have to go to a funeral."

"Right," Clemi says. Is he not the most completely awkward person ever?

"Do you smell something?" he asks.

Clemi's cheeks flush, and she feels a wash of embarrassment. Hot yoga was indeed hot. She has never been this sweaty in her life.

"Like burning plastic?" he continues.

She is presumably burning fat, not plastic. At least, she hopes that is the case. She sniffs the air, and indeed he is not wrong.

"It does smell like burning plastic. Also, smoke."

A moment later there is a piercing, bleeping sound. Then an automated voice: "Fire alert. Please evacuate the building. Fire alert."

She and not-Malcolm look at one another, then at the cubbies where the shoes are stored. They grab their respective sneakers and race down the steps, then out the door just as the fire crew begins to stream into the gym.

The evacuees seem excitable this time. Not only is an alarm blaring, but it seems possible there might even be a fire. Word is, the heat from hot yoga melted some plastic or caused a small electrical fire. No one is quite sure what happened, exactly, but definitely there is smoke. Not-Malcolm does not seem particularly interested in this though. He is stuck on the Hinckley Hilton.

"So, should we go together? To your event? Or should we meet there?"

Clemi had nearly forgotten about this plan amid the excitement of the fire alarm.

"Since it's a work thing for me, I need to be there early. Can you meet me there? Is that okay?"

"Sure. Text me the details," he says. "Let me AirDrop my contact."

"I don't even know your name."

"Colman."

"Seriously?"

"Yes. Why? Is that problematic? I was named for my great-uncle."

"No, it's a great name. It's just funny, the coincidence."

"I'm not following."

"People keep mistaking you for Malcolm, but your name is Colman, and like . . . that's just the same bunch of letters mixed up."

"Well, not really, because you'd need an extra *m*."

"Sure, but still, it's kind of weird."

"And then, what do you do with the *n*? It doesn't have a place in the name *Malcolm*."

"That's true, but still kind of close, don't you think?"

"Also, an extra *l*."

Not-Malcolm, who turns out to be Colman, is looking at Clemi like she has lost her mind. He is apparently a literalist. No room for fudging things, throwing in an extra consonant or two. Whereas she is on the lookout for the poetry of things.

"And what name do you go by, esquire?"

"Ah, so you are a humorist!"

Not-Malcolm looks at her blankly.

"I'm pretty far from being a lawyer right now," she explains. "Just entertaining the idea. My name is Clemi."

"So I'm going to assume this is you: Clemi's phone."

"Indeed."

She hears a ding, and Colman's contact info appears.

"Okay, just text me the details," he says. "I can't wait to see the hotel."

She watches him walk away, this lanky enigma. What in the world has she just done, inviting not-Malcolm to the gala?

Is she so desperate that she wants River to believe she has a date? Possibly, but it's not a need-to-know question. It may not even be a want-to-know, for all she knows.

Chapter 16

WHEN CLEMI DROPPED by the apartment two weeks earlier to pick up the keys and get her plant-watering instructions, Fiona had been in a rush. She was "late for a drink with Ilana Rusk," she'd said, in a tone suggestive that Ilana Rusk, whoever she might be, was a name to be name-dropped. Fiona had seemed distracted, still busy accessorizing, selecting earrings, holding up scarves in front of the mirror, tossing the rejects on the bed. She then began digging through the many compartments of her oversized tote, searching for keys and lipstick. The bag had at least three zippered pouches that extended from what looked like bungee cords, which made locating anything something of a scavenger hunt. Clemi half wondered whether this bag had other attachments—a mini screwdriver or a nail file, maybe even a leaf blower, because you never know.

Clemi had apologized for the intrusion, even though Fiona had been the one to set the time for the visit. The outcome was that Clemi received what amounted to a drive-by tutorial on the care and feeding of the plants: *"Mist this one, do not overwater that one, rotate these ones on a daily basis so that all sides get equal amounts of sun."* This is not to suggest that Fiona is casual about her plants. They were evidently *not* impulse purchases, not randomly acquired PLU codes of greenery tossed into her cart en route to the checkout line at Trader Joe's—which, as it happens, is where Clemi acquired her one and only plant, a philodendron, which was supposed to be easy to care for, yet expired within a week nonetheless. ("Root rot," her then-roommate had pronounced, harsh words that had felt like an indictment.) Fortunately, Fiona had not asked for references regarding Clemi's horticultural abilities when she invited her to plant-sit.

This time, Clemi is determined to a better job, to keep these plants not only alive but thriving. She is in the midst of tending to a finicky orchid when, outside the window, she sees a cat.

It's a large cat, brownish and greyish, with a very long tail and piercing green eyes. The cat looks a lot like Immanuel and is sitting in a tree. Not just any tree, but the only tree in this otherwise concrete, antiseptic development. She might say the cat is staring at her, but she is aware she is projecting. Stare at something, and it will likely stare back, or appear to stare back, even if it is a cat in a tree that is at least five hundred feet away.

She also knows that, barring some miracle, this cat is not Immanuel. Yet who doesn't love those stories that occasionally make headlines about animals swimming across oceans, then trekking hundreds of miles to reunite with their owners, or in this case, the programs director at a literary nonprofit the cat has known for all of a day? Whatever the explanation or lack thereof, there is a cat in a tree outside, and Clemi feels some moral compulsion to see whether it needs help, if only to prove she is a person who cares about cats, notwithstanding how she has failed to keep track of the only one that has ever been put in her charge.

Still discombobulated from yoga, her hair swept into a style that, in keeping with her surroundings, might best be described as a potted plant, she heads out into the lobby, down the stairs, and onto the street. Outside the mood is festive. Only ten minutes have passed since the fire department gave them the all-clear to go back inside, but many of the residents have remained. Pizza boxes are strewn about, as are beer cans, one of which she accidentally kicks into the gutter. It's a party out here. One she has not been invited to.

She approaches the tree and stares up at the cat. It is very high up, parallel to Clemi's fifth-floor apartment, and she wonders how she can help the creature down. People in movies typically call the fire department in these situations, which seems a bit extreme, especially given that they have only just left.

"Hey, cat!" she calls up to him. He seems to hear her, although that might be her imagination. "Immanuel?" she tries. She is well aware this is not Immanuel, but where's the harm in calling him that because you never know? "Not-Immanuel?" she corrects herself, even though a name is a name to a cat, or so she thinks. It's all in the intonation, or at least it was with the chocolate Lab they had when she was growing up. You could ask Zoey if she wanted to do the laundry, and she would wag her tail excitedly and drool the same way she might if you were offering her a treat.

"Immanuel, are you okay up there? Do you want me to call for help?" she tries again.

"That's Moma," says a male voice, startling her.

"MoMA? Like the museum?" She is still staring up at the cat.

"Moma like your mom. Because she's a mom."

"But you pronounced it like the museum."

"Look, don't ask me, I'm just repeating what I heard from someone else a few minutes ago. I don't know how this cat spells its name. If it's pronounced *momma*, it would have two *m*'s."

"Obviously." She turns to see who is driving this absurd conversation and lets out an involuntary little scream when she sees it is a clown. Of course it's a clown, because this is evidently her reality now. She lives in a clown world, as if her life has become a video game populated by nothing but clowns. Also, cats.

"It's okay," he says. "I don't know why people get so freaked out, but it's become a whole thing. Almost like it's suddenly cool to hate on clowns."

"No, sorry, I don't hate on clowns. It's just . . . well, you are unexpected. And it's hard to explain, but I've been dealing with a lot of clowns lately. Not in real life, but in an intellectual sort of way. I'm being haunted by clowns, pursued by them. Like there's a plague of clowns all of a sudden. Sorry. I don't mean that in a bad way necessarily."

The clown is looking at her with what is possibly a smirk.

"A plague?" he asks.

"No, really, I didn't mean it like that. I was thinking more along the lines of what might be the collective noun for clowns."

"The collective noun?"

"You know, like a herd of sheep. A murder of crows. A swarm of bees."

"Oh, sure. Like a parliament of owls. Or a shrewdness of apes."

"A shrewdness of apes?"

"Yes. That's what it's called."

"How did I not know that? Is it because they are . . . shrewd?"

"Obviously. But I'm still stuck on a plague of clowns. That hurts."

"Apologies. That's not what I meant. It's just that they are plaguing *me*. I'm studying for the LSAT, and the first problem, on the very first page, involves clowns, and I can't get my mind around the whole thing. The question might as well be in a different language. Maybe I should give up on law school already. Cut my losses. Not that they are insubstantial."

"What do you mean?"

"I mean the prep book was nearly fifty dollars. Of course, I got my staff discount, even though I'm not working at the bookstore anymore . . . don't tell anyone though. They shouldn't have given it to me . . . The book ended up being not quite thirty dollars, but if I was a more honest person, I would have objected. But then they would have had to void the transaction and start over."

The clown is surprisingly attentive, nodding its head occasionally, like a therapist.

"That's only the tip of the iceberg, given all of the dishonest things I've done the past two days," Clemi continues. "I'm not fit to be a lawyer. Either morally or intellectually, I guess. Especially morally. More specifically, ethically. And, now that I think deeply about it, definitely intellectually as well."

Now the clown reaches into its pocket and hands her a tissue. Clemi is somewhat mortified to feel a tear trickle down her cheek. She seems to be having some sort of breakdown here beneath the tree. She is reminded of the cat and looks up. It is nestled in the crook of a giant limb, licking its paws.

"Sorry, it's just been a lot. I don't know why I'm dumping this on you."

"No worries. It happens a lot. An alley, by the way."

"An alley?"

"Yeah, it's odd, I know. Sometimes you might hear other things, like a mutiny. Or a pratfall. Or a truckload."

"Still confused."

"The collective noun for clowns."

"Oh, right! Why an alley?"

"Because that's where they used to get dressed before a performance, maybe?"

"Funny, that makes me think of the LSAT question."

"What do the legal minds want to know about us clowns?"

"It's all about your—their—arrival times at the circus. Like, how no clown arrives at the same time as any other clown, and no clown arrives more than once that day. And each clown wears either green or red, but not both."

"Anything else?"

"I don't remember exactly, but, like, two of the clowns that arrive before one of the clowns wear red. And this one arrives before that one and before that other one, et cetera. Something like that."

"That sounds like fun."

"Ha. It is a form of torture for me, but I'm glad you think so. So, here I am already obsessing over clowns, and then I'm at the gym doing yoga, trying to forget about the stupid clowns—no offense—and then I see a clown in an apartment across the street. Two clowns, actually. One of them was having a smoke. Wait . . . duh . . . was that you? Do you happen to live in one of those apartments?"

"I don't live there, but my cousin does," he says, pointing to the spot Clemi was monitoring during yoga. "He's the smoker, not me."

Not-Immanuel emits a meow, and they both look up.

"Anyway, if you don't mind my asking, which study guide are you using? I have one too, but the book I have doesn't have a clown prompt. Yours sounds better."

"You're taking the LSAT?"

"I am. I'm registered to take it in September. What about you?"

"I haven't signed up yet. I figured I'd just look at the book first. So you're a clown, but you want to be a lawyer?"

"Does that surprise you? Do you think clowns aren't smart or something? Anyway, the clown gig is very part-time. It's just a hobby."

"Oh, so sorry. I didn't mean it like that. Truly." Or did she perhaps mean it like that? Is she inadvertently microaggressing against clowns?

"What do you do when you are not being a clown?"

"I've got a couple other part-time gigs. One of them is at a law firm doing administrative stuff. And I just took a second job at a restaurant to earn some extra cash. What do you do?"

"I work at a literary nonprofit."

The clown's face lights up. "Which one?"

"It's currently called WLNP. Washington Literary Nonprofit."

"Oh, wow, my mother used to be on the board. She was the president for a while when I was a little kid, back when it had a different name."

"No way!"

"Maybe you know her. Janet Silverman. She's not on the board anymore, but she still goes to the luncheons and such."

"I've only been there a few days, so I don't know anyone."

"She was long gone before all the racism and anti-Semitism

stuff surfaced. But you're lucky. If I had a cool job like that, I wouldn't be applying to law school."

"It sounds better than it is," Clemi says. "The job, I mean. It's a little complicated right now. That's so weird about your mom. What are the odds?"

"DC is a small town. Everyone knows everyone. Anyway, I've got to run. It was nice to meet you."

"Yes, you too!" she says, reluctant to end her conversation with the very nice clown. She gets the sense that he is possibly kind of adorable, but it's hard to tell with the makeup and the fake nose.

"Good luck with the clowns," the clown says.

"You too!" she says absurdly.

"And it looks like our work is done."

"What do you mean?"

The clown points in the direction of not-Immanuel, who has now descended from the tree and has settled on a bench.

"Okay, well, goodbye for real. I've got to run."

Clemi watches him walk away. He is wearing black running shoes and carrying his clown shoes in his hand.

"Hey, clown!" she calls. "Do you have a name?"

"Zeke."

"Zeke? No way!"

"Is there a problem with my name?"

"No, it's just that one of the clowns in the prompt is named Zeke."

"Prompt? Oh, you mean on the LSAT question?"

"Yes. I can't remember exactly what you are up to, but I think you are arriving before or after Xochitl, or Ursula. You are wearing either red or green, obviously."

Zeke the clown examines himself. "I'm wearing both red and green."

"You are indeed."

She begins to laugh. Zeke laughs too. They laugh for a moment and then look at each other. She is half tempted to ask for his number. A quarter tempted to invite him to the gala. She imagines herself showing up with a clown on one arm and not-Malcolm on the other. She's pretty sure she will need all the fortification—from the River situation, as well as from whatever chaos lies ahead—she can get.

Friday

Chapter 17

THIS MORNING, THE day of the gala, Clemi is determined to preserve her strength, to not leave this apartment until she must. She will even forgo her usual morning visit to the corner for overpriced coffee and instead apply her admittedly challenged logic skills to mastering Fiona's complicated coffee maker. The various lights and buttons on the gizmo are about as straightforward as the cockpit of a Boeing 737. Ditto for the backstory of why Fiona has this ridiculous machine—something to do with her ex-boyfriend, a multimillionaire financier who decided to go back to his wife, then left Fiona with this machine as well as an automatic pod replenishment plan she can't seem to cancel since the account is not in her name.

Fiona hadn't been exaggerating when she said a lot of coffee had piled up; the enormous bowl full of colorful aluminum caffeine-infused capsules is spilling over onto the counter, and two unopened boxes sit in the cabinet beneath.

Clemi pokes around the uncooperative device and finds, or thinks she finds, the spot where the capsules go, but it takes a few dry runs to get the thing to produce. She has been told by many people that she is an old soul, and perhaps she is, because she doesn't understand what was so wrong with the aged Mr. Coffee she used to have, handed down to her by Mrs. Bernstein, her former boss at the bookstore. Nevertheless, as she has also been told, *she's a smart girl who will figure it out.* And finally, she does.

She takes the magnificent coffee, steaming inside a yellow, artfully distressed mug that claims, from the stamp on the bottom, to have been hand-thrown in a studio in Tivoli, New York, and settles into one of Fiona's stunning leather chairs, a Ludwig Mies van der Rohe MR Adjustable Chaise Longue evidently. Fiona had let this name drop too, multiple times, without ever saying who Ludwig was or what the *MR* in the name stands for.

She rotates the Ludwig Mies van der Rohe MR Adjustable Chaise Longue to get a better view out the window, where she is able to see directly into the yoga studio. It's like some upside-down world from this perspective, staring out across a landscape of some thirty people holding tree pose. Here she is, in someone else's apartment drinking coffee from someone else's mug, looking out onto the lives of others, contemplating the alternate versions of herself, the self she might be.

Who is she anyway? This is not a convenient time for an existential crisis, but said crises, alas, cannot be scheduled like dental checkups. Existential crises build slowly, imperceptibly. You are unaware of them, blinded to them until it's too late. Consider here and now. This existential crisis, the one she is clearly in the grip of, began days ago, slowly, and was cresting, it seems, while she was talking to that clown. What is she doing with her life? What is her point? What was she made for? Why is she persevering with this job? Trying to pull off this gala, participating in the writing of a rubber check? Coming up with a somewhat devious plan to get Sveta to pay for her own air travel?

Is this all in the name of trying to impress her mother? Or is it to meet Sveta Attais, who may or may not be a prima donna, what with her first-class air travel demands? And while she is at it, why not throw into the mix the questions of whether she should go to law school, and how she would pay for it? And where she will live in six months, when Fiona returns from her writing residency?

Also, is that leaf discolored? Might that plant be in early-stage leaf spot?

She will not do this, will not self-destruct. At least not today! Instead, she will use what little time she has this morning to study for the LSAT.

She reaches for the book and picks up a pen, determined to figure out what is going on with Zeke, who, now that they have met, is her primary-focus clown. Maybe that's what she needed to figure this all out: some human connection.

Her scholarly endeavors are interrupted by the ringing of her phone. She doesn't recognize the number. Generally, she screens her calls, but given what lies ahead today, she figures she'd better answer because it could be the hotel, or the caterer, or Howard calling from a new, or different, phone.

Or it could be Sveta. And it is.

"My darling Clementine," the familiar voice trills.

"You landed!" Clemi says before it occurs to her that there are many possible scenarios in which Sveta might be calling to say she did *not* land. Maybe the plane was diverted due to thunderstorms, or turbulence, or someone being ill on board. Or maybe it ran late back in Casablanca and she missed her flight—in which case, two new first-class tickets might need to be procured.

"I did! We got in about an hour ago. Thank you. The flight was perfect, although Vlad did not especially like the breakfast they served. He's not an egg person, which I should have mentioned to you, but oh well, too late now. He made do."

"Oh, so sorry," Clemi says. "How is your back?"

"My back?"

"The pinched nerve?"

"Oh yes, thank you for asking! It's much better. But really, I don't think I would have made it if I'd been unable to recline."

"Very glad to hear that." Clemi does not wish a bad back on Sveta, of course. Neither does she want to think she—or rather WLNP—has been unnecessarily mugged.

"Did you get to the hotel?"

"Yes, we are here now. Thank you again for your help. We are going to take a nap, then get ready for tonight. I still get nervous at these events, believe it or not."

It had not occurred to Clemi that a person might be nervous while accepting a literary award. So remote is the likelihood of her finishing a novel, let alone winning a literary award, that she has never paused to consider any downside. Not that a case of nerves is a condition that can't be overcome. She once heard an author talk about having scored a prescription for beta-blockers, which can apparently have a calming effect on authors and even some nonauthors.

"You'll be great, Sveta," says Clemi. "Nothing to worry about."

"You are a dear. Listen, can I talk to Howard? I still cannot reach him, which is concerning."

You and me both, Clemi does not say.

"He's not available right now," Clemi says as if he is in the next room, possibly on the toilet, or otherwise momentarily indisposed. "But I can help you with . . . whatever."

"It's a little delicate, I'm afraid."

"Anything you tell me is confidential," Clemi says. "I'm here to help. That's my job."

Things may not be going so well at WLNP, yet here she is, Sveta Attais's confidante, her darling Clementine. At this rate, they will soon be BFFs.

"I suppose. I mean, what choice do I have?"

Okay, so maybe not BFFs.

"It has to do with Vlad," Sveta continues. "I explained the situation to Howard last week. Vlad's family life has not been straightforward. His father is a cad. I threw him out about a year ago and have filed for divorce. Never mind Akhil's many personal indiscretions—don't get me wrong, that was not okay—but what I could no longer abide were his shady business dealings. He was bringing all sorts of unsavory, so-called business partners into the home. I didn't want Vlad exposed to any of this . . ."

"I see," Clemi says. "That's a lot."

"It is a lot, and it has been difficult for poor Vlad. Oh, how I hate Akhil. I don't want anything to do with him anymore, although I fear I'm stuck with his name now that I've written two novels under Attais and won your lovely little prize, to boot. Don't ever change your name, Clemi. Do you understand?"

"I do understand," she says, although this particular problem seems as far away as winning a prize.

"He needs a lot of attention."

Vlad or Akhil? Clemi wonders but does not ask.

"And he has some minor behavioral issues. Nothing terrible, just normal eight-year-old stuff, plus a little extra." *Ah, Vlad. Vlad who is eight.*

Clemi is afraid to ask what constitutes minor behavioral issues, never mind "a little extra."

"When Howard called to tell me I'd won the prize, I explained I might need to bring Vlad, but I wasn't sure at the time. My sister had originally said she could watch him if he came . . . She lives someplace called Bethesda. I think it's in Maryland. But now she has her own conflict. Her mother-in-law is ill, and she has to hop on a plane to Savannah tonight, so . . ."

"I see," Clemi says again, starting to get nervous.

"I'm so glad you understand. So, you won't mind watching him?"

"Watching . . . ?"

"Vlad. Just keeping an eye on him. During the award ceremony, but also this afternoon. He's a little discombobulated from the long flight, and I am too. I need to pull myself together. This winning-an-award situation is all so much more stressful than you can imagine."

"So you mentioned," Clemi says. She does not mean to be hostile, or maybe she does a little bit. Who wouldn't love to experience the stress of winning an award? Also, is she seriously asking Clemi to babysit?

"I'd love to help, but I'll be working, helping to run the event. Could you ask anyone else? Maybe your sister knows someone?"

"She does not. Do *you* know someone?"

"I mean, it's short notice."

"I will need references, of course. I realize there's no time for formal written references, but a text will suffice. And it would be great if they could come to the hotel soon. I need a nap."

Now Clemi adds to her list of questions what constitutes *soon*.

"Tell whomever you find that he's very easy. They won't even notice him."

"I thought he had some behavioral issues."

"Of an extremely minor nature."

"He's just a little extra."

"Exactly."

Clemi is so flustered, she is not entirely sure how the phone call with Sveta concludes. She only knows it is over, and that now she is responsible for finding someone to care for Vlad. To watch him do whatever, soon. Her social connections in DC pretty much revolve around the bookstore, so she puts out the word by texting a few booksellers. You would think all of these bookish people would jump at the chance to make some extra money, especially when she tells them that the child in question belongs to the Chestnut Prize award winner. But all she gets are nos. Perhaps it would help if she could disclose it was Sveta's child, but as far as she understands it, the winner is meant to be kept on the down-low until the award is presented tonight.

She then has what seems like a brilliant idea: Skylar, who of course knows the identity of the winner, has children, so perhaps she can help. She sends a text:

Know anyone who can watch Sveta's kid?

Skylar's reply is instantaneous.

Three laughing/crying emojis, followed by:

Hell no.

Her third response is more tempered.

Wish I could help but the kids will be with my ex.

Clemi wonders what Skylar knows that she does not. She drops into a google search the words *Sveta Attais* and *Vlad*. The results that pop up look dodgy, as if clicking on the links could result in a hammer reaching out from inside the computer and whacking her on the head. But she can see from the headlines and introductory snippets of text that Vlad was supposedly responsible for some $52,000 in property damage to the Hôtel du Cap in Antibes. He and Sveta had stayed there three years ago for the Cannes Film Festival premiere of her first novel's film adaptation.

Likely this is just malicious gossip. Otherwise, this story would be popping up on more legitimate websites, like *People* magazine or *The New York Times*. Or so she assumes. She likes celebrity gossip as much as the next person, but how the media covers it is not her area of expertise.

The original plan, the one where she spent a leisurely morning drinking coffee (limited edition, master-crafted single origin from Costa Rica, according to the information on the pod), rereading *The Marrakesh Social Club* while reclining in a Ludwig Mies van der Rohe MR Adjustable Chaise Longue, pretending she is a person who could afford a Ludwig Mies van der Rohe MR Adjustable Chaise Longue, or even a person who knows the difference between a Ludwig Mies van der Rohe MR Adjustable Chaise Longue and an IKEA Boinga-Boinga chair, is now shot. Ditto for her plan to get her nails done, one of her secret bougie luxuries. Her nails are nothing special either before or after the thirty-dollar expense, but that's not the point. She finds something cathartic, even rejuvenating, in the contemplation of colors, the consideration of the range of possibilities, the ways she might change, or maybe tweak, the world's perception of who she is until the polish begins to chip and fade. That said, she usually selects a hue so bland as to be unnoticeable.

But a manicure is not in the cards today, and it is nearing the time she had better pull herself together—take a shower and get dressed early so she can head over to the hotel to meet this Vlad child, figure out what she is meant to do with him. She considers the many hours she has spent poring over Sveta's stunningly beautiful prose, thinking about how Sveta is the only writer in the world she has ever wanted to meet, how she left her perfectly good job at the bookstore (okay, low-paying, long hours, high-stress job, perhaps) to work at WLNP chiefly for the perk of meeting Sveta Attais. Now here she is, already wondering how quickly she can stick Sveta Attais and her "a little extra" son on the next flight to as-far-away-as-possible.

Outside the window, the yogis stream out of the studio, making way for the noon Pilates fusion class, if the app on her phone is accurate. She watches the mats being cleaned and rearranged, and a few minutes later, the new students arrive and take their places on said mats. One of them settles in the front row and looks out the window. She seems to be staring directly at Clemi. Clemi stares back. How she wishes she were there, staring back at herself here. Her thinking is beginning to scramble, and the day hasn't even properly begun.

Chapter 18

ALTHOUGH IT'S ANOTHER beautiful afternoon, with the tulips in bloom and the cherry blossoms a spray of pink on the sidewalk, Clemi decides to call an Uber rather than walk, given that she is wearing her best dress. The car deposits her at the hotel's main entrance, where she takes a deep breath and steps through the revolving doors that spit her out into the now-familiar lobby.

The place is bustling. Several guests who may or may not have just gotten off the large bus idling at the entrance are queued up in front of the registration desk. And a dozen or so people are seated in the lobby, some apparently using the space as a de facto meeting room. Others stream in and out of the restaurant, creating a hum of what the captions on a television show would likely call "indistinct background noise."

Attire is a hodgepodge of what looks like tourist garb—shorts and sneakers, baseball caps—but a few people look like they are already dressed in evening wear. Clemi hopes she is appropriately attired. When she'd asked Howard how to dress for the dinner, he had provided unhelpful and sometimes contradictory answers:

"*Dressy or dressy-ish,*" he'd said at first. "*No real dress code. But maybe along the lines of cocktail attire. Or more like cocktail-ish. I suppose you could even get away with business plus.*"

Then, the next day, in response to a telephone inquiry from a donor, she overheard Howard say the words "black-tie optional," which to Clemi sounded a little more intense than cocktail-ish or business plus.

Howard had then gone on to animatedly describe his own dress code faux pas when he once attended a White House State Dinner for the president of Canada.

"*Yes, of course I meant the prime minister,*" she'd heard him say into the phone. He rolled his eyes at Clemi conspiratorially, as if to signal that the person on the other end of the phone was ridiculous for thinking Howard didn't know the difference between the titles for heads of state. "*I couldn't find my cuff links anywhere. I had to run to Brooks Brothers at the last minute.*"

This recollection stirs up some nostalgia for those brief few carefree days when she and Howard shared an office, when they exchanged light banter between cat-free desks like characters in a workplace sitcom. Not to mention the days when Clemi had taken Howard at his word, had not thought to question whether he had really been invited to the White House and possibly spent some time chatting about books with Justin Trudeau. She had even allowed herself to imagine that perhaps, by virtue of working for WLNP, she might one day be invited to a State Dinner too.

Still, Clemi had found Howard's lack of clarity about what to wear somewhat surprising. Hadn't WLNP, or rather the Arthur Muller Foundation, been hosting this gala for something like fifty years now?

She doesn't want to get it wrong. At least not egregiously so, as she did back when she worked at the bookstore and had been invited to a cocktail party in New York, a rooftop gathering at the home of an executive at one of the big-five publishers. She'd been sent last-minute to fill in for her boss, who had come down with a bug and was too sick to attend. Mrs. Bernstein had paid for Clemi's train ticket and put her up in a nice hotel, even given her a per diem for food. But Mrs. Bernstein had been similarly vague in relating the dress code. *"Casual,"* she had said. To Clemi, casual meant jeans and a t-shirt, so she thought she was stepping things up when she'd put on a denim skirt with a new pair of strappy sandals, and even bought an expensive-for-her peasant top from Anthropologie.

Oh, how she had been misinformed! She thought this would be a gathering of booksellers—generally a freewheeling, leaning-toward-bohemian sartorial bunch. But it was not. The gathering was of New York publishing types. Mostly tall, thin people dressed in black, men and women alike. It was not a dripping-with-money situation—you could imagine these people had perhaps been the spawns of journalists or educators, and not railroad tycoons—but it was intimidating and somewhat depressing nonetheless. Clemi had felt she did not belong, even though she sort of did.

Twice that evening she had been mistaken for the host's babysitter, which makes Sveta's suggestion that she take care of Vlad a little triggering. But she did learn one important lesson from the New York debacle: When in doubt, wear black.

Clemi looks around the lobby and reminds herself of the layout, then finds the bank of elevators that lead to the guest rooms. She enters and presses the button for the tenth floor. A moment passes. The lift seems to not be moving. The doors reopen, and indeed she is still on the lobby level. A young woman wearing a hijab, with two small children in tow, enters and nods at Clemi, then presses her keycard to the pad on the elevator and hits the button for 11. Ah! She needs a keycard to make this thing move! Clemi quickly taps the 10 again and smiles at the woman so as not to give the impression that she is basically hitching a ride. Which she is. Still, "No need to call security," she wants to tell this woman, who may or may not be eyeing Clemi with suspicion. Clemi is not a criminal! She is a good person! An honest person! In the short history of her life to date, she has mostly not committed bank fraud!

It is 3:00 p.m. She has exactly one hour to sort out the Vlad situation. Then, she is meant to find Skylar in the ballroom at four to meet the interns who have volunteered to help, and to talk with Penelope, whose team will be prepping food and setting tables. In Howard's absence, Clemi is apparently the point person for questions, which is a terrifying thought given that she is the person least likely to have answers. Her party-planning expertise involves knowing how to order pizza. Now she is overseeing a gala for 242 glamorous Washingtonians who are paying, at minimum, $800 per plate.

Her lack of expertise should hardly matter, she reassures herself. This event is a well-oiled machine that will run itself. Plus, Skylar will be there, ditto for the interns, and the caterers are managing most of the logistics. Penelope is one of the most highly regarded caterers in town; go to any party and ask who is providing the food, and chances are, it is Penelope.

So, really, what could go wrong?

Ha! Clemi is aware that even hoping things will run smoothly is akin to a jinx. As her late grandmother would have said, it's a *kinehora* to think something is good, or even that it might not be a total catastrophe. Throw salt over your left shoulder. Say "tfu tfu." Spit once per *tfu*, again, over the left shoulder, or it will not work. Burn something in effigy. Perform a ritual dance around a bonfire. Do whatever you need to do—just don't, for the love of God, believe for a moment that things might go well.

In any event, before she expends all her nervous energy on the dinner, she must first deal with Sveta. Keeping an eye on this Vlad child might not have been part of the original plan, but Clemi is determined to make it work. What choice does she have, really? Besides, she has watched many women multitask, have their babysitting arrangements fall through, and still meet deadlines. With or without Vlad by her side, she will meet Penelope at four. With or without Vlad, she will—somehow or another—get through the evening.

She does a quick mental body scan, adjusting the straps on her dress, running her fingers through her hair, pulling the lip gloss from her bag, and applying a fresh coat. She remembers how, at her cousin's wedding last year—a splashy affair in the Hamptons—Clemi had worn this same dress. She had done everything in her power to look her best and had even gone to Drybar to have her hair styled into something called a Cosmo, then had her makeup professionally applied. Why? Because her mother was going to be there, and she hadn't seen her mother in more than a year.

After pulling her into a stiff, awkward hug, Elena had stepped back to assess her daughter. Clemi had thought, given how much time she had spent preening, that her mother would comment on her appearance, that she would at least grudgingly acknowledge that she liked Clemi's shoes, hair, or dress.

"Stand up straight," her mother said. That was all. Although Clemi had been a little bit crushed by this, she had obeyed.

Yes, she is aware it is not a healthy thing that her mother continues to hold this much power over her. Clemi is, after all, twenty-six. But this command had made an impression. Today, no matter what happens, she is going to stand up straight. Or at least try. She hesitates a moment when she arrives at Sveta's room, pops a breath mint, and knocks.

Sveta swings opens the door, and Clemi is so startled by her appearance that she is momentarily speechless. Sveta is even more stunning than her author photo. She is nearly six feet tall. Her bearing is so regal, she ought to have a crown atop her head. Her long dark hair is sculpted and braided and sprayed into a complicated gravity-defying shape that makes Clemi think of a bird of paradise, which happens to be an advanced yoga pose she cannot fathom either. (Truly cannot so much as decipher what limb goes where.)

Sveta smells of sandalwood and bergamot, of first-class air travel and of literary success. Even wrapped in a hotel-issue terry cloth robe, wearing no makeup, Sveta is the most striking, elegant woman Clemi has seen in her entire life.

She pulls Clemi into an embrace as if they are dear old friends, and this time when Sveta exclaims, "My darling Clementine!" Clemi does not bristle. *Call me whatever you like*, she thinks deliriously. *Just don't ever let me go.*

Sveta ushers her into an enormous suite with a breathtaking view of the city. She can see the Capitol. She can see the

Potomac River. She can see planes hovering in the sky. She also sees an enormous gift basket of fruit and cookies, a bottle of champagne chilling in an ice bucket, a room service tray with silver platters of food, and several elaborate flower arrangements set in vases.

"Thank you for this," Sveta says, gesturing to all the finery in the room. "Such generosity! So much more than I expected. So kind of you to upgrade us to a suite! And all this food!"

Ah, this is an upgrade. That, at least, makes more sense. But . . . is WLNP footing this bill? That is very generous of them. *Of us.* Or, at this point, possibly of *her.* Clemi hopes the room has been prepaid, because it seems unlikely that whatever credit card is on file is going to work upon checkout.

"I have to warn you, Vlad is a little out of sorts. Jet-lagged, no doubt. He did not eat his breakfast or his lunch. I'm hoping you might be able to get some food in him. Otherwise, he'll be cranky. And trust me, that is not something you want to see."

From what Clemi has glimpsed online, she believes this is likely true.

"No problem, but I should explain that since Howard is unable to be here tonight, and unless our board president shows up, I will have to step in to give the welcoming remarks. Also, I'll need to greet the guests as they arrive. I'm basically the interim executive director." Normally she would not say something this obnoxious-sounding and grandiose, but she wants Sveta to understand that she is a person with a job. She is the ED pro tempore, not a babysitter. Or maybe not *only* a babysitter. At least not tonight.

Sveta tears a limb of grapes off the vine and studies it, then plucks a single green orb, wipes it on a napkin, and pops it in her mouth. It's not clear if she has registered Clemi's protests.

"So, I guess what I'm saying is that it might be hard for me to watch Vlad the entire evening," she continues. "I wonder if we might ask the hotel if they can help? They must have babysitting services, or maybe they have a recommendation?"

"Surely you are not suggesting I leave Vlad with a *stranger*."

"Well, no, but I'm sure they are properly vetted, so not strangers to the hotel, at least."

She's not so sure at all. What does she know of hotel babysitting services? She's tempted to point out that she, too, is a stranger, but knows this will not likely help the cause.

"Well, what if I watch the person who watches Vlad?"

"Darling, that's adorable. But that's exactly what I will be doing. I'll watch you watching Vlad, so we don't need to layer on a third person. Do you see?"

Clemi does not see. Or rather, she does see. She sees there is no way out of this situation.

"And not to worry. You can still do all the things you need to do. Now, if you don't mind, I am exhausted beyond words. I've reached the stage in my life where those long flights just wipe me out. Especially with a child to entertain. You'll understand someday when you have children. I need to get some rest."

Before Clemi can respond, an adorable boy with a curly, thick mop of hair comes screeching into the room. He stops abruptly just before crashing into the credenza that holds two of the flower arrangements, which is a very good thing. Clemi thinks of Road Runner, the cartoon character who moves at high speeds and then stops on a dime, leaving a trail of dust and gravel in his wake.

Vlad is wearing orange high-top sneakers with fluorescent light-up soles. The rubber appears to be springy. Just looking at them makes Clemi want to jump. Something on his person, Clemi is not sure what, makes a high-pitched, highly annoying squeak that is painful on the ear. She wonders whether it's the shoes. In Vlad's hand is a large stuffed something that is orange and yellow and has a ring of fluff, or maybe feathers, around its neck.

"You must be Vlad! And who is that?" Clemi asks, pointing to the toy. She hopes to win him over before he has the chance to declare her an enemy combatant.

"You must be Vlad! And who is that?" The toy is now speaking, evidently. And it sounds like a mechanical version of Clemi, which is highly disturbing.

The boy looks up at her with his big brown eyes and long, enviable lashes and begins to laugh. He sets the toy on the floor, and Clemi can see it is some variety of poultry. A duck, perhaps. Or maybe a chicken. It begins to toddle on the ground, shaking its head from side to side, and then says again, more loudly this time, "You must be Vlad! And who is that?" It then begins to laugh.

"What the what?" Clemi says, stopping herself from uttering the curse word that is on the tip of her tongue.

"Oh, ignore that," says Sveta. "That's just a toy his grandmother bought him at the airport before we left."

"It has a recording device?"

Sveta nods affirmatively. "It connects to an app, so you could even use it to take notes in a pinch."

Clemi doesn't want to make too much of this, but really, this is not cool. Sure, she knows he's just a kid messing around with a toy, but this thing has just recorded her without her consent, which feels a little icky.

"He will tire of it quickly. By tomorrow, he will have moved on to something new," Sveta continues. "In fact, we saw something in the gift shop when we checked in. A panda, I think. You could go get him that if you'd like."

"I want a panda!" Vlad says.

"If you behave for dear sweet Clemi, maybe she will get you a panda."

Clemi wonders whether she is meant to pay for said gift-shop panda.

"I want the panda right now!" Vlad says, stomping his little foot hard enough for the room service tray to wobble. His high-top sneaker lights up purple and orange, punctuating this demand.

"Not now, but if you are a good boy for Clemi, she will take you to the shop tomorrow. Maybe she will buy you some candy too."

Tomorrow? Clemi would like to tell Sveta that tomorrow she will be long gone. Although, well, perhaps not quite. She will at least tie up loose ends, help get them to the airport at a minimum.

She takes a moment before responding to any of this, reminding herself that Sveta is one of the most highly regarded authors in the world—her hero, her role model—and that she ought to remain calm and go with the flow, be kind and accommodating to this child.

"What is the name of your bird?" Clemi asks, squatting down to Vlad's eye level.

"It's a chicken and his name is Homer."

"Homer like Homer Simpson?"

"Um, Homer as in have you heard of *The Odyssey*?" Vlad responds. He then pushes some button on Homer, which not only increases the volume but does something to Clemi's voice that seems to translate it into a different language, followed again by Vlad's cackling laugh.

"Now you speak Portuguese!"

Clemi is still stuck on the Homer situation. "Are you reading *The Odyssey*?"

"He read it last month. Now he is on a spy novel binge," Sveta says as Vlad plucks his chicken from the floor and approaches the tray bearing the split of champagne. He picks up a glass and takes a sip.

"Vlad, no!" Sveta snaps. "You've had enough already. Do you remember what we discussed? You need to behave well for our new friend Clementine while Mummy accepts her award."

"I have an idea. Let's read a book!" Clemi remembers from her bookstore days that refocusing the conversation is better than just saying no. If a customer asked for a book they did not have in stock, for example, they would either say, "We can have that here in two days," or "If that's the book you want, you might prefer this one!"

"We've been traveling for a million hours, and I've already read a million books."

"Okay. Fair enough. Why don't we . . . watch a movie?"

"I already watched a movie."

"What about another movie?"

"I already watched another movie."

"I'm going to take a nap," Sveta announces. "But first, give me a hug," she says to Vlad.

The boy approaches his mother, and she wraps him in her arms. "I love you I love you I love you," she says.

"I love you too, Mommy."

Sveta begins to lift him up, which seems impossible. He is not a large child—in fact, he is rather thin—but he is no longer what Clemi would consider to be a liftable size. He wraps his arms around his mother's neck and his legs around her waist, then gives her a kiss on the cheek.

"Oof!" Sveta says, setting Vlad back down on his feet and rubbing her lower back. "I keep forgetting. I need to stop doing that! You are getting so big, my darling."

Clemi would never wish back pain on a fellow human being, yet she is relieved to see that the back pain is for real. This whole doting on Vlad situation is both a little much and surprisingly touching.

Nonetheless, as she watches Sveta enter the bedroom and shut the door, leaving her in charge of this wild child, Clemi cannot quite believe this is happening.

Chapter 19

THEY ARE GETTING ready to go to the gift shop for a snack—an absurd, even obscene thing to do given the amount of food in the suite—when Vlad asks for the passcode to Clemi's phone.

"You have a text from Skylar," he announces. "Would you like me to read it to you?"

"How and why do you have my phone?" She had popped into the restroom for a minute, and he must have taken it out of her bag.

"Do you want to give me the code so I can read the text to you or not?"

"Maybe not? Please give me the phone."

The chicken repeats the command at a too-loud volume. "Please give me the phone," it says, or rather, squawks.

Clemi is predisposed to finding the good in every person, but this boy is proving a challenge. She wonders if this high-energy state is his norm, or if he is wired from travel and possibly too much sugar. She can't help but think of Ezra Pound, hopping around the tennis court like a manic bunny rabbit. That's what

Vlad reminds her of. Not Ezra Pound, obviously, but a bunny. An Energizer Bunny. She would like to find, and then remove, Vlad's battery pack, or at least switch his power mode to low. And what she would like to do to the talking chicken is unspeakable. She entertains visions of locating a knife and ripping out his stuffing. Setting him on fire. Drowning him in the tub.

Vlad locks eyes with her for a moment like he's going to protest, but then he breaks into a beatific smile and hands over the phone.

"What does it say?" he asks.

"*We're here. Remind me what you want us to do about the silent auction cards.*"

"What does that mean?"

"Oh crap, I almost forgot about that," she says, ignoring the question. "Let's go, Vlad. I need to go to the ballroom, and you need to come with me."

Unsurprisingly, Vlad has some ideas about possible activities that do not involve going to the ballroom, all of which might accurately be called *noncompliant*: going to the Spy Museum, buying a hoverboard for overnight delivery since he just realized he left his in Morocco, or playing a game of chess.

Clemi agrees to the game of chess—even though, much to her embarrassment, she does not know how to play.

"That's okay," says Vlad. "I'll teach you."

They proceed to line up the pieces in an order Clemi is pretty sure has nothing to do with the actual game of chess. Then Vlad takes a pint-size toy robot from his backpack, knocks all of the pieces off the board, and announces, "I got your queen. You lose. Let's get out of this place."

Clemi feels like she might cry, not about this chess game,

but about all this chess game symbolizes, i.e., a complete loss of control.

———

Just outside the ballroom they find four bright-eyed, well-dressed young people gathered around Skylar. They are listening attentively, some of them typing notes into their phones. These are likely the interns, or so Clemi assumes. The *temp* interns is what she means. The ones who have volunteered to help with this event. Not like Skylar, the intern intern. Or at least the oldest of the interns by some twenty years.

Age is not the only thing that distinguishes Skylar from the others. She is notable for her amount of bling. This may be a glitzy affair, sure, but Skylar is more appropriately dressed for the Oscars. She wears a full-length sequined gown with a racy slit up the side, is draped in diamonds, and is balancing quite impressively on ridiculously high stiletto heels.

Skylar notices Clemi and Vlad, and she then waves them closer.

Vlad at least makes a good first impression, what with his floppy hair, his high-top light-up shoes, and the stuffed chicken pressed to his chest. He looks angelic, even. And hey, maybe he is! He's a spirited kid! That Hôtel du Cap story? Probably just a rumor. Clemi doesn't believe everything she reads.

"Come join us," Skylar urges. "I was just telling everyone about the incident last year. Establishing proper protocols should anything like that happen again." She turns to Vlad and puts her hand on his head like he's a puppy. "Aren't you the cutest thing ever?"

"This is Vlad," Clemi says to the interns. She is just about to explain that he is Sveta's son when she remembers the winner has not yet been publicly announced, and she is not sure what has been shared with the volunteers.

"And hi, everyone. I'm Clemi, the new programs director. I don't know anything about the incident, so I probably ought to listen in too."

"Sorry, Clemi. I forgot that you haven't met everyone. This is Sarah, Vikram, Biff, and Lili." She nods toward each intern as she says their name, and they each give a little wave in return.

"Hey, my man," says Biff, giving Vlad a high five. "Glad you came to help us!"

Biff? Perhaps Clemi misheard. She looks at the name tag printed in a large font attached to the lanyard around his neck. His name is indeed *Biff*, which is surely short for something. Biff is buff. He looks like a surfer, or like someone who would play one on TV. He is tall, tan, and shaggy, with very white teeth. He is muscular too. His biceps are practically bursting through the sleeves of his shirt, which seem a size too small.

"Hey," Vlad replies, sounding surprisingly timid. He seems quite taken with Biff. Enchanted. Or perhaps just intimidated. Biff motions Vlad over and whispers something in his ear, and Vlad's face lights up brighter than his shoes.

"Sure," Skylar cuts in. "I was telling them about what happened last year when a certain board member's husband started hitting on the award winner."

"Seriously?" Clemi says. "I can't believe it." She's not sure why she says this, given that she believes this entirely.

"Believe it," Skylar commands. "He's a serial philanderer. Everyone knows that. He was also hitting on me. But that's a whole other story. We have a history. It's complicated."

This disclosure is followed by a moment of collective awkward silence.

"But in his defense, he was extremely inebriated. And it became a whole thing. We couldn't find ... er ... this gentleman's wife. To this day, I don't know where she disappeared to that night, but anyway, who here remembers how we managed the situation?"

Sarah raises her hand. "We called an Uber for him."

"Exactly. But what was the problem with that?"

"He refused to get in."

"Right again. And why?"

"Wrong kind of car."

"Bingo, Sarah. So what is the lesson, should something like that happen again?"

"Call Uber Lux."

"Bingo again! Except you have to use your judgment," Skylar explains. "It depends on *who* needs a car. Pro tip: Try to use *their* app so WLNP isn't paying for the ride. We're trying to keep a cap on expenses right now."

Clemi appreciates this nod toward solvency, but it's not like the difference between a thirty-dollar and a fifty-dollar Uber ride is going to matter right now, given how this entire Ponzi scheme of an enterprise seems poised to collapse.

"Anything else we should know?" Vikram asks. "Since I think Sarah is the only one here who worked the event last year."

"No, I think that covers it," says Skylar. "The rest is just about checking people in. You have the guest list there, in alphabetical order. Don't forget to hand each guest a silent auction card, though . . . Oh, wait, I almost forgot. Clemi has something she needs us to do."

Biff is now playing with Vlad's chicken, and the two of them are stifling laughs. Probably they have just recorded Skylar and translated her into who knows what . . . Nepali, maybe. Clemi is grateful Vlad has made a friend, but she gets the sense that Biff might not be the best influence.

"Yes, thanks, Skylar. Before we hand out the silent auction cards, we need to make a quick adjustment. I know it's late to be doing this, but we only have about three hundred cards, so I hope we can get through this quickly. If you look at the bottom of the card, you'll see Javier Jiménez-Jiménez's name. Very unfortunately, Mr. Jiménez-Jiménez has passed."

"Dude, that's so sad," says Biff.

"That *is* sad," says Lili. "We were assigned his book, the one on totalitarianism . . . I forget what it was called . . . in my graduate seminar on totalitarianism."

"*On Totalitarianism*," says Clemi. "That was the title."

"No, actually, I think it was *The End of Democracy*," says Lili.

"I think that was a different book. On the same subject."

"Hmm . . . maybe. But I'm pretty sure Jiménez-Jiménez also wrote *The End of Democracy*. I mean, I could be wrong but . . ."

Lili is now pulling out her phone to check, and Clemi thinks perhaps she has finally met her booknerd match.

"Regardless, yes, it is a big loss," Clemi agrees. "So what we need to do is remove his name from the program."

Five pair of intern eyes look to her to elaborate on how this is meant to be accomplished.

"I'm not sure what the best option is," Clemi says. "I'm open to ideas. The thing is, if we cut his name out, we'll lose all of the copy about WLNP on the back."

"Also, it will look stupid," Vlad offers, which is not untrue. "Why don't you take a black Sharpie and just cross out his name?"

"I suppose," Clemi says. "Although that seems a little dark, given that he has just passed. I don't think we should actually, like, strike him out."

"Why is *cutting* him out better?" Vlad asks.

"No, you're right. I suppose we could just leave the card as is and put a sign at the silent auction table explaining why this particular item has been deleted. Although *deleted* is probably not the right word. The more I think about it, a sign might be the most tasteful way to go." She can't quite believe she is having this discussion with an eight-year-old.

"Leave it to us," Skylar says. "We'll figure something out."

"Totally," says Biff. "That's what we're here for. Let us all ideate on this for a bit, and we'll come up with a plan."

"Fantastic. Thank you all so much. I'm going to find Penelope and see what needs doing inside. Come on, Vlad."

"I'm going to stay here and help Biff ideate," Vlad announces. "Biff says it's okay."

Clemi is not going to leave this child with this child. But Skylar cuts in. "We'll all keep an eye on him, honey. Just go do your thing." She pulls another chair up to the registration table. "Here, Vlad. Come sit right here. You can sit next to Biff. We'll put you to work."

Clemi is not sure what she thinks of this plan, but already he is seated at the table, Biff on one side, and on the other, Sarah, who—with her no-nonsense shoulder-length hair, her simple, elegant black dress, her practical shoes, and her expertise in stuffing drunk philanderers into Ubers—seems like a responsible human being, not to mention one who can possibly do a better job of maintaining her patience with Vlad than Clemi can.

"You're right," Lili says.

"About what?"

"Jiménez-Jiménez wrote *On Totalitarianism*, but not any of the five books called *The End of Democracy*. I'm deeply embarrassed."

"Easy mistake," says Clemi, feeling more gratified than she should.

Chapter 20

THE TRANSFORMATION OF this cavernous, soulless, corporate space into a glittering, sparkling ballroom is, to Clemi's eye, nothing short of miraculous. Penelope's team has strung lights overhead and filled the place with elegant floral arrangements. The room smells like gardenias, somehow, even though what she sees looks more like clusters of purple and white hydrangeas. Elegant block print cloths are draped over each table, and calligraphed name cards are set in front of each place setting. The array of silver cutlery is somewhat intimidating, with all the extra forks and spoons no one will likely know how to use, even if they are certifiably posh human beings.

Clemi looks up at the stage and sees a podium, then says a silent prayer to the gods of travel on Dr. Jolly's behalf:

May your flights be smooth. May your connections connect. May the customs agents grant you easy passage. May your luggage arrive. May the lanes of the Capital Beltway traffic part.

Never has she wanted to see anyone quite as much as she would like to see Dr. Jolly in precisely two hours. Should he fail to arrive, and in the absence of Howard, Clemi may be expected to rise from the table, walk to the stage, mount the stairs without tripping, welcome everyone to the dinner, and thank them for their support. Surely she can manage this. It's not as if anyone will expect much from her. She can introduce herself as the new programs director and simply explain that . . . well, probably best to not explain anything. Just a simple welcome should do.

Still, the possibility of getting through this without something going wrong seems about as likely as her winning a gold medal in Olympic ski jumping.

Penelope spies Clemi, but rather than greet her, she stares. Or maybe she glares. Whatever she is doing, it is completely unnerving. Clemi wonders whether her little bit of makeup has smeared, or if her hair is sticking up strangely. Maybe she has some goop hanging from a nostril, or a big wiry hair sprouting from her chin.

Penelope speaks at last. "I'm usually a good judge of things," she says. "I'm not sure if I'm more upset about my radar being off, or about the check."

"I don't know what you're talking about," Clemi bluffs, even though she knows exactly what Penelope is talking about.

"The check is what I'm talking about. I thought you were trustworthy."

"I am. Absolutely. What about the check?"

"Okay, let's not play this game. There is a problem with the check you wrote yesterday. It's called *insufficient funds*."

"What? That's incredible!"

What Clemi really means is that it seems incredible that Penelope would already know this. Having been on the receiving end of a bad check once, she did not learn of the problem until her own rent check bounced a week later. That was about four years ago, however, and she supposes that rapidly advancing technology has made it harder to commit bank fraud.

"Do you need proof?" Penelope pulls her phone from her pocket and begins to open her bank app.

"It's okay. I mean, I believe you. Of course I believe you. I just don't understand how that could have happened. Let me try to reach Howard again. Like I said, I'm new on the job. But I'm sure there's a reasonable explanation, and we can sort it out tomorrow. Or maybe Monday, being realistic."

"Normally, per our contract, we would walk out the door right now. Our work would be done. The only reason we are still here is because I don't want to make a scene. The Panamanian ambassador and her husband are here tonight. I'm catering their daughter's wedding this fall, and since it's a huge event, I think they want to see us in action. Otherwise, I assure you, we would already be long gone."

"You have my word: You will be paid. I don't understand what happened with the check, but we will make it right."

Clemi sounds so convincing, she is almost convincing herself.

Penelope's scowl remains, but she switches subjects. "While you are here, I have some questions about dietary restrictions and preferences."

"Sure!" Clemi says, aware that she sounds a little too chirpy. "Happy to help!" As if she can help. As if she knows anything about the dietary restrictions and preferences of even one single guest. Although, that's not entirely true. She knows Vlad likes his chicken nuggets fried to a crisp and that he is not a big fan of eggs.

"Can you look over this list and be sure we have it right? I must say, in all my thirty years of catering high-profile Washington events, I have never had to make this many accommodations."

"Really?" Clemi asks. "I had no idea."

Penelope is not done complaining. "I mean, I'm used to the allergies. That's not a problem. We always have the nut allergies and the people who can't eat dairy, the allergies to nightshades—no problem. And I'm completely on board with the kosher meals, the halal meals, the vegetarians, the pescatarians, the vegans. But I don't know what I'm supposed to do with this guy. He is one of your board members, evidently, and he only emailed about an hour ago, which is rather late. Plus, I don't even understand what he's saying."

"Who is it?"

Clemi is not sure why she bothers to ask. She doesn't know most of the guests, and there's not much she can do about whatever it is he wants.

Penelope looks down at the sheet of paper in her hand. "Percy Garfinkle is his name."

"Oh, him. I don't know him, but I remember Howard saying something about him. I forget what."

"Well, he has some very complicated—and like I said, *last-minute*—requirements."

"Like what?"

"Like he wants his meat cooked to specific and somewhat unusual temperatures. And he does not eat pork. Not for religious reasons, he says, but because he cannot abide eating the meat of pigs since they are highly intelligent animals. He has opinions about octopi as well."

"Oh boy, I'm so sorry."

"I'm far from done," says Penelope. "He dislikes mushrooms, brussels sprouts, broccoli, and beets. Also, saltwater fish."

"Um, wow. That is a lot. I don't know what to say."

"What are we supposed to feed this man?" Penelope asks.

"I mean, it sounds like he will be able to eat a number of things, as long as they are cooked to specification, right?"

"We aren't going out on a limb to accommodate this guy. Like I said, I don't mind the allergies. But his fussiness is just fussy. I can't do that to my staff."

"Well, maybe we just go vegetarian for him, but no beets, broccoli, brussels sprouts. Or just give him a lot of bread. Any chance you are serving a freshwater fish option?"

"We are having sea bass. But I'm not sure if it's freshwater or saltwater. None of that seemed relevant when we planned the menu."

"I mean, I'm not a caterer, but it must be called sea bass for a reason, right?" Clemi asks.

"No, the thing is, it's both. Some sea bass are saltwater and some are freshwater."

"No way! That's so unexpected!"

Penelope does not reply. Her displeasure at sea bass sui generis, at Clemi, at Percy Garfinkle, at the bounced check seems about to erupt. Her mouth opens as if she is ready to spew hot lava, but she is mercifully interrupted by a young suited waiter who taps her on the shoulder to ask about the placement of a new batch of floral arrangements that has just arrived on a wheeled cart.

While they are discussing this, someone on the stage says "test, test, test" into the microphone, which is set at an ear-splitting volume. At the same time, there is a tap on Clemi's shoulder. She flinches. For all she knows, it's the FBI or whoever it is that arrests people who write bad checks. But it's Skylar.

Clemi is so happy to see a potential ally—or perhaps, more accurately, a coconspirator—that she throws her arms around her and gives her a hug even though she only saw her about two minutes ago.

"Easy, easy," Skylar says. "My hair . . ." She disentangles herself from Clemi's embrace and takes a step back. "You okay, Clemi?"

"She is not okay," Penelope says. "She is in trouble. All of you are in trouble. Your guests are the most high-maintenance bunch of people I've ever dealt with, not to mention that the check she wrote just bounced."

"Oh my gosh," Skylar says. "That's impossible! Although . . . wait a minute, Clemi, did you write the check from the *old* TD account?"

Clemi has no idea where Skylar is going with this since she's the one who helped her with the check, but she seems to have a plan.

Before Clemi can respond, Skylar turns to Penelope, lowers her voice, and says in a confidential tone, "She's new. She doesn't have a clue about what's going on. And Howard had a family emergency, so we're scrambling a bit. But you know WLNP. We always make good."

Clemi winces but is happy to be thrown under the bus if it gets her out of this mess, at least for now.

Penelope looks skeptical. Her lips, accented by a shiny pink gloss, begin to move, but then stop. Clemi imagines her recapping all the reasons WLNP might not *always make good*, which could turn into a complicated rant, but what she actually says is more straightforward:

"I don't believe you. Not a single word. But we're professionals. We will follow through on our commitment, and then, if the finances aren't sorted out on Monday, we will get a lawyer and sue your ass. And I'll take it to the press. You'll be reading about this in *Washingtonian*. And in *The Washington Post*. It will be on CNN. It will be on Fox News. You've messed with the wrong person. With your history, you'll go down hard. Mark my words!"

Clemi is not sure that a bounced check to a caterer is going to make the national news, but this does not seem to be a statement that needs correction.

"Penelope, you are making too much of this," Skylar says. "You did such a beautiful job at my second wedding, and I think you know that even if I have to write a check out of my personal account, I will do it."

Penelope's expression changes from contempt to confusion. She stares at Skylar, then lets out a little squeal and throws her arms around her too. "Oh my God. Skylar Hymowitz? Or is it Skylar Rockefeller? I mean . . . wait . . . Papadopoulos? I'm so sorry I didn't recognize you. You changed your hair!"

"Yes, well, I changed my name too. A couple of times. Now it's Skylar Papadopoulos again. But yes, it's still me."

"So good to see you! How's your mom?"

"Mom is the same. She's on a cruise with her new boyfriend."

"Wait, she has a *new* boyfriend? She's not dating that cute barista anymore?"

"Good grief, thank goodness that one's over. I haven't met this new guy though, so not sure if this is better or worse."

Buff Biff leans his head into the room with an announcement. "Your friend Vlad just told me he is bored, so he went back to the room. He said to tell you not to worry."

"Seriously?" Clemi says. "You let him go? He's only eight. He shouldn't be running around the hotel on his own."

"I mean, yes? I'm sure he'll be fine. He was super helpful. Very quick study, that kid. He got through redacting almost all of the silent auction cards, then said he is jet-lagged and needs a nap."

As if, Clemi thinks. As if Vlad is going to take a nap. As if she doesn't have enough to contend with tonight.

"I'll be right back," she tells Penelope.

"No way. I need you. I've got, like, fourteen more questions for you. I haven't even begun. I'm a little confused about who is sitting at table twelve. Also, someone just texted that they are allergic to ice."

"Allergic to ice?"

"Yes, and I don't know who sent the text."

"I'll try to figure it out. But in a minute. I'll be right back. I need to find Vlad."

"I've got it," Skylar says. "Don't worry about a thing. I can manage."

"Just tell me what you know about the ice person," Penelope yells to Clemi as she turns to leave.

"No idea," says Clemi. "It's probably a typo. Maybe he's allergic to . . . lice?"

"I mean, who isn't?" says Skylar. "My kids, you cannot imagine. It's a total nightmare, and trust me, it doesn't matter where you send them to school. We pay $48,000 a year for private school, but they come home with lice. We might as well send them to public school to get ordinary lice, right? I suppose he could have meant mice too. But, obviously, we aren't going to be serving mice. Not for $800 a plate."

Chapter 21

CLEMI STEPS BACK out into the hallway. Standing upon the expanse of the dizzying commercial-grade martini glass carpet, she looks in both directions, trying to remember which way to go. She is still contemplating ice, lice, and mice. What might this person have meant? She runs through the alphabet as she makes her way through a dimly lit corridor, hoping she is headed in the right direction.

Dice? Nice? Rice? Rice! He must be allergic to rice! She is tempted to turn around and run back into the ballroom shouting, "Rice! Rice! Rice! Don't serve him *rice!*" But she doesn't have time. She has to find Vlad before Sveta wakes up from her nap and realizes Clemi is incapable of keeping an eye on her son. Also, she needs to get him dressed for tonight. She sends Penelope a text instead. It reads, simply:

Rice!

Eventually she finds an escalator. Who knows if it's the right one, but it hardly matters, as long as it goes up. Everything in this maze of a hotel seems to somehow connect. She weaves through the lobby and over to the elevators, and again she presses the button only to go nowhere. It is like the movie *Groundhog Day*; she will have to live this day over and over and over until she gets it right, and one of the many things wrong with this awful day is that she is still without a hotel keycard.

She contemplates joining the line at the front desk to explain her keycard situation to the concierge but is saved by the arrival of a guest approaching the elevator. The man seems in his late forties, with a receding hairline and bit of a hairy belly peeking through a shirt that has popped a button. He looks a little sad. Not like he is about-to-burst-into-tears sad, but more like life has given him a beating. Like maybe he's mid-divorce, fighting with his soon-to-be ex about who gets the Vitamix and how often he can see the dog. He's what Clemi and her college friends used to refer to as "Sad Dads." They can be observed sitting at bars, loading up on half-priced beer and happy-hour appetizers, something preposterously called "Oriental-style snack mix" set out for them in little bowls like birdseed for cockatoos. This particular Sad Dad is pushing, or rather dragging, a roller bag that is—sadly—missing a wheel. Garments are pushing through the partially opened zipper like an abscess.

"Thanks for holding the elevator," he says. He seems winded, a bit besieged. "You're a lifesaver. My flight was late, then I almost missed my connection, and don't even get me started on the traffic coming in from Dulles. I still need to shower and change, and I haven't even written my remarks yet."

"Remarks?"

"Yeah. For a dinner tonight. I have to give the welcoming remarks. I wasn't sure I'd even make it. All this running around, it's getting to be too much at this age. In fact, I had an epiphany on the flight. This is going to be my last year as board president. It's bittersweet, of course, and there are things I'm going to miss, but it's time. I feel it in my bones. You know how you can dither about something for years, and all of a sudden, it becomes crystal clear?"

"Goodness," Clemi says. "Are you Dr. Jolly?"

He looks at Clemi, astonished.

"I mean, I have been called that, actually. How did you know? I've been called many things, some of them far worse over the course of my career. You cannot imagine how cruel people can be. Which is part of why it's time for me to step down. Anyway, sorry, not sure why I'm dumping all of this on you."

"Oh, no problem. I get it." She thinks she gets it, but really, she is mildly confused. What's so wrong with calling him by his name? "I'm Clemi. The new programs director, by the way."

"Oh, very nice to meet you! I'm pretty out of the loop these days, not sure who is even on staff, so forgive me."

They are still standing in the going-nowhere elevator, and Clemi wonders if he is ever going to press his keycard to the pad.

Now a family of five begins to clamber in. They are speaking a language Clemi does not recognize, but which sounds possibly Icelandic. Or Norwegian. Or Swedish. Something about it is suggestive to her ear of someplace cold.

The door remains propped open while they await the arrival of a sluggish teenager named Brittany. They call her name repeatedly. "Brittany!" Then something in the possibly Nordic tongue. Then, "Brittany! Brittany!"

Brittany finally appears. She wears earbuds, too-short cutoffs, and a Minnie Mouse t-shirt, and she looks pissed off.

Clemi and Sad Dad are now squashed against the back of the elevator car, and Clemi is marveling over this coincidence of running into the board president in the elevator. She is feeling hugely relieved.

"Can someone please press 10?" she asks.

"And 7," Sad Dad Board President adds.

The elevator has just begun to move, but unbelievably the doors open again. Now they are on the second floor, and an extremely large man with an extremely large suitcase pushes his way in.

"We are going up," Brittany's father explains in accented English.

"No problem," says the new occupant. "I'll ride up with you. Then down."

Clemi is now completely squashed against the back wall. She takes a deep breath. She might as well enjoy what air she can before they run out. She is beginning to experience a moment of déjà vu. She is fishing for a memory. Something comedic, perhaps? Vaudevillian, even? Something involving a lot of people being shoved into a car so small that it is physically impossible to contain them all, and yet in they continue to go. She envisions people standing on the sidewalk, waiting for a ride, and then a tiny car pulls up and they pile in, and one of them pops his head through the roof.

Where is this image coming from? She squeezes her eyes shut. Weirdly, that helps. She remembers! It's a GIF River recently sent her when the Metro was diverting the trains onto one track because of construction. The cars were completely packed.

The elevator stops on the sixth floor. Brittany's family needs to get out, which means the large man with the large suitcase needs to relocate to enable their exit. There is a shuffling about of bodies that reminds Clemi of the puzzle game Rush Hour, where one must strategically push plastic cars and trucks about on a grid to facilitate the exit of a particular vehicle. But then, confusingly, some members of Brittany's family step back in. Their rooms are evidently on a higher floor.

The mom props the elevator door open with her back as they converse in a mash-up of English and whatever else they are speaking. Dinner arrangements may be the subject, and whether to meet in the lobby or at a nearby hamburger joint.

There is some disagreement about this. Some faction of the family, it seems, would prefer Chinese. The elevator door begins to bleep in protest, as does Sad Dad Board President.

"For the love of God, some of us are in a hurry!" he says.

Clemi makes a mental note that he is a grouch.

"Okay, Amelia, don't forget we're in America now," the father says. "Go to your room with the kids and call me before this madman pulls out a gun."

At long last they reach the seventh floor, and the board president makes his way past the remaining family members and the large man with the large suitcase.

"See you soon," he says to Clemi.

"Yes, see you at dinner!" She is still a little puzzled. His schlumpy physical appearance is not suggestive of a person who writes about beauty, but she supposes that's on her. Just because someone is interested in the subject of looking one's best doesn't mean that they, themselves, need to present well.

"You dropped something," says the large man with the large suitcase, bending over to pick something up off the ground.

Clemi thinks, at first, that he is talking to her, but he hands an object to the departing board president that is red and round. It appears to be a small Styrofoam ball, but Clemi has a condition that might be called "clowns on the brain," so to her, it looks like a nose.

Chapter 22

EN ROUTE TO Sveta's suite, Clemi spies the remnants of someone's room service lunch languishing on a tray. It appears to be a club sandwich, grotesquely large, with multiple layers of bread that no human mouth could reasonably accommodate. Bits of turkey, bacon, and tomato peek out tantalizingly from the edges. Beside the half-eaten sandwich is a pile of fries. Clemi's stomach rumbles. Breakfast had been a single overly ripe banana lousy with brown spots. And in her hurry to get to the hotel, she forgot to eat lunch. Then she was too distracted, and polite, to help herself to anything from Sveta's room service tray, even though enough food was there to feed a dozen people for lunch.

She reaches the suite and is again stymied by the problem of the keycard—a stupid oversight on her part to not have asked Sveta for a key. She knocks and waits, knocks and waits, to no avail. She texts Sveta. There is no response. She calls her but it goes to voicemail.

A member of the housekeeping staff emerges from the room next door with an armful of sheets and towels.

"Perhaps you can help me?" Clemi asks. "I'm locked out of the room."

The young housekeeper looks at her with an expression best described as a laughing/crying emoji.

"Go to the front desk with your ID, and they will give you a new card."

"I will, but it's sort of an emergency. I've lost a child."

"You've lost a child?" This gets the woman's attention.

"Yes, have you seen a boy, about yea high?" Clemi puts her hand parallel to the ground, just below her armpit. "Dark hair. Possibly holding a stuffed chicken?"

The woman switches to Spanish. "¿El diablo pollo?"

Clemi's Spanish is not as strong as it ought to be given her many years of study, but she understands the question.

"Yes, that's probably him. Apologies if he did anything wrong. He's not a bad kid. He's just a little . . . extra."

The housekeeper's face has gone pale. She goes back inside the room and shuts the door.

Defeated, Clemi begins to knock again. This time Sveta appears. She is still wrapped in the hotel-issue robe, her hair now a little mussed.

"So sorry! I hope I didn't wake you!"

"Can I help you?" Sveta replies.

Clemi admittedly did not love being called *my darling Clementine*, but that was certainly preferable to this icy greeting.

"I just . . . Vlad," she says, deliberately vague. "He wants to . . ." For the life of her, Clemi can't think what to say without letting on that she has already lost track of this woman's son.

"I told him to just buy whatever he needs in the gift shop. And it's late enough in the day that he probably doesn't need sunscreen, but you can be the judge of that."

"Oh! No problem." Clemi is grateful for the tip. Vlad must be at the pool.

"But as long as you're here, why don't you take his clothes for the gala so you don't have to come back up to the room?"

"Do you want me to come in and get them or . . ."

"Sweetheart, is everything okay?" she hears a male voice ask.

Ah! This now makes sense. Sveta is *entertaining*.

This disembodied voice is sexy. Or maybe it's not. Maybe it's just a regular voice. It's the thought of what she has just interrupted—bodies entwined between high-thread-count sheets—that is sexy.

"It's fine! It's just the babysitter. I'm dealing with it," Sveta says.

Just the babysitter. Yup, that's me, Clemi thinks.

Clemi would like to get out of here quickly. She repeats the question about how to best procure Vlad's clothes.

"Whatever you prefer," Sveta says. "Although I suppose you might as well grab them now from his room." Sveta steps aside for Clemi to enter.

As Clemi makes her way to the small room where Vlad is meant to sleep, she glimpses the man from behind as he retreats to the bedroom wrapped in a towel. He has a nice back. Long and muscular.

Clemi is not generally a reader of novels with hunky, scantily clad men on the cover, but right now she is thinking she might want to pick one up in the hotel gift shop. This unexpected scenario has her feeling a little unhinged.

She sees in Vlad's suitcase a neat stack of t-shirts and trousers, a nest of socks. She retrieves what look like his dress pants and a dress shirt. As she rummages in the suitcase for dress shoes, something lights up and begins pulsing electronic noises. She jumps back, startled, until she realizes it's just another in his collection of noise-emitting toys. She also sees copies of *Smiley's People*, *The Spy Who Came in from the Cold*, and *Tinker, Tailor, Soldier, Spy*.

She is both surprised and not surprised. Given the preternatural talents of his mother, Clemi wouldn't be shocked if Vlad was already at work on a novel. Or the second in a trilogy, for that matter. That said, he seems too smart to set himself up for a life of creative despair.

She tries to stop herself from the rabbit hole into which she is beginning to descend about what to do with the rest of her life. Should she really go to law school?

"Are you finding what you need?" Sveta mercifully interrupts. She is standing at the door, her arms akimbo. Clemi doesn't need to be clairvoyant to get that Sveta would like her to hurry up and leave.

"Yes, I'm good. Although do you have a small bag, like a tote or something, I can put all of this in?"

"Sure. I'll get one." Before turning to leave, she steps back and stares at Clemi for an unsettlingly long moment.

"Everything okay?" Clemi asks.

"Yes, I'm just wondering, is that what you're planning to wear tonight?"

The answer is yes, but given the intonation of the question, Clemi supposes it ought to be no.

Still, she has done the best she can. A simple black dress, simple black flats, a light application of makeup. Not only is she on a budget, for goodness' sake, but from what she knows of WLNP's finances, she might not ever get paid.

"Might I make a suggestion?"

"Of course," Clemi says. Normally she bristles at suggestions, since they typically come from her mother. She hopes Sveta is not going to tell her to stand up straight.

"I'll be right back," Sveta says.

Mr. Sexy calls for Sveta again, now referring to her as "darling." Sveta replies that she needs a minute. Clemi would like very much to get out of here.

Another moment passes as she stands awkwardly in Vlad's room, half hoping for a glimpse of Mr. Sexy, the other half hoping she does not see him at all.

Clemi's phone dings. It is Penelope, replying to Clemi's earlier text:

Rice?

"It might be easier if you come in here," Sveta shouts. Clemi tracks the sound of her voice to the enormous bathroom, which is lit up like a cruise ship. "Let's turn you into a princess."

"That's not necessary," she says, suddenly a little frightened, not to mention unsettled by the implication that she is currently, possibly, a frog.

"I don't really want to be a princess. That's not me."

"Who is me?" Sveta asks sincerely.

"I mean . . . I don't know," Clemi says. "I'm just not particularly glam."

"Ha! Well, you will be now."

Sveta isn't fooling around. She begins by handing Clemi a pair of shoes. They are a touch too big, but a close enough fit: silver sparkly heels that make her feel, if not like royalty exactly, then at least a grown-up. Sveta then hands her a stunning black sheath.

"I have a couple of extra dresses. I just came from a wedding," she reminds Clemi. "So I have all sorts of clothes."

Given that Sveta is nearly a foot taller than Clemi, it seems unlikely that the dress will fit—and yet it does. The fabric clings so tight, it seems to suck up the length. It looks . . . not bad! Now Sveta begins working her over with a curling iron. She applies makeup, first a base of primer and foundation, then some sparkly blush. She then moves on to the eyes.

"Open," she instructs, which is hard to do when someone is wielding a mascara wand. "Wider."

Clemi is glad her eyes are forced open wide, because otherwise she would have missed the glimpse of the large cat on the window ledge. The cat is there for an instant, and then is quickly gone.

"Is that *a cat*?" But what would a cat be doing on the tenth-floor window ledge of the Hilton Hotel? It seems impossible.

"Stop talking, darling. You're going to mess this up. But no, it's not a cat. We're too high up for cats."

Clemi is quite sure she just saw a cat, however, and wonders whether what Sveta says is true. Yet Sveta sounds quite certain. Maybe Clemi is seeing things. Maybe she's feeling the side effects of the allergy meds again, except instead of clowns this time, with cats:

In rare circumstances, .02 percent of patients report seeing felines in unexpected places, particularly on window ledges of hotel rooms on high floors.

Sveta steps back to assess what she has done to Clemi. "You do look stunning, my darling. Let's just get you some lipstick. If this whole novel-writing thing goes bust, perhaps I will become a makeup artist."

"You are in no danger of going bust," Clemi says. She looks in the mirror and is startled. She doesn't know if this new look is good or bad, but it is certainly not subtle.

"Wait, there it is again!" Clemi says. Whatever it is, it's in motion. A blur of grey. A long curly tail, pointy ears, whiskers—all of the standard cat parts go by in a whoosh.

Sveta approaches the window and looks in both directions. "I don't see it, darling, but I see a big fat pigeon. Do you usually wear glasses? Maybe you thought it was a cat because it's such a big bird?"

"No. I have twenty-twenty vision. It was a cat."

"It couldn't have been a cat, unless it was a flying cat. Now, if you don't mind, you should probably go check on Vlad."

Clemi knows cats don't fly, but she wonders whether there is some variety of cat that is possibly more aerodynamic than your baseline cat. Her knowledge of cats is pitifully low.

"We had a cat at the office that disappeared. It might have squeezed through the window, which I accidentally left open a crack, but it was pretty high up and . . . well, I'm just hoping it got down okay. If that's what happened."

"Don't be ridiculous, darling. To think this is that same cat would be crazy. Cats are a dime a dozen. I wouldn't overthink it—they all look more or less alike."

Clemi considers calling her out on this remark, which sounds a bit speciesist. Cats come in all shapes and sizes, and in a wide variety of colors, from what she has observed.

"I mean, I know cats don't really fly, but there must be a reason they say cats have nine lives. I don't know much about them. I'm allergic."

"Percy is highly allergic too. He just told me he has an ice allergy. Imagine that!"

"Wait, what? That's Percy?"

"How do you know Percy?"

"I don't. But I was just talking to the caterer, and she mentioned that someone has an ice allergy. I thought maybe it was a typo. How do *you* know Percy?"

"We met earlier today, in the elevator. And it's not a typo. It's a very serious condition, apparently. And I'm glad the message made its way to you since Percy told me he forgot to mention some of his food particulars when he RSVPed."

Clemi is on information overload. All she can think to say is, "So not rice!"

"Not rice?"

"Hang on a sec." Clemi pulls out her phone and texts.

Not rice. You were right. It's ice!

Penelope texts back:

WTF? Where are you?

"Okay, well, enough of this, darling. Now I need to get dressed myself. And don't forget that Vlad needs some dinner before the dinner."

"Can he not eat dinner at the dinner?"

"He's a picky eater, remember? You'd better take him to the restaurant before the event. He likes his chicken nuggets crispy. Just charge it to the room."

Chapter 23

AND THERE IS Vlad, splayed like a starfish on a lounge chair. He is wearing tiny aviator sunglasses and orange swim trunks that still have the sales tag dangling from the waistband. In his hand is half of a coconut, and between his lips is a straw. He looks relaxed and confident, like an early investor in Nvidia stock.

"What the hell?" Clemi blurts out.

"Back at you," Vlad replies. "What happened to your face? And why are you wearing my mom's dress? Aren't those her shoes too?"

Clemi had almost forgotten about the makeup. She wonders what level of insulting it would be to Sveta were she to go into the restroom and wipe it all off.

"Your mom gave me a makeover."

"You look spectacular," Vlad says.

"Really?" Clemi blushes. Maybe this look is okay after all. On the other hand, what does it say about her that she's gratified by a compliment from an eight-year-old?

"Here. Sit here," Vlad says, pointing to the lounge to his right. "The other chair is taken."

Clemi looks to the right and sees an empty lounge chair, as

well as an astonishing full-on view of the Washington Monument. She also sees a young woman in a straw hat and a striped tankini who is reading an Emily Henry novel. Clemi would like to occupy some parallel universe in which she, too, is relaxing by the pool rather than corralling a recalcitrant child. She would order some fries and an iced tea and ask this woman whether she prefers *Beach Read* to *Funny Story*.

"Someone was lying there, but he got a call and left abruptly. I'm pretty sure he's coming back though. He left his drink." Vlad raises the coconut to demonstrate.

"You're drinking his drink?"

"Just sampling. It's pretty good. A little too fruity, but not bad. Would you like one?"

"Does it have *alcohol*?"

"It does, but I'm sure we can get you a virgin if you prefer."

Who is this child? Amenable, conciliatory Vlad is certainly preferable to bossy, bratty Vlad, but this is not okay.

"Let's get you a Coke," Clemi says, removing the coconut from his grip. "We can also order you some dinner. Or better yet, let's get you dressed—I've brought your clothes—and go inside to the restaurant."

"But I thought we were going to have dinner at the dinner?"

"Well, that's what I told your mom, but she wants you to eat first. Besides, I don't especially want to sit by the pool. It's hot out here, and as you just noted, I'm already dressed for tonight."

"Sure, Clemi. In a little while. But first, I want to see if this guy comes back."

"Which guy?"

"The guy I just told you about. The gentleman who is, or was, sitting there drinking his drink, which you ought to put back over there." Vlad points to the small table between the lounge chairs. "He told me he lives in Texas and is here to meet his grandson for the first time."

"Oh, how nice," Clemi says, setting down the coconut drink. Like she gives a hoot about the gentleman who has been sitting here, who is visiting from Texas and is here to meet his grandson for the first time.

"Listen, seriously, I need to get back to the ballroom and check in with the caterer again. I've still got a lot to sort through. I was hoping you might change into your regular clothes. I've got them right here," she says, holding the tote bag, which sports the name of Sveta's publisher.

"Okay, Clemi. Chill for a minute. Let's just see if he comes back."

"Why do you care?"

"I don't think he's really here to see his grandson. Although perhaps he is."

"Okay, again, who cares?"

"Is there a specific term for when someone is undercover, but part of the cover is true?"

"What even are you talking about?"

"You know, like when a spy's claimed background actually mirrors his real background. So it's a little easier for him to stick to his bona fides?"

"Ah, I see. I forgot you are deep in a Le Carré phase. But you are asking the wrong person. Not my area of expertise."

"And you know this how?"

"I saw the books in your suitcase. When I was getting your clothes."

"Ah, so you're spying too."

"Seriously, enough, Vlad. I've got a lot on my mind. I can't deal with this right now."

"Well, anyway, I'm getting off topic because I don't think he's a spy. What I really think is that he's FBI."

"FBI? Why do you even think that? Plus, why would an FBI agent be here, at the pool?"

Now Clemi scans the area, looking for the man who is possibly FBI. She does not see anyone who might pass as either FBI or as a grandfather from Texas, but she sees a small girl in a purple bikini with her thumb in her mouth, a pasty-looking man in a Dodgers baseball cap and polka-dot trunks, and a woman in a colorful sarong who is shouting something to three young children who are about to jump in the pool, each one clutching a different-colored Styrofoam noodle.

Maybe all of them are FBI.

Clemi knows it's ridiculous, but she has a highly developed sense of guilt. She thinks about the bounced check. Is that an FBI matter, she wonders? Surely the FBI has more pressing concerns, given all the arms dealers and cyber scams and drug problems, the art forgeries, catfishing, pig butchering, and corrupt politicians. What would they care about one little, tiny bad check issued by a flailing nonprofit to a snooty society caterer?

"Well, for one thing, he was lying by the pool wearing a suit. And kind of a cheap one, at that."

Clemi is tempted to ask him how he knows a cheap suit from a not-cheap suit, but then remembers this is a kid who flies first-class.

"Look, I don't know what he's doing here. I'm just extrapolating from what I heard him say when he got the call. Before he walked away."

"*Extrapolating?* That's quite the word. I think in this case you might be overextrapolating, however. Why do you think he's FBI?"

"He sounded kind of agitated. He was being all friendly and nice to me, and then once the call came in, he started using the f-word. He said some other things I'm not supposed to say. Do you want to listen?"

"Listen?"

"I recorded it. I mean, the chicken recorded it."

"The chicken? Oh, right!" El diablo pollo. Now she notices the chicken's plush red beak poking out from beneath Vlad's towel. She wonders if this is even legal, to record a stranger speaking on his phone, minding his own business, sipping from a coconut, poolside. Never mind a stranger who is possibly an FBI agent. Then again, what level of naïve might it be to expect any privacy in this world?

"I do not want to listen. Plus, you shouldn't be recording people without their consent. Look, Vlad, it's five fifteen. I'm not kidding around. I need to get back to the ballroom to help with the setup, and that means you need to change." She holds up the bag again. "I have your clothes right here."

"Do you have everything?"

"I'm pretty sure I do."

"Shirt, trousers, tie."

"Check. And I've got your socks and dress shoes."

"Not going to wear those, just for the record. Do you have my underwear?"

"Um . . . it's possible I do not."

"Good going, Clemi."

"Apologies. Maybe you can make do?"

Ignoring her, Vlad presses whatever one presses to make the chicken speak, and the voice of the grandfather from Texas issues from the speaker located beneath the chicken's tail feathers.

"His assets were frozen by the Brits. He was getting desperate. His property taxes were overdue, he had tuition bills to pay . . ." Then there is a long pause. "I know his kids are grown, but he had a mistress and a whole other set of kids. Three more, all in posh schools. His wife didn't know. It was f%$#ing extortion." Another long pause. "Herring, I think . . ." Pause. "Herring, like the fish . . . Listen, I'm at the pool. I have to call you back from a secure line."

Clemi feels a little jolt of anxiety. "Did he just say *herring*?"

"Yes, herring," Vlad says. "It's a fish."

A waiter whom Clemi had not previously noticed is suddenly standing at the foot of her lounge chair.

"Indeed! A herring is a forage fish, mostly belonging to the family of Clupeidae," he says.

"Oh sure," Vlad says. "I've had herring. It's good on crackers, with a bit of horseradish on top."

"Herring?" Clemi repeats, astonished. Herring as in the bank password? Herring as in the financial advisor?

"Apologies, but we do not have herring," the waiter says. "At least not poolside, as far as I'm aware. I'm pretty new, though, and they do change up the menu from time to time, so I can check if you'd like!"

"No, that's okay. But thank you!" Clemi says.

"Are you sure?" Vlad asks. "I mean, now that you mention it, herring sounds pretty good. And it's not a problem, you know. You can just charge it to the room. The people giving my mom the award will pay."

"No, really. But thank you," Clemi says again to the waiter. "We don't need anything right now."

The waiter leaves, and then Clemi, despite her better instincts, asks Vlad to play the recording again.

"Ab-so-*lute*-ly!" Vlad says, enunciating each syllable with what sounds like glee. He depresses the button on the chicken, but nothing happens. He tries again. "I think it might be out of juice," he says. "I need to plug it in somewhere."

"Well, that's another good reason to go inside. We can go into the locker room and charge it up while you get dressed. I'm sure they have an outlet."

"We need to go back to the room, Clemi. Obviously I can't get dressed without my underwear."

Clemi runs a variety of possible scenarios through her mind about how to best procure Vlad's underwear, but he is already belly flopping into the pool, splashing her in his wake, and she is beginning to give in to the fact that he is the one in charge.

Chapter 24

AGAIN, THEY WAIT in the elevator, going nowhere. Vlad, wrapped in a towel, shivers in his orange trunks, clutching the stuffed chicken. His big brown eyes are trained on Clemi, as if she is going to remedy this situation, get this contraption to move, make it so he is no longer cold and wet. She is reminded that this small tyrant causing her so much grief is just a little boy, and this chicken, without its recording superpower, is in fact just a toy.

What has happened to her executive function? Three days ago, she was a highly organized person. Now she lurches from catastrophe to catastrophe, forgetting to do simple things like asking Sveta for a keycard.

She and Vlad wait patiently as a young mother in a pink sundress approaches the elevator. She is pushing a double stroller and has a newborn in one of those complicated-looking kangaroo pouches across her chest, but just as she is about to enter, someone calls to her and she switches direction.

Vlad looks up at Clemi as if realizing, at long last, that she is yet one more useless adult, then pulls from his wet pocket a keycard that he presses to the pad. They ride in silence to the tenth floor, then exit and make their way down the hallway. Just as they are about to turn the corner to the wing that leads to the suite, they hear what sounds like a *meow*.

Then there is a second *meow*, this one undeniably emanating from a cat, and they both swivel their heads toward the propped-open door of a guest room. On the unmade king-size bed is a king-size cat, and fresh linens waiting to be put on.

"Here, kitty," Vlad calls softly.

Startled, the cat leaps off the bed and onto the balcony, the door to which is open.

"Well, that explains it," Clemi says.

"Explains what?"

"Why I saw a cat on the window ledge a little while ago. Outside your hotel room. Your mother told me it was impossible, but I *knew* it was a cat. It looks exactly like Immanuel. But that *is* impossible. I mean, what would he even be doing here? How would he have gotten himself here?"

"Who is Immanuel?" Vlad asks, entering the open room.

"Just a cat I know." She follows Vlad hesitantly. She doesn't want to add trespassing to her possible rap sheet, but the door is open—really two doors are open—and this cat might escape back onto the window ledge. Even more, she is in pursuit of a child, so really, she is just doing the responsible thing.

The cat is now crouched on the corner of the balcony, staring off into the middle distance, perhaps taking in the view.

"Is that really you, Immanuel?" Clemi asks, bending down to pet him. "It really does look like you. Do you remember me? We were office mates?"

"It looks like his collar has a tag," says Vlad, checking the name. "Yup, it's Immanuel. Like the guy who wrote *Hamilton*."

"That's Lin-Manuel." Clemi is tempted to point out that she has finally scored a point against this genius child, found something she knows that he does not, but that seems possibly beneath her. Or at least it ought to be. "This is kind of amazing," she says. "I don't understand what he's doing here. Anyway, let's go back inside."

"It's a lot warmer out here," Vlad says.

"Good point. It's true, this room is freezing. Let me get you a dry towel."

Clemi walks into the bathroom, which is still steamy from a recent shower. She sees a toothbrush and a razor by the sink and feels a little creeped out that she is invading someone else's space, quite possibly Howard's. But to hell with Howard! Howard, who has left her holding this bag full of holes. Howard, who has presumably drained the WLNP bank accounts. Howard, who has pilfered the family finances, depleted his children's college funds.

But if this is really Howard's hotel room, what in the world is even going on?

She finds a dry towel on the rack beside the shower and brings it to Vlad, then wraps it around his shoulders.

"Eat your food, Immanuel," Vlad says.

Clemi hadn't noticed that in the corner of the balcony sit two coffee cups. She bends over to look, and one appears to be filled with some mushy, gooey substance that resembles macaroni and cheese. In the other coffee cup is a liquid that looks a little yellowy. She doesn't know why, but she dips a finger in the liquid and puts it in her mouth.

"Apple juice," she says. "Why would anyone give a cat macaroni and cheese and apple juice?"

"Because they don't know what cats eat maybe? I love cats, but my mom won't let me have one," Vlad laments. "But now I do!"

"Do what?"

"Now I do have a cat."

"This is not your cat, Vlad. It belongs to my boss."

"Your boss isn't very good at taking care of his cat, feeding it macaroni and cheese. I think I can give it a better home."

"That's not how the world works, Vlad."

He looks confused. That is apparently how the world works for him, or at least it has so far.

"If this is your boss's cat, where is your boss?"

"That's an excellent question. I don't think this is my boss's room. I wonder if . . . I don't know. It's crazy, but maybe someone stole the cat? I may not know much at this stage, but I'm close to certain that Howard would never feed Immanuel macaroni and cheese."

"Here's another idea. Maybe the cat checked himself into the hotel," Vlad suggests.

Clemi pauses to consider this possibility. She imagines Immanuel standing patiently in line at the front desk, then, at his turn, putting his paws on the counter and handing over his credit card.

This whack-a-doodle thought is followed by another even crazier one. What if Immanuel *is* Howard? What if he's been transformed into a cat? Maybe she's been asking all the wrong questions. Perhaps this is why the cat is eating human food. She is not a big reader of fantasy, but she knows at least some of the tropes. Maybe he's fallen under some spell? Or taken some magical pill?

She kneels and looks a little more closely at Immanuel. He does look a bit like Howard, now that she thinks about it. Or at least they have similar eyes, and they are both hard to read.

Her phone dings, and she sees a text.

Here!

Colman! She almost forgot about him. He is early. She is not really in a position to deal with him right now. What was she even thinking by inviting him, or rather, allowing him to invite himself?

Where, here?

I'm in a restaurant. At the bar. It's called McClellan's.

Um, I'm in the middle of something.
Will meet you there in about 10 minutes.

"Okay, let's go, Vlad."
"Wait, what's this?" he asks.
"What's what?"
"On the floor," he says, pointing toward the bed, toward a pair of boxer shorts and some ripped-up paper.

Vlad squats and begins to lay out the many pieces of shredded paper on the carpet, moving them about like jigsaw puzzle pieces, which he does with alacrity. Maybe she should ask him to take the LSAT for her. Within seconds he has put together what looks like a ransom note.

"'You want cat back you keep quite. Or say by by.'"

"Quite?"

"I think they mean *quiet*. This person can't spell."

"Or maybe English is not their first language," Clemi says, suddenly frightened.

On the other hand, this could be Howard's room after all. Maybe he has paid the ransom and rescued the cat, which he has now brought here. This might make sense given that he was kicked out of his house, so possibly he was forced to get a hotel room. At least now he can be here for the gala tonight. But if that's the case . . . well, none of this makes much sense. Why is the door propped open?

Just then a housekeeper appears, the same one Clemi spoke to earlier. She gasps when she sees Vlad. At least the chicken is in the tote bag, out of sight.

"Seriously, Vlad, let's go. Right now!"

"We can't leave the cat. Someone is going to kill him!"

"We don't know that for sure. Maybe he's been rescued and brought here for safety."

"Yes, but maybe not."

Clemi does not know what to do. The gala should begin in less than an hour, so the cat ought to be low on her list of concerns. Plus, this child needs to get dressed, and Colman is waiting for her at the bar. On the upside, at least she can cross making opening remarks off her list now that the board president is here.

Chapter 25

THEY FIND A tie in the closet and loop it through Immanuel's collar to form a slipknot and a makeshift leash. It's a powder-blue number adorned with tiny horseshoes, a few of which have a bemused-looking horse mugging on the lip of the U, as if it is in on some private joke.

They exit the room, and Clemi watches Vlad lead, or rather attempt to lead, Immanuel down the hall. The cat is not a fan of this method of ambulation. He wants to do what he wants to do. Mostly he wants this thing around his neck to be off. Every few steps he decides to take a break. It takes some coaxing, including picking him up and setting him back on his feet, but eventually they make it to the suite.

Vlad pulls the keycard from the pocket of his still-damp swim trunks, but Clemi stops him and knocks.

"We don't want to barge in," Clemi says. "In case she's getting dressed." But what she is really concerned about interrupting is not suitable for Vlad's ears.

"Well, hello again," Percy booms. Or at least she assumes this is Percy. She has only glimpsed him from the back, wrapped in a towel. He looked better from the back than from the front, alas. He has a too-large face that is oddly askew and a hard-to-not-stare-at unibrow.

"Sveta, the babysitter is here," he calls. "And you must be Vlad! I've heard so much about you!"

Vlad looks puzzled. "I haven't heard anything about *you*. Who are you? And what have you heard?" he asks while retrieving his chicken from the tote bag and plugging it into an outlet. Although Clemi is not a fan of this chicken, nor in favor of recording people without their consent, she sort of gets the impulse. Something about this guy seems a little off—or perhaps she is just feeling protective of Sveta.

"Oh, all good things," Percy says, clearly bluffing. "But what I hadn't heard is that you have a cat! And what a cat that is. Get this cat some Ozempic!" He begins to laugh at his own not-funny joke.

"Sveta, darling," he tries again, more desperate this time. "Your boy is here with his entourage."

"Entourage?" Sveta replies, entering the room. She looks like a goddess. She wears a skintight, floor-length batik dress that manages to look seductive without giving a hint of anything away. Clemi wonders if this perfect fit is the result of an expert seamstress, or whether Sveta's body is simply so perfect that it conforms to any size.

"He has brought his cat. As well as his nanny," Percy says.

"His *cat*?" Sveta is fussing with an earring—a delicate gold filigree that could be representative of coagulated flower bouquets. Clemi would need to inspect them more closely to confirm this theory. Sveta seems to be having trouble jabbing the thing through her ear. She drops the post, then squats and digs around in the carpet, looking for it. She is now at eye level with the cat, and they study one another in silence.

"Sweetheart, where did you get a cat?" Sveta finally locates the tiny metal object and affixes it to the back of her lobe. As she rises from the floor, she yelps. "Oh, my back!"

Percy rushes over and begins to massage her back before she brushes him away.

"Please, darling, don't touch. That might make it worse." She is hunched over in pain.

"Can I get you something?" Clemi asks.

"Thanks, I'll take a couple of Tylenol in a minute. Did you eat dinner yet, Vlad?" Sveta presses her hands to the small of her back, self-massaging.

"No. I came to get my underpants. But I'll have a snack while I'm here," he says, approaching the buffet table, the contents of which seem to have multiplied in the last half hour. Vlad plucks a piece of chocolate off what looks like a replica of the hotel. "This is so cool, Mom. Where did it come from? I'm going to eat the roof!"

"It was sent by . . . someone," says Sveta, not looking very happy about this gift, or this someone. She is distracted by something on her phone and does not comment as Vlad tears another chunk off the chocolate hotel.

"Sadly, I don't like chocolate," says Percy.

"That is sad," Vlad agrees. "Are you allergic?"

"No, I just don't like the taste of it. But I am allergic to ice."

"Ice! That's so cool!" says Vlad. "I've heard of that. It's called cold urticaria, right?"

"How do you even know this?" Clemi asks.

"It was in a book I read," Vlad continues. "The husband was accused of murdering his wife, but as it turns out she died because the air conditioner was set too low and her throat swelled up. Because of the cold. See? You can either get all itchy from the cold, like hives, or you can get really sick and faint or even die!"

Immanuel has rolled over. His paws are in the air like he is seeking attention, playing dead, pleading for someone to remove this Hermès noose from around his neck.

"As a person with this affliction, I must say that sounds kind of improbable," Percy says.

"It's improbable, I agree. It was not a great book. A little color-by-numbers, if you ask me. But it's a nice twist on the classic ice-as-weapon trope," Vlad opines.

"That reminds me of the brain teaser involving a man found dead in a locked room with a pool of water on the floor," says Percy. "How did he die?"

"Oh my God, this sounds like one of the logic questions in my study guide."

"You're taking the LSAT?" Percy asks.

Clemi can't help but notice that Sveta, who appears to be texting with someone, now looks even more distressed.

"Yes, maybe, why?"

"Which study guide do you have?"

"I don't remember the name. Smithson, maybe?"

"Bingo. Right answer. My second cousin once-removed owns Smithson Study Guides, so let me know if you need any help."

"Help with . . . ?"

"You know, your score?" he says.

Is he really suggesting what Clemi thinks he might be suggesting?

"The murder weapon was an ice pick," says Vlad.

"You're making an assumption there. Did he commit suicide?" Percy asks.

"Well, sure," says Vlad. "That's a possibility. But the private investigator will have to sort that out."

"Fortunately, my cold urticaria is not that severe. But I don't want to take any chances."

Clemi is only half listening. She is still fixated on what seems to have been an offer to rig her LSAT score. Do people really do that? It should go without saying that she would never explore this option, and yet... well, she has already been involved in the writing of a bad check. What's a little tweaking of the score? She banishes the thought before it has time to grow roots.

"It can be unpredictable though. I once had a bad flare-up when I was dining on a yacht owned by Prince Richard. What an amazing evening. Beluga caviar, 1959 Dom Pérignon on tap."

"The Duke of Gloucester? I didn't know he was the yachting type," Vlad says, retrieving this odd piece of information from who knows where.

Percy flinches. Either he did not know that Prince Richard is the Duke of Gloucester—assuming this is, in fact, true—or he doesn't like being interrupted. Or maybe he is making this story up. This reminds her of Howard, or at least of the little bit of him that she knows. She wonders if something in the WLNP water makes everyone feel the need to boast.

Now Immanuel hops onto the sofa and begins to dangle backward off the cushion, sliding headfirst toward the floor, slowly, like a Slinky. Clemi thinks this is a reasonable response to the conversation and is tempted to follow suit.

"Listen, Vlad. You're going to catch a cold if we don't get

you out of that wet bathing suit. Plus I'm running late. My friend is waiting for us in the bar."

"I will wait here," Percy says. "I shall be escorting my lovely date to the dinner to accept her award."

Sveta has gone into the bathroom to find the Tylenol, but she can evidently hear the conversation. "Please, go on ahead! I'll see you downstairs."

"No, darling. I will wait for you."

"Percy, I insist."

"Absolutely not. That would be ungentlemanly."

"Go," she says. "Now." She sounds like she is telling the cat to scat.

"Well, I suppose I ought to go on ahead since I'm hosting a table of VIPs, including the chair of the Folger Shakespeare Library and one of the directors of Chase Bank."

"Bye!" Vlad says.

"Okay, farewell!" says Percy, still not going anywhere.

"Bye!" Clemi adds, hopefully. This man is truly insufferable. What is Sveta thinking?

Vlad takes the chicken's leg and pumps it up and down in a mock wave.

Percy finally begins to back out the door. Once it clicks shut behind him, Clemi and Vlad look at one another and begin to laugh. They laugh and laugh and laugh, and then Sveta walks in, still staring at her phone and looking like she's just seen a ghost.

Chapter 26

VLAD SPOTS HIM at the far end of the bar, where he is sitting on a high-top swivel chair drinking a beer and staring down at something, the menu perhaps.

"Hey, I see Malcolm Gladwell over there. I should go tell my mom!"

"That's not Malcolm Gladwell, but how do you even know who Malcolm Gladwell is? Is there anything, or anyone, you don't know?"

"Good question. Let me think a second. Nope. Nothing I can think of."

"Nor are you lacking in self-confidence."

"I'm not!"

"Admirable to a point," Clemi says as they make their way through the bar, which is bustling with happy-hour enthusiasts—a hodgepodge of tourists, locals dropping in after work, and what appear to be conference attendees sporting lanyards around their necks. She catches Colman's eye and waves to him as she and Vlad make their way through the crush of day-end revelers.

"You didn't answer my question. How do you know who

Malcolm Gladwell is? Please don't tell me you read his entire canon on the flight."

"I met him at the Jaipur Literature Festival last year."

"Of course you did. Probably you met my mother too." It is only just occurring to her that she and Vlad have in common these larger-than-life mothers, except in his case it appears to have enabled his confidence and in her case it has had a largely deflationary effect. Vlad is too distracted to follow up on her mother reference, which is just as well. She'd hate to hear that they had breakfast together in the hotel or such and became great pals, although it wouldn't surprise her to discover that everything in her life, even this babysitting gig, comes full circle to her mom.

"Look at that guy!" Vlad now points to someone with a mop of rainbow-colored hair sprouting from his scalp like tiny springs.

Clemi freezes. This weird clown situation just goes on and on and on. The instructor in the creative writing workshop where she first met River talked about this, how once you learn a new word, you begin to see it everywhere. She said it was called the frequency illusion. Maybe this is what is happening with the clowns. Probably they have always been in abundance, but before this stupid LSAT question burrowed inside her brain, she had not spent much time, if any, thinking about them. She might see them at the circus, or at a children's birthday party, or read about them in a book—but apart from that, she has never given them much consideration.

Also, she is making an assumption. Maybe the guy has some strange genetic condition, and this is his real hair. Or maybe he dyed it blue and red and purple, and every other color on the spectrum, because he likes attention.

"It's not polite to point at people, Vlad."

"Sorry," he says, but the apology sounds a little forced.

Vlad runs to Colman and, without any preamble, presents him with the cat, now stuffed inside his mother's gigantic tote. Her bag is quilted and puffy-looking, like a down parka but with handles. It looks a lot like Fiona's bag, the one Clemi was fishing through the night she came to the apartment for the plant-sitting tutorial, the one that reminded Clemi of a Swiss Army knife, what with all of its unexpected gizmos. As with the clowns, now that she knows this bag, she sees it everywhere she goes, weighing down the shoulders of women.

It is also evidently a great cat carrier; Immanuel seems happy in there, his head peeking up through the handles.

Colman, as awkward as he is with Clemi, seems entirely comfortable with Vlad.

"Well hello, child! And hello, cat! Why are you in a bag in a bar?"

"Do you remember me?" Vlad asks. "I remember you."

"I'm sorry. I do not."

"Didn't we meet in India?"

"Oh, maybe. Were you at the Pearl Tech Conference in Bangalore last spring?"

"Um, no. I was at the Jaipur Literature Festival."

"Interesting," says Colman. "Perhaps we crossed paths in the airport."

"That's probably what happened," says Clemi, eager to be done with this conversation. "Sorry we took so long. We had to go back to the room so Vlad could change, and we got embroiled in a conversation with a board member. Don't ask."

Unsurprisingly he does not ask.

"Why are you all the way back here?" Vlad asks. "It looks like you're hiding. And what are you reading?"

"I am hiding, yes. And I'm reading a book."

"So you are!" Clemi doesn't mean to sound so excited, but she wonders if perhaps he has changed his tune about books. Alas, he has not. He holds up a travel guidebook.

"Why are you reading that?"

"It has all this info about Reagan's limo. The one they stuffed him into after the assassination attempt. Did you know the bullet ricocheted off the car before it hit him? It's the same limo that Nixon used."

"That's a grim thing to be reading."

"Also, this hotel now has something called 'the President's Walk'?" Colman does not wait for an answer before continuing. "Did you know he's a musician now?"

"President Reagan? I don't think he's alive," Vlad says.

"No, John Hinckley Jr. He's been trying to play gigs, but every time he announces he'll be somewhere, the venue starts getting harassed and they have to cancel."

"Isn't he in jail?" Clemi asks.

"No, he was declared legally insane. He was sent to a psychiatric hospital, but they released him about ten years ago."

"Who are you talking about?" asks Vlad.

"The man who tried to kill President Reagan. He shot his press secretary, James Brady. Also a police officer and Secret Service agent were killed."

"Why did he want to assassinate the president?" Vlad asks.

"Hinckley wanted to impress Jodie Foster."

"The actress? I met her at Cannes when the adaptation of my mom's book premiered."

Clemi is not sure how much more of Vlad's name-dropping she can stand. Perhaps he should join the WLNP board.

"Yes, that's her," Colman says. "He was stalking her for a while. He seemed to think shooting Reagan would help win her over. I don't quite know how that was supposed to work, but he was obviously not well.

"He also had a lot of extreme political views, which I didn't realize until reading this. He was involved for a brief time with the Nazi Party in Dallas. And he also founded something called the American Front that was a white-supremacist organization—"

"*Really?*" Clemi interrupts.

"Yes, that's how he wound up in a psychiatric hospital here in DC. St. Elizabeths."

"No way. That's bizarre."

"The whole thing is bizarre."

"Yes. But also Arthur Muller used to visit St. Elizabeths. And he was a Nazi too. *And* a stalker. He wasn't committed there; he just played tennis with Ezra Pound—but Ezra spent something like ten years there, maybe more. I wonder if they knew each other! Maybe they even played tennis together. Did John Hinckley play tennis, I wonder?"

"No idea. But I doubt they would have overlapped if he was playing tennis with Ezra Pound, who would have died well before the assassination attempt. Anyway, who is Arthur Muller?"

"Muller was the founder of our nonprofit, but he's gone, erased, expunged, so don't worry about it."

Colman does not look like he is especially worried about it.

"Well, even if they overlapped, not all Nazis know each other," Vlad says knowledgeably. "Where is this secret walkway? Is it near where my mom is getting the award?"

"I don't know. This isn't the best book. It doesn't have a lot of detail."

Colman sets the book down on the counter and looks at Clemi. "You look different," he says. "It's strange."

"Um, *strange*? That's not exactly what I was going for."

"No, I didn't mean that you look strange like an alien species or something. Just, something is different. I don't know what."

"Do you mean *species* or *specimen*?" asks Vlad.

"I hope I don't look like either," Clemi says. "I'm dressed for the event tonight, so I'm wearing a dress. And I have on makeup."

"Oh, I see," says Colman. "That makes sense."

It's a good thing Clemi is not fishing for a compliment, because none is forthcoming.

An older couple approaches, their eyes trained on Colman. "Would you mind taking a selfie with us?"

"He needs some privacy right now," Clemi says, waving them away.

"That's why I'm all the way in the back," Colman says. "Someone else happened to be reading *Talking to Strangers*—this Malcolm guy sure wrote a lot of books—and they asked me to sign their copy."

"Yeah, my mom gets that all the time," says Vlad.

"Okay listen, everyone. We ought to go. I need to get back to the ballroom," Clemi says.

"But wait, my mom said I should get dinner before the dinner."

"I know, but do you really need dinner before the dinner?"

"It's probably a good idea so I don't get cranky. How about some chicken nuggets?"

"Seriously? Fine, but what if we order them to go? What else do you want? Fries? Something to drink?"

No answer. She looks around, and Vlad is not there. Colman is back to staring at his guidebook.

"Where'd he go?"

"Who?"

"Vlad."

"The kid with the cat?"

"Yes, that's the one."

Colman points downward, and Clemi sees him crawling along the filthy floor.

"What on earth are you doing?"

But he is already too far away to hear her. Then on the floor she sees not just Vlad but Immanuel, who is now out of the tote bag and prancing in the other direction.

"Oh, geez," Clemi says, squatting down in her dress and heels. There are bits of food on the floor, a couple of napkins, a straw, a Metro fare card, a condom, still in its package, thank goodness. It's sticky down here, and it smells like feet and beer. She is trying to keep one eye on Vlad and the other on the whoosh of grey cat.

Just then she hears a scream from across the room, followed by the sound of tableware crashing to the floor. A man jumps up from his seat and lets out a loud string of obscenities while wiping liquid off his lap. A waitress rushes over with a stack of napkins. What looks like a pretty good cheeseburger lies on the floor in a puddle of its own ketchup.

"Calm down," his female companion urges. But she, too, has been splattered with food.

The man does not calm down. In fact, he does the opposite. "What the hell is this animal doing in here?" he asks, furious. "Don't try to tell me this is a comfort animal or some such bull."

Clemi rushes over and scoops up Immanuel. "I'm so, so sorry. I can explain." She's not sure why she says this, because she's not sure she can explain.

"Are you not familiar with DC Law 22–91?" says the female companion.

"Um, no, not specifically, but—"

"It's called the Dining with Dogs Act of 2018. It's still in effect," she says.

"Okay, but . . ." Clemi has no idea how to finish the sentence, which is okay because Vlad cuts in.

"It's not a dog, it's a cat," he says, grabbing Immanuel and stroking his head. "You poor, poor thing. I'm sorry these people were so mean to you."

The man starts toward Vlad like he's going to hit him, and the woman pulls him back.

"Stop it, Joe, you're overreacting. He's just a child. And we have bigger fish to fry."

"Speaking of fish, would you like some herring with your burger?" Vlad asks.

Now both of the food-flecked diners look at Vlad with widened eyes.

"What did you just say?" asks the woman.

"How do you eat your burgers in Texas?" Vlad inquires. "And how's your grandson?"

"Texas?" the woman asks. "Our grandson? What the hell is happening here, Joe?"

"Please, Charlotte, let me handle this. I don't know what he's talking about. Clearly, he has me confused with someone."

"Okay, Vlad, let's go," Clemi says. The man is so angry that he looks on the verge of a cardiac event.

"Maybe this will refresh your memory," Vlad says. He produces the chicken, which he must have pulled from the tote bag, and before Clemi has a chance to stop him, he hits the play button.

"His assets were frozen by the Brits. He was getting desperate. His property taxes were overdue, he had tuition bills to pay . . . I know his kids are grown, but he had a mistress and a whole other set of kids. Three more, all in posh schools. His wife didn't know. It was f%$#ing extortion . . ."

"What the hell! Give me that thing," he says, lunging toward the stuffed chicken.

"Joe, again, he is just a child. And it's just a toy. It's on you for not being more careful with classified information. This isn't the first time you've gotten us into trouble."

Joe glares at Charlotte, who is presumably his professional partner. Then he grabs the chicken and tears the head off. But it keeps talking. The recording device is in its butt. He throws it to the floor and stomps on it multiple times, then pours his glass of water on it.

A small crowd has formed around the table. People have whipped out their phones and are recording the scene. Vlad has begun to cry, which Clemi had not thought possible.

Charlotte picks up the chicken's head, which is now sticky

and wet, and hands it to Vlad. Vlad holds it close to his chest for a moment and tries to compose himself.

Colman has now joined them. He is holding his book, looking befuddled.

"Wow, are you Malcolm Gladwell?" Charlotte asks. "I really loved *Blink*. I think about it all the time. It informs my every decision."

Chapter 27

EVEN IF CLEMI were stoned, which is not something she is inclined to be (life is confusing enough as is), she could not have conjured a scenario that would send her racing through the Hilton Hotel in Washington, DC, wearing Sveta Attais's slightly-too-long dress and slightly-too-big shoes, and holding the hand of her adorable but confounding enfant terrible son who—because he is a little extra—happens to have a cat stuffed inside a bag. And not just any cat but her boss's cat. A very large philosopher cat at that, who is wearing an equestrian-themed Hermés tie and who might or might not be a hostage in a situation that possibly involves the FBI. And that's not even accounting for a decapitated and now-decimated stuffed chicken recording device, a Malcolm Gladwell doppelgänger, and clowns. So many clowns.

"This is completely nuts," she says to no one in particular. "We're characters in some screwball comedy."

"A Noël Coward play, perhaps," says Colman.

Colman, she would like to say, you are such an odd duck, now with the dated theater references. She wonders what else goes on inside his brain.

"Were he the author of this play, soon someone will be rushing through the hotel with their hair on fire, wearing nothing but underpants," he says.

"Be careful what you say," Clemi advises. "I have enough to contend with already."

As they ride the escalator down, someone on the adjacent escalator going up shouts to Colman, asking for a selfie. Clemi waves them off like she is his publicist, which at this point she sort of is.

They wend their way through the corridors and to the anteroom of the ballroom, where some of the early bird guests are already assembled, waiting to check in.

Vlad tugs on Clemi's hand, signaling toward an older woman who is wearing a dress with an enormous green-and-blue feathered bodice that might have been harvested from an actual peacock. It's impolite to stare, Clemi knows, but she is struggling to determine whether this is the handiwork of a famous designer, or the sort of thing one might find at a pop-up Halloween store.

The peacock woman is talking to a rail-thin woman in a bright red, too-short chiffon dress with a giant bow at the waist.

"Look," Vlad says. "That's the ambassador to Panama."

"The peacock or the box of Valentine's Day candy?"

"The candy," Vlad says.

Clemi considers asking him how he knows this, but really, what's the point? This child seems to know everything and everyone, including his new BFF Biff, who is seated behind the check-in table. Vlad runs to greet him, his sneakers emoting with colorful delight. Biff motions for Vlad to come behind the table and sit in the empty chair next to him. Clemi is not so sure this is a good idea. She gets the sense that Biff might not be the best caretaker, plus the idea of Vlad assisting in the checking-in of guests is worrying, but it at least takes him off her hands for a while.

The ambassador to Panama approaches them excitedly. Clemi puts out her hand to shake and begins to introduce herself as the new programs director at WLNP, but the ambassador only has eyes for Colman.

"It's absolutely amazing to see you," she says. "It's been twenty years, yet not only do you look the same, but everything you said is still true. Truer than ever, really. In fact, my husband and I were just discussing analysis paralysis at dinner last night. The more information we have, the less we understand. Especially when it comes to politics. Wouldn't you say?"

"It's funny you should say that," Colman begins. "I was just thinking about—"

"Wait! Wait!" the peacock says. "Let me find a pen. I want to write this down."

Skylar sees Clemi and rushes over, pulling her off to the side. "Sorry, it's still a little early, but you know our guests: hard to keep them at bay. We just had a bit of an incident," she says. "A couple of the guests—a Russian gentleman and someone who is maybe Salvadorian?—I think they are the spouses of those two," she says, pointing toward a pair of women dressed in simple black sheaths, who seem unaware of the behavior of their husbands. "They crashed the bar and are pouring drinks for the guests. The bar is not supposed to be open yet, and Penelope is having a cow. I think a few people are already drunk."

"Oh boy. Off to a good start."

"Is that your date?" Skylar asks, pointing toward not-Malcolm, who is now engulfed in a circle of women, several of whom are taking notes. "Good job, Clemi."

"No, he's not my date. He is a friend from yoga."

"If he's not your date, would you introduce me? I'm a huge fan. Okay, I'm not really. I mean, I would be, I could be, I just haven't read him yet, so it's not like I have an opinion one way or another. But I'm sure he's brilliant. I can't believe he's your friend from yoga. Why didn't you mention that? You could have brought him! Oh, wait, you already did!"

"So what's the deal with the silent auction?" Clemi asks, redirecting the conversation.

"Didn't Howard walk you through all of that?"

"Actually, he did not. He was going to on Wednesday, but then, you know. He went wherever it is that he's gone."

"Right. Okay. Well, the plan is to start corralling people into that room," she says, pointing to the right, "in about five minutes, just as soon as the waitstaff is ready to start. There will be cocktails and passed apps. And then the guests can write their bids with little notepads and pens and put them in the box on each table. That part will last about forty minutes, at which point we'll ring the chime and herd everyone into the ballroom to start the dinner and the ceremony."

There is a tap on Clemi's shoulder, and she sees someone familiar. Then again, so many people look familiar lately that she is beginning to doubt her ability to distinguish one human from another.

"Is there a room where I can leave my things?" the familiar-looking man asks, nodding toward a small roller bag that is missing a wheel. "I have my change of clothes in there." This bag is also strangely familiar.

Change of clothes for what? she wonders, given that he is wearing a suit and tie.

Clemi is still staring at him, trying to make the connection.

"So, is there a greenroom, or even just a private spot where I can go over my remarks? How long do I have? Oh, also, what's my cue? Will someone introduce me, or should I go up there and introduce myself?"

"Oh! It's you!" It's the Sad Dad from the elevator. The board president. Boy, does he clean up well. He could certainly still pass for a Sad Dad, but at least his shirt is properly buttoned—no more hairy belly peeking out—and what remains of his hair is now combed. "I have no idea, but surely there's a greenroom. Come with me."

She pulls him into the ballroom, again struck by the transformation of this once-sterile room into something out of a fairy tale, especially now that the lights have been dimmed and the candles on each table are twinkling.

They make their way to the stage. Clemi has been behind enough stages at enough venues in her time doing events at the bookstore that she is confident in the existence of a greenroom back there, somewhere. She spies Penelope in the corner of the room, talking to the waitstaff, but does her best to avoid her given that the likelihood of a pleasant encounter is zero to none, especially given the latest situation with the bar crashers.

On the stage is a podium, with the WLNP logo affixed to the front, and the step-and-repeat banner behind it. They ascend a ramp on the side of the stage, and Clemi leads him behind the curtain. They walk down another hallway, and she opens a door and finds someone sitting on the toilet. "Whoops, sorry!" she says. "Wrong door."

She opens another door and indeed finds a dressing room with a sitting area, a television, and a mini refrigerator filled with water bottles.

"Perfect," he says, collapsing into a chair. "I'm going to decompress back here. So, just let me know when it's time."

"You sure?" Clemi asks. "I mean, I don't know how this works, exactly, but don't you want to mingle before the program begins? Talk to donors and whatnot?"

"Good lord, no! I am not a mingler. This is why I can't do this anymore. Time to let someone else take over. I mean, you might wonder why I went into this business," he continues. "And that's a fair question! I agree it's counterintuitive, but you'd be surprised to learn that a lot of us are shy."

"Sure. I get it," Clemi says. She has no idea what he's talking about, but now is not the time to explore the psychodynamics of nonprofit board presidents.

"Should I at least show you where you'll be sitting so you can know where to go after your remarks?"

"No, no, I remember it all from last year. I mean, we were in Toledo last year. But if you've seen one hotel ballroom, you've seen them all. Believe me, I've done this so many times, it's rote by now . . ."

"Toledo?"

"It's a city in Ohio."

"Oh, sure. I mean, I know where Toledo is. Unless you meant Toledo, Spain."

"I went there once. With my wife. My ex-wife, that is. We are divorced. She took the house and the kid and the dog. Bled me dry."

"I thought so," Clemi says. She didn't mean to blurt that out, but she is nonetheless pleased with her powers of perception, her ability to identify the Sad Dads of this world.

"You thought so, what?"

"Toledo, Ohio," she bluffs.

"Yes, Toledo, Spain, was ages ago, back before Jimmy was born. It was our third anniversary. We did two weeks in Spain. Barcelona. Madrid. The beach in Nerja. I know Toledo isn't on everyone's bucket list, but I've always had a thing for marzipan."

"Marzipan? That's got something to do with Toledo? Why did I think that was a German thing?"

"Common assumption. Not entirely wrong, but the first known reference to marzipan was from Spain. Toledo specifically. In the early 1500s."

"Who knew?" Clemi says. "Listen, if you need anything, just text. Give me your phone number, and I'll call you so you'll have my number. The silent auction has just begun, so I'd better be sure everything is cool."

"Okay, cool," he says.

"Cool," Clemi repeats as they exchange contact info, but she's not sure how cool it is. As she walks away, she realizes that she's still confused. Why was the last awards ceremony in Toledo? She'll have to ask Skylar about that. It's not something Howard thought to mention. Maybe there are two ceremonies, one in DC and one on the road. That makes sense, maybe.

Something about this feels a little off. But then Clemi is probably being overly sensitive. Because without question, something about this entire WLNP situation is decidedly off.

Chapter 28

AS CLEMI ENTERS the room, now packed with smartly and in some cases less smartly dressed patrons of the literary arts, Vikram, one of the young interns, hands her a silent auction card. He seems to not remember that she is the programs director and not a paying guest, which she supposes is a backhanded compliment. Her status has transformed from middling admin and babysitter to a princess in the able hands of a fairy-godmother-literary-rock-star with a curling iron for a wand.

She studies the card.

WLPN SILENT AUCTION
Promoting Literature That Is Prophetic in Vision

- Private lunch at the Tabard Inn with Ellie Grossman, author of *The Snowbirds*

STARTING BID: $800

- Dinner for four at Masseria with *The New York Review of Books* editor Renata Chakrabarti

STARTING BID: $2,000

- Weekend in Vail condo, sleeps five, use of snowshoes included

STARTING BID: $10,000

- Catered dinner party for ten with Booker Prize–winning author Francis Ruben

STARTING BID: $10,000

- Private lunch with superagent Lilian Getter; pitch her your ideas for a book

STARTING BID: $5,000

- Bring five friends to lunch with SURPRISE public intellectual. ~~Javier Jiménez-Jiménez, philosopher, historian, and staff writer at The New Yorker~~

STARTING BID: $12,000

Ha! *Surprise public intellectual.* That would not have occurred to her. She had assumed they would simply be scratching through Javier's name. She supposes this is a good fix; it at least buys them time. People can bid, and then they—whoever *they* are, given that she is planning to be long gone after tomorrow—will still have time to find a public intellectual after the event. In fact, this solution is kind of brilliant.

"Hello, Clemi!" says a tall, elegant, very slim man. It takes her a moment to place him—everyone is out of context, looking somewhat different now that they are dressed up—but mercifully it clicks.

"Mr. Samaraweera! So good to see you!"

"Are you feeling well? I know you were having some breathing problems."

"Oh, I'm fine. Thank you for asking. The allergy meds are a little strong but . . . fine, other than . . . this," she says, waving her arm around the room.

"It looks like things are in good order. At least on the surface. Did you speak to Howard?"

"Nope. Not a word."

"Well at least you reached Herring, I assume."

"No. Why? Did you?"

"No, but I thought I saw him earlier in the lobby."

"Seriously?"

"Well, I don't know for sure. I've never met him in real life, but I once saw a picture on LinkedIn, and he is rather, shall we say, well . . . hard to miss."

"Hard to miss in what way?" Clemi pulls out her phone. "What's his proper name? I want to find his profile."

"I'm not completely certain, but in any event, don't bother. He's erased himself, it seems. He's now a complete enigma online. But he's easy to spot. I don't want to be disparaging, but he looks like . . . a herring."

"He looks like a herring? What does that even mean?"

"Good question. I guess he's a little scaly? Which again I mean in the nicest possible way! He has beady eyes. And grey hair. He looks a little bit like Albert Einstein if Albert Einstein were a forage fish."

"Is he in here?" she asks, studying the room.

She looks around and sees some two hundred people wearing their finest, smiling their brightest, holding their cocktails and lipstick-stained wineglasses, kissing one another on the cheeks, picking hors d'oeuvres off trays proffered by waiters dressed in black. She sees people who look like socialites, including a couple of women so thin and wealthy-looking that they seem to have stepped off the pages of a Tom Wolfe novel. Social X-rays, he called them. She sees people who in some hard-to-pinpoint way—perhaps because of their ten-thousand-dollar watches—look like financiers. And she sees some who bring an international flair, such as one woman wrapped in a stunning purple sari—diplomats, perhaps. And she sees some who look like writers, a style she'd be hard-pressed to define in terms other than less-wealthy-looking than the rest of these flagrantly wealthy-looking guests.

She does not see anyone who looks like a herring.

"Not that I'm aware of," says Mr. Samaraweera. "I saw him in the lobby when I arrived. I was going to introduce myself, but he looked very preoccupied. In fact he was crawling around on his hands and knees, looking under the furniture."

"Oh, how odd," says Clemi. "Do you think he was looking for Howard's cat?" she asks.

"Why would he be looking for Howard's cat?"

"Well, remember how I told you on Thursday that the cat... the one that was in the office but disappeared? I thought at first it might have squeezed out the window, or that Howard took him. But now I think it was kidnapped."

"Why would anyone kidnap a cat? You can adopt them for free at the shelter. Or there's a new cat café I just read about. You can get them there too. Or on my neighborhood listserv. So many free cats!"

"I think it's more complicated in this case. Howard is very attached to his cat, apparently. And I just saw him—the cat, not Howard—here."

"Here where?"

"*Here*. Vlad has him. We took the cat. From what might have been Herring's room. Which is why he might have been crawling around, looking for it."

"And Vlad is . . ."

"Sveta's son. I'd better go check on him."

"Sveta's son? Why is he here?" she hears him say, but she is already across the room.

Having established that Vlad is still on good behavior, still seated at the check-in table, still under the spell of Biff, Immanuel nesting peaceably in the bag on his lap, she now scans the room for Colman.

A waiter evidently thinks she is looking for a drink and sticks a glass of white wine in her hand. Is she supposed to drink while taking all of these allergy meds? Probably not! But what's a little sip?

A different waiter presents her with a spray of tiny fish tacos, which are more delicious than they look. She can taste the garlic and chiles, which call for another sip of wine. As the waiter walks away, she calls him back and plucks three more from the silver platter.

A bespectacled man who looks a bit like Woody Allen turns to her and says, "There you are! Amanda and I were just talking about you!"

She has never seen these people before, at least not insofar as she is aware, but she smiles and nods. "What were you saying?" she asks, emboldened by two mere sips of wine.

"Remember that dinner party a couple of years ago, on New Year's Eve?"

She does not remember that dinner party a couple of years ago, on New Year's Eve, but she gives a noncommittal nod, curious to see where this is going.

"Amanda thinks it was Martin who started the fight."

"The fight?"

"Well, you're right. *Fight* might be too strong a word. The brouhaha."

"Well, it might have begun as a brouhaha," Amanda cuts in. "But it certainly became a fight. For the love of God, there's still a dent in the refrigerator from where she kicked it."

"I mean, who could blame her? When Sherri showed up with the baby, my God! Did you know the baby was his?"

This question seems to be intended for Clemi.

"Sherri?" she asks.

"Wait! I think you had just been sent back to the car to get the diaper bag when the fight began, weren't you, dear?" asks Amanda.

Ah! Her glam makeover aside, she is pretty sure she is once again being mistaken for someone's nanny. She smiles politely, excuses herself and says she'll be right back, procuring three pieces of sashimi from a tray before she slips away.

So many people are packed into this room that it is difficult to move. She remembers her boss at the bookstore once quoting someone named Sally Quinn who called these kinds of parties Rat F**ks, which was evidently meant to be a good thing: Pack the room with so many people they can't move, ply them with alcohol, serve only salty foods, keep them away from water, and everyone will get very drunk and have a hell of a time.

Where is Colman? Clemi is not especially tall, so in this crush of people she can only see what she can see, which is mostly the shoulders of a lot of festive, chattering, well-heeled people holding wineglasses, eating hors d'oeuvres. She feels responsible for Colman. He is so socially awkward that she should not have left him on his own, but she had to lead Sad Dad back to the greenroom and had little choice.

As she makes her way toward the back of the room, she overhears someone mention Sveta's book, which is gratifying to hear, a much-needed reminder of what this evening is about. Although Sveta has not yet publicly been named the winner—that will happen at the dinner—she is one of three finalists.

Howard had told Clemi that in the past, they had feted all three finalists at the gala, but this year they are trying to cut costs. He had said this before Clemi had reason to question the finances.

Clemi eavesdrops on these presumptive kindred bookish souls for a minute, then wishes she had not.

"Sveta who?" she hears a large man in a bow tie ask an elegant middle-aged woman wearing a full-length chiffon number adorned with butterflies.

"Sveta Atta or Ataba, or Entebbe, or Entebbata, or something like that? Some Indian name, I think. Maybe it's Arab?"

"Oh, her, yes, I think she's Serbian."

"I know it's not appropriate to say this," the woman says, making air quotes around the word *appropriate*. "But I miss the old days."

"The old days?"

"You know what I'm saying. I mean, I'm probably being surveilled by the cancel culture police right now—I wouldn't put it past them to have cameras in here—but back when this was called the Arthur Muller Foundation, no one was tied up in knots trying to be all 'progressive.'"

"Surely you're not suggesting . . . I mean, wasn't Muller a Nazi?"

"Nazi, schmatzi. I'm just saying, when is the last time someone named, say, *Bob White* won a prize?"

"Actually, I think Bob White won a National Book Award last year for his memoir about growing up Black in Greenwich, Connecticut."

Clemi wishes she had not paused to listen, but she supposes it's better to know what is going on in some people's heads. Or is it? What might be the harm in giving herself a break for one night and enjoying the evening? As if that's a remotely possible thing.

She continues to move toward the corner to see whether Colman is back there entertaining guests with grim details of assassinations—she last heard him talking about the bullet-resistant glass on presidential limousines—when there is a tap on her shoulder and she turns to see River.

River. Oh, River. She is not so superficial as to be attracted to a boy just because of his looks—let us not forget that he is an unqualified jerk!—and yet it is difficult to not be mesmerized by his piercing green eyes, his thick tousled hair, his jaunty smile, by the way he places his hand on her back and pulls her in for a kiss that is heading toward her lips but swerves at the last minute and lands on her chin. Which is a good thing! She no longer wants to kiss River because he is an unqualified jerk!

"Where's Augusta?" Clemi asks. "Oh, wait. I mean Martha."

"Martha is already at the table," he says. "Her feet are hurting. She has some issue. Plantar fascist something."

"Plantar fasciitis," Clemi corrects.

"Sure," he says. "Anyway, it's a thing that happens when you're old."

"She's not that old, is she? I mean, I think she's in her fifties? Anyway it can happen when you're not old too."

"Why are we talking about Martha's feet when we could be talking about how gorgeous you look?"

Clemi blushes despite herself. But River is already moving on. He has the attention span of a flea and has already exhausted the subject of how gorgeous Clemi looks.

"Excuse me a sec, Clem. I see someone I know. I had no idea Malcolm Gladwell would be here."

"You know Malcolm Gladwell?"

"Well, I mean, I don't know him exactly, but I know someone who knows him. I'll be right back."

He is gone before Clemi is able to set him straight.

She looks toward the back of the room but sees only more shoulders. She tries to follow River, snaking her way through the crowd, to no avail. She has lost River, and still can't find Colman, but she sees the flashes of a camera, and she sees a woman standing on a chair, trying to get a better view. The woman is wearing precariously high heels, and her face is so powdered, her hair so white, her lipstick so red, that she looks like she belongs on the set of a ballroom drama.

A waiter refills the glass in her hand as Clemi continues to push her way through the mosh pit. It is beginning to feel like the point in a movie where the director jumps the shark and drops in some sort of surreal dream sequence.

She is a tiny fish in a sea of people. A wee speck in the universe. A cog in the literary-adjacent machine.

Mercifully an intern arrives with a gong, signaling that it is time for everyone to move inside and find their seats before Clemi can think the next ontological thought.

Chapter 29

MARTHA THOMAS IS not at all what Clemi expected, although if pressed, she can't say what she might have expected, given that Clemi has not spent much, if any, time thinking about Martha Thomas. Because her own mother is a literary agent of the Martha Thomas ilk, Clemi tries to spend as little time as possible thinking about literary agents, period. Which is yet one more reason to avoid the entire trying-to-write-and-publish situation and to go to law school.

But this Martha Thomas, she is really something. She is dressed in a sleeveless jewel green number that highlights biceps so ripped, she could possibly lift a garbage truck. Her long grey hair gives her a steely awesomeness. And she rocks a shade of red lipstick Clemi can only aspire to have the nerve to someday wear. Like Augusta, she is at least thirty years older than River. What in the world is Martha Thomas doing with this wispy albeit adorable twit? Granted, Clemi fell for him too, but then she is a mere mortal, not an esteemed literary agent.

Clemi introduces herself, then takes her seat at the table, where she is flanked by Vlad and Colman. Next to Colman is someone named Patrice von Trapp, evidently no relation to the von Trapps of *The Sound of Music*, but who seems to enjoy the confusion and is currently mid-conversation about the beer selections at the von Trapp brewery in Stowe, Vermont. She is chatting with the gentleman next to her, whom Clemi just overheard talking about his own recent visit to Stowe, which somehow morphs into a discussion of the increasingly high costs of maintaining his racehorses and the high property taxes in Middleburg, Virginia, where he evidently lives. Then there are Martha and River, and rounding out this table is Percy, who was just awkwardly slotted in when Sveta made it clear she did not wish to have him at her table, where he had situated himself by swapping around the place cards and creating no small amount of seating arrangement chaos. One glitchy thing with this year's WLNP cost-reduction plan—flying in only the winner and not the finalists—is that Sveta is already here, seated at a table. But since she was not at the predinner reception, few people seem to have noticed. Besides, even if they have, Clemi gets the sense that the granting of a literary prize is largely beside the point; people are here to see one another and to be seen, and not because they especially care about who is named the winner of the Chestnut Prize.

("*I made an error of judgment,*" Sveta had whispered when she'd asked Clemi to disappear Percy from her table. "*Please don't get the wrong idea about me—I haven't been with another man since Akhil and I separated, and, well, I thought it would be a good distraction, that it might calm my nerves.*")

River is leaning in to Martha Thomas, whispering in her ear. Now Martha Thomas stares at Clemi across the table.

"Wait, you're Elena's daughter?" she says. "What are the

odds? I was at your mother's baby shower! Oh my lord. How's your mom?"

Oh boy. This is not the conversation Clemi wishes to have right now. But it is too late, completely out of her control. Martha Thomas is standing up and insisting everyone at the table shift seats so she can be next to Clemi. River looks crushed.

"Tell me everything," Martha says. "I haven't talked to your mother in years. Not since she stole Avis Ratner from me. I'd worked with her on three sets of revisions, and then *poof*—she tells me she's switching agents. But I'm over that now. So is she still in New York? Or wait, she moved to London, right?"

This is fine, Clemi tells herself. Surely she can find a way to smile and make small talk about her mother. It's not as if they are estranged. It's just that she is working pretty hard to make her own way in the world. Anyway, Clemi can answer her questions nicely, and she won't be sitting here long. In just a few minutes she will need to pop up and give the board president his cue, so she might as well enjoy being a dinner guest while she can.

Besides, she is still ravenously hungry despite having stuffed into her face at least a dozen appetizers, the mini Peking duck rolls being her hands-down favorite. Decorum aside, she begins to attack the salad as soon as the waiter sets it down—a dainty plate of arugula dusted with pomegranate seeds and what looks like goat cheese, pine nuts, and pear.

River has at least recovered from being abandoned by his agent and is attempting to chat up Colman. "The stickiness factor, what a completely life-changing concept," she hears him say. He seems to be reading from his phone, having probably brought up Gladwell's Wikipedia page.

Colman is still flipping through his guidebook.

"The walkway must be over there," he says to Clemi, pointing toward the stage. "The back door presidents and other VIPs can use to get in and out of the building without public exposure."

"That's so cool," says Vlad.

"Here's another cool thing," Colman says. "Did you know that when Reagan survived, it broke a twenty-year curse?"

"What do you mean?" asks Vlad.

"Beginning in 1840, every president in twenty-year intervals died in office."

"No way!"

"William Henry Harrison, Abraham Lincoln, James A. Garfield, William McKinley, Warren G. Harding, Franklin Roosevelt, and John F. Kennedy."

"Wow, so if Reagan had died, we'd still be under the curse!"

"Okay, no one really believes this," Clemi says.

"That's crazy. I represented books on Garfield, Roosevelt, and Kennedy," Martha says.

"Crazy!" Clemi agrees, even though it does not seem that remarkable a coincidence.

"Are you thinking of becoming an agent too?" Martha asks.

"Oh lord, no," says Clemi. "I'm the programs director here, as River might have mentioned."

"Yes, he also said you're a writer. That you met in a writing workshop."

"Well, yes, but I'm thinking I might switch gears and take the LSAT. I bought a study guide."

"Feel free to send me some pages," Martha Thomas says, ignoring this.

"Pages? Of the study guide? Oh, you mean of what I've written... Thanks, but what I have is kind of a mess, and like I said, I think I might go to law school. The whole business seems kind of rough."

"Well, I'm not going to fight you on it, but it's an open invitation. Anything for Elena's daughter."

This offer seems loaded, a possible gift horse. "Anything for Elena's daughter" sounds highly suspicious, like she might become a pawn in the agenting blood sport that is Martha Thomas versus her mother. But this is how the world works, sort of, sometimes, maybe a little bit. She will take it into consideration.

"I'm honored," Clemi says.

"River knows how to find me."

"Can I go look around the hotel?" Vlad asks. "See if I can find the secret walkway?"

"Absolutely not!" Clemi snaps.

The cat in the bag on Vlad's lap begins to stir, and she hears a little whimper from inside. "And please keep an eye on Immanuel. If he gets out of that bag one more time, I swear..."

"You swear what, Clemi?"

"I don't know, exactly, but it's not good. He shouldn't be here in the first place. And he shouldn't have been at the bar either."

"That's not Immanuel's fault. And it's not my fault, either."

"Well, it wasn't *not* Immanuel's fault," Clemi corrects. "I'm not assigning blame, but it wasn't *not* Immanuel's fault. And it wasn't *not* your fault," Clemi continues, getting confused, herself.

"You shouldn't use double negatives," Vlad scolds, avoiding the larger point.

"You are right, but that doesn't mean I'm wrong."

"But you are wrong, Clemi. I mean, Immanuel should not be in the hotel in the first place, and I'm not the one who brought him here, so you can't blame me for the fact that he got out of the bag in the bar."

"Sure, Vlad. I don't want to litigate this. I've lost track of what we are even trying to say. So whatever you say. You're always right."

Does she sound exasperated? Yes, she does. She is not proud of the fact that this child has won the battle, has completely worn her down. She is grateful that this conversation was presumably not recorded, thanks to Joe the FBI agent who stomped to death the stuffed chicken. Now that she thinks about it, she wonders where Joe and Charlotte are.

She looks around the room to see if they are lurking in any corners, while also keeping an eye out for a man who looks like Einstein if Einstein were a forage fish. She sees none of them, but she sees Sveta, three tables over, beckoning to her.

Clemi excuses herself and makes her way to Sveta's table, but en route she is hailed by two local writers with whom she is familiar from her time at the bookstore—a dashing writer of historical thrillers and his husband, and an author best known for her endless self-promotional efforts whose Instagram features reels of her sitting at her desk and typing, occasionally sharing tips on throwing elegant dinner parties. Clemi stops to greet them and exchanges small talk about her new job.

When she finally arrives at the head table, Sveta motions her over and whispers in her ear. "Thanks for keeping that man away from me," she says, nodding in the direction of Percy. "I learned just before dinner that Akhil is somewhere in the hotel, which is deeply upsetting."

"Akhil . . . your husband?"

"The very one. Keep him away from Vlad. Also, I don't particularly care what becomes of that Percy man, but Akhil has a jealous streak, so it's really best if Percy just stays in his corner."

"Oh dear, sure. I'll do my best."

"Bless you, child," Sveta says. "You're a gem. And how is Vlad? Did he eat dinner before the dinner?"

"He did not. We got a bit distracted. But I promise he'll eat now."

"Also, please tell Percy to stop texting me."

Clemi feels for Sveta, who is clearly nervous and under a lot of pressure. She gets that Sveta made a bad decision, opening herself up to this Percy dude. Still, she is reminded of a t-shirt she once saw in a bar at a ski resort that said, "Just Because I'll Sleep with You Doesn't Mean I'll Ski with You." Except in this case, it means "I Won't Sit Next to You at a Gala Dinner."

"I'll do my best," she says.

As she is turning to head back to her table, the lights dim and the video begins to play. Clemi has almost forgotten about this part of the evening. She hasn't seen this before and is curious to learn what she can about this organization. Alas the three-minute video has all the depth of an infomercial for teeth whitening. There are clips of past winners accepting awards, and of Howard bloviating about Literature That Is Prophetic in Vision without any indication of what that might actually mean. Unsurprisingly, there are no references to Arthur Muller, to Hyman Berkowitz, or, for that matter, to any current or former board members. The footage at least provides a brief interlude in which to sit down and eat.

As Clemi sticks another forkful of salad into her mouth, she hears a tapping at the microphone. Someone on the tech staff is testing the mic, and Clemi realizes she's already botching her job; it's time for the welcoming remarks. She rushes backstage and finds the board president. He is fast asleep on the couch.

"It's time!" she says loudly. But he seems to be out cold. She pushes gently on his shoulder and tries again. "Dr. Jolly, wake up!"

His eyes pop open. "Why are you mocking me?"

"What do you mean?"

"I don't understand why you persist in calling me that. Years ago they called me jolly, but that was a joke, and it was a little mean-spirited, I think, because I'm not."

"Not what?"

"Not jolly."

"So who are you?"

"I don't know. I guess I'm dour. Do you get it? Opposites?"

"I guess I get it, but what I mean is, what is your name?"

"Simon."

"Simon?"

"Yes. Simon Brinkley."

"I thought you were the board president."

"I am."

"Well... hmm... I'm new. Obviously, I'm a little confused, but it's time. Let's go! I'll walk you to the stage."

Sad Dad Board President, who is rather confusingly not named Dr. Jolly, reluctantly stands up and pulls himself together.

He's a little rumpled now, but whatever. There's not much to be done about that, so out they go.

Clearly something is very wrong, but since it's not clear to Clemi at this point what she ought to do, she leads him to the microphone. Back at her table, she finds that her salad has already been whisked away.

Simon Brinkley, board president, begins to speak but is entirely inaudible, which is possibly for the best. The AV tech rushes back to the stage and fiddles with some wires, to no avail. A moment later, a new microphone is produced. He tries again. He spreads out his notes on the podium and looks as if he might begin to cry. He is so nervous it is painful to watch, but finally he begins to speak.

"GOOD EVENING! As board president, it is my honor to welcome you this evening."

There is a somewhat hesitant round of applause.

He clears his throat and continues. "Each of these past several years, as we have gathered, whether here in this beautiful hotel or at other similarly beautiful hotels around the world—and a huge thank-you to our hotel sponsors, as well as to Moffett Vineyards for so generously donating the wine . . ."

Clemi's eyes dart around the table. No one said anything to her about donated wine. Are they drinking Moffett wine? No, they are not.

The board president, aka Simon Brinkley, is starting to find his groove. "It is always a challenge at these dinners to strike the right tone, to find words that are celebratory yet acknowledge the very real struggles and horrors unfolding outside these doors. This is an especially fraught time in this fragile world..."

What the hell? Does he think he is giving the State of the Union Address? Who is this person? Something is clearly very wrong. There must be a way to get him off the stage before people actually begin to pay attention. Right now, mercifully, all she hears is the clanging of silverware.

"It has also been a fraught time in our profession. The way intentions are so easily misconstrued..."

Uh-oh. People seem to be putting their forks down and listening to his words.

"This is meant to be a festive evening, but we nevertheless must strike a somber balance and remember that our profession continues to be in crisis."

Someone claps, and others join in.

"We all know this is a calling," he continues, seemingly energized by the response. "No one enters this line of work unless it is burning a hole deep inside them. But that doesn't mean we shouldn't be treated with the respect that we deserve...

"It is impossible to earn a living wage in our once-dignified, indeed *revered* profession. And opportunities have plummeted over the last ten years. There are a number of contributing factors, which I know you know, and which we will be discussing when we break into workshops tomorrow, so I won't belabor them now."

Workshops? Tomorrow? She might not know a lot about WLNP or about this gala, but she knows there are no workshops tomorrow, that there has been no wine donation, and it is finally dawning on her that a huge mix-up has taken place. This man might be the board president, but of the wrong board. Nevertheless, he is now on a roll.

"We are becoming an endangered species. Nearly as endangered as the Sumatran rhino!"

"I saw one of those once, in Sumatra!" Vlad shouts enthusiastically.

"Shhhh," Clemi says, putting her finger to her lips.

"As the western lowland gorilla," the board president continues.

Now Vlad stands up in his chair, waving his arms. "I saw that once in the Congo!"

"Vlad, this is not the time," Clemi whispers. "Here, eat a bread roll," she says, stuffing a miniature brioche in his mouth.

"Coulrophobia is nothing new, of course, and it's not the entire explanation for our declining employment..."

Coulrophobia? Clemi has never heard of coulrophobia. She leans over and asks Vlad if he knows what that is.

"It's a fear of clowns," Vlad explains. "I don't have that, but I know someone who does."

Skylar is now at the table, squatting by Clemi's side.

"WTF?" Skylar asks.

"I don't know. What is even happening? I mean clearly he is the wrong board president. My bad, I guess. I'm so sorry."

"He's just in the wrong ballroom," Skylar says.

"What do you mean?"

Simon Brinkley is still talking, now waxing rather eloquently about the need to sacrifice for the sake of one's art. Someone in the room begins to cry.

"I mean, he's a clown."

"I see that."

"No, I mean he's really a clown. A *clown* clown. In the professional sense."

"Oh my God."

"There is a clown convention down the hall. In the other ballroom. The National Association of Clowns. He's *their* board president."

"No way! Is that why I keep seeing clowns everywhere? I thought this was a bad dream. I'm so sorry. I ran into him in the elevator. He said he was the board president, and I thought . . . well, I wasn't thinking obviously. I just made an assumption. Just more evidence that I'm not a good candidate for the LSAT, because I cannot think logically." This would have qualified as a need-to-know situation, as opposed to nice-to-know situation, though the former fully encompasses the latter. "Oh my God, what do I do?"

"What are you even going on about? Take a deep breath, Clemi. He's winding down anyway, and everyone is into it. Let's just allow him to wrap up. I'll escort him off the stage in a minute. I don't think you can do anything at this point."

He is indeed winding down, and then he is done, thank goodness. But before he leaves, he tosses into the audience dozens upon dozens of round red Styrofoam noses. People jump up from their chairs and scramble to get one, jostling with one another like he's launching t-shirts during the seventh-inning stretch at a baseball game. He then exits the stage to wild applause.

"I've got him," Skylar says. "You just get up there and tell everyone to enjoy their main course, and that we'll continue the program after dinner and announce this year's award winner."

Clemi nods, grateful that Skylar has a plan.

"And put some muscle into it. Try to sound excited."

Chapter 30

CLEMI DOES PUT some muscle into it! She tries to sound excited! And she *is* excited, about Sveta anyway, even though she can't fully get a handle on who Sveta is. Clemi has run the gamut of emotions trying to better understand this woman, this brilliant writer who vacillates between lovely and vulnerable and surprisingly entitled. Not to mention her "extra" son, who is equally confounding in a different, rather exhausting way.

Nevertheless, for anyone who can write like that . . . well, Clemi will cut her a little slack. And despite herself, Clemi is developing quite the soft spot for Vlad.

As Clemi descends from the stage, she notices something odd in the middle of the room. The catering cart, which is covered with a cloth, appears to be moving about on its own. She stares at it, puzzled. Perhaps Penelope's business is using cutting-edge technology in the form of self-driving catering carts. Next thing you know, little robots will appear to clear the salad plates and refill the wineglasses, to pacify cranky dinner guests whose meat is undercooked.

She watches for a moment as the thing maneuvers about, cutting figure eights around the tables. The cart isn't stopping anywhere, nor does it seem to have a plan. She wonders if the cart has gone rogue. Then it begins to emit tinny music like a Good Humor truck.

It's a single refrain, a remix of ABBA's "Dancing Queen." Clemi suspects the music is not coming from the cart, exactly, but rather from a cell phone in close proximity. She walks to the other side of the cart and sees through a gap in the cloth curtain that a figure has contorted itself into the bottom shelf of the contraption. Maybe one of the waiters got caught in there and is somehow stuck?

"Are you okay in there? Can I be of help?" she asks.

Now that she is up close, she sees that two hands on either side of the cart are paddling at the floor, propelling the thing as it begins to move away.

"Hello in there? Are you stuck?" she tries again.

"I'm fine, thank you very much," the cart replies.

She knows this voice!

She lifts the cloth and sees her boss twisted into what can only be a painful knot. He is wearing a rumpled shirt and torn jeans and is not dressed in anything even remotely approaching business plus.

She squats to get a better look. "Howard? What the hell?"

"I can explain."

"Explain which part? I mean, I don't even know where to begin with the questions. You have no idea what's been going on. Although then again, you probably do, given that you created this mess."

"Just give me a chance to explain."

His phone is at it again, blurting out the ABBA tune, again from the top.

"Can you turn that off, please? It's incredibly annoying."

"Can you do it? It's new, and I've never had an iPhone before. I don't know how it works."

Clemi takes the phone and depresses the sound button. "Wait, what happened to your other phone? Was that really you texting about the cat food or . . . ? It sounded like you were in trouble."

"It was me. But I was on the run, literally. Herring showed up outside my house unexpectedly. He flew in from London and wanted more money. He was blackmailing me, making all sorts of horrible threats against my family. Then I realized he had hacked into my phone and had my location thingamajig turned on. I don't know how to turn it off, so the only thing I could do was stick my phone in the garbage disposal. Which was sort of a moot step since I had just received notice from Verizon that my bill was delinquent and they were about to close my account. So that, at least, was serendipitous timing."

"So whose phone is this?"

"My mom put me on her plan."

The thought of Howard on his mother's cell phone plan makes Clemi a little sad. She imagines this woman, whoever she is, unable to retire now that she has added her forty-something-year-old son to her phone plan, and imagines him back home, snuggled beneath a Spider-Man quilt in his childhood bedroom, while his mother scrambles his eggs and does his laundry.

"How are you even squashed in there? Just squatting like this is killing me," she says, standing up straight and rubbing her lower back.

Now she sees Skylar gesturing to her frantically. Clemi acknowledges her with a nod, and then returns to a squat. At least yoga has made her a little more limber than she was a week ago.

"Okay, well, this is not the best time to chitchat," she says to Howard. "I have to deal with all this." She waves her hands dramatically.

"Really, I can explain."

"It had better be good, because I don't know why I'm even still here, trying to pull off this circus. Literally, Howard, it's a circus."

A waiter approaches and looks at her strangely. "You okay down there? Did you drop something?"

"No, I'm fine! Thought I'd lost my phone, but it's right here!" She holds Howard's phone up as proof, then hands it back to him. "You'd better find another spot. You are doing about as good a job at hiding as a dog under the bed with its tail sticking out."

"Speaking of which, where's my cat? Herring sent me a cryptic message. I think he nabbed Immanuel."

"Don't worry. We have him back. He's safe."

"Oh thank God. Thank you, Clemi. I don't know what I'd do—"

"Save it, Howard."

She leaves and begins to walk back to her table, having forgotten to ask the most critical question: What in the world is he doing here?

Now Clemi sees the FBI agent, Charlotte, chasing Simon the Sad Dad Board President, who was evidently backstage changing into his clown costume when she burst in on him. He began to run, not sure what was happening but completely terrified, wearing only a polka-dot shirt with ruffles and fuchsia boxer shorts. Clemi turns back toward the ruckus, trying to process what is going on. The FBI is here, presumably, on account of the presence of Herring, who is apparently somewhere in the hotel. And from what she gathers, Howard has been funneling money to Herring, who was blackmailing him... and somewhere along the way Immanuel became bait. It's not much, and it still doesn't add up, but it's more than she understood a few minutes ago.

Presumably the FBI is after the board president believing that he, too, has been siphoning funds. Not only do they not understand that this is the president of a different board, but also that in the case of WLNP, the board president likely has no idea what is going on.

"You've got the wrong guy!" Simon Brinkley shouts. "I'm just a clown!"

Agent Joe, who has just entered the ballroom, confirms this, shouting to Agent Charlotte, "Not the clown! We want the fish! He's over there!" He points toward the far corner of the room near the exit. Clemi can't help but notice that Joe has catsup stains on his shirt.

Clemi looks toward the back of the room and sees a squat man with grey hair that is sticking up in all directions as if he has just been electrified. She does a double take and is not sure if it's the power of suggestion or not, but the man definitely looks like a fish with his grey scaly skin and bulging eyes, except he definitely has two legs in lieu of a fish tail.

The man who can only be Herring sees the agent rushing toward him and makes for the door.

Clemi considers the FBI agents, reflecting on every bad thing she has done in her life, from sneaking a tortoise into work once, to participating in the writing of the bad check. She then begins to back up stealthily, returning to her seat, where Vlad is regaling the table with an amusing anecdote to do with Jaroslav Hašek.

"The Rangers goalie?" Martha asks.

"No, the Czech writer. He is best known for writing *The Good Soldier Švejk*. But he once had a job as an editor at an animal magazine and was getting pretty bored. Or he thought maybe his readers were getting bored. I forget which. Anyway, he started to invent animals, and then he'd write stories about them to keep things fresh.

"The board president's reference to the rhino and gorilla reminded me of how Hašek made up something called the Gruesome Guzzler. He wrote that it lived in the sea from 10:00 a.m. to 4:00 p.m. Then it emerged and spent the rest of the day eating children."

"Eating children?" Martha practically screams, then composes herself and apologizes. "I'm so sorry," she says to the table. "It's just that the idea of an animal eating children is rather upsetting. But then I remembered this is all pretend. Vlad, you are the most remarkable child!"

"I know!"

Clemi is waiting for Martha to offer to represent him too.

Now Herring is back in the ballroom, sluicing around the tables, with Charlotte still in his pursuit. Then he is back out the door, somehow managing to elude this woman who is half his age and in possession of a gun.

Vlad jumps from his chair and starts to run after them, his sneakers lighting up like the Fourth of July. He accidentally crashes into a waiter who is pouring wine into the glass of the

Panamanian ambassador. Red wine spills all over her dress, alas. Clemi adds a dry-cleaning bill to the accumulating pile of WLNP debt. She is not sure how much more of this chaos she can take.

"Vlad!" Clemi calls. "Come back here right now! What are you even doing?"

"Can you watch Immanuel?" he asks, ignoring her.

Clemi returns to the table and finds the tote bag, but when she lifts it, it is surprisingly light. She cannot believe Vlad has lost the cat again, even after her warning just a few moments ago.

"Excuse me a minute!" she says to no one in particular, racing after Vlad. He is as slippery as the cat and seems to have again disappeared. She looks around the lower floor lobby and sees only a couple of guests who appear to be en route to or from the restrooms.

She asks them if they've seen a child, and a woman in a pink tulle frock points a finger in the direction of the escalator.

"Thank you!" Clemi says. "Any chance you saw a cat?"

"The one wearing a Hermés tie?"

"Yes! That's the one."

She points the same finger in the opposite direction.

Clemi hesitates. Should she run after Immanuel, or Vlad? Vlad, of course, whom she now spies at the top of the escalator. He is chasing after Charlotte, who has just alighted from the top step and is running through the lobby in pursuit of Herring, who apparently realizes he is about to be apprehended and darts into the revolving door. Bad move. There is an FBI agent standing on the other side. His only choices are to surrender or to keep swimming around in circles in the glass door.

He goes around in some ten loops before emerging dizzy and disoriented, then falls to ground as he is cuffed.

Immanuel now enters stage left, looks at Herring, and stops in his tracks. He arches his back with his hair standing straight up and makes a loud hissing noise before turning and running back in the other direction, leaping onto the escalator and bounding down the moving stairs.

Exasperated, Vlad turns and follows.

"Wait a minute, that's my tie," says Herring. "One of my favorites!"

"You aren't going to be needing that tie for some time," says Charlotte. "Although I take that back. You might want to wear it in court."

Chapter 31

"LET'S GO, VLAD," Clemi says once she catches up to him in the downstairs lobby. "Your mom is about to get her award!"

"No way. Not without Immanuel."

The cat is now heading toward the wing that leads to the swimming pool. He then pauses and crouches behind a giant poster board for a forthcoming travel convention. He looks terrified.

"You poor thing," Clemi says. "That awful fish man won't ever bother you again." She has no idea what Herring might have done to the cat, but presumably he wasn't giving Immanuel a lot of TLC. She picks him up despite her better judgment, less worried about allergies than about soiling Sveta's beautiful dress, which is instantly covered in cat hair. She then takes Vlad's hand and leads him back to the ballroom.

By the time they arrive the lights are dimmed. The room is awash in an electric blue. The candles twinkle on the tables. On the stage Sveta stands regally, smiling magnanimously.

Clemi has to admit that Penelope is a catering genius. If she ever gets married—not that she is a girl who sits around planning fantasy weddings, especially since she is too busy planning fantasy careers—she might aspire to something like this.

Sveta was announced the winner a moment ago—by whom Clemi has no idea—and now people are on their feet. Lights from iPhone cameras are flashing. Sveta nods her head, soaking in the adoration. She is so radiant that Clemi half expects her to grab the microphone and begin belting out a Beyoncé tune.

Now Percy rushes to the stage and hands her a bouquet of flowers, which she graciously accepts, although Clemi detects a subtle grimace.

Then Mr. Samaraweera steps onto the stage, shakes her hand, and presents her with the check. This strikes Clemi as a little tacky, like something from an old-school game show, but she supposes this must be WLNP protocol. They each hold one end of the envelope containing the check and pose for photos.

The problem that is about to occur might in other circumstances pass unnoticed until a later date—award winners do not typically stop glowing and blushing and air-kissing in order to check the name, or amount, on the check—but in this case, Mr. Samaraweera says aloud, "And huge congratulations, Vivian Adebayo, winner of this year's WLNP Chestnut Prize for Prescient Fiction!"

Sveta's face is now a slow-motion triptych of emotion. Her smile flattens, then fades, then a mask of confusion settles in. Murmurs move through the audience, although perhaps some of them have not paid enough attention to the name of the winner to notice what has just occurred.

It takes Mr. Samaraweera a moment to understand too. Perhaps it has less to do with him being more knowledgeable about multivariable calculus than the difference between two literary icons, and more to do with his being unaware of the depths of the malfeasance at WLNP.

Sveta stands there awkwardly, attempting, again, to smile, which is the only reasonable thing to do.

Now a tall, rugged, rakishly handsome man in an exquisitely tailored suit rushes to the stage and kisses Sveta on the cheek. He, too, hands her a bouquet of flowers.

"I'm so proud of you, my love!"

Sveta's rictus is putting in some overtime. She's a pro and is not going to cause a scene, even though Clemi is pretty sure this man must be her estranged husband, aka the cad, aka Akhil. Now Sveta bows graciously and invites Vlad onto the stage. Vlad, back in possession of the cat, now sticks Immanuel in Clemi's arms again as he runs to the stage and leaps toward his mother.

"Thank you, my dear Vladislav. I could not have written this book without you. You are my inspiration. My sun and my moon." She begins to pick him up, then winces, presumably because of a twinge in her back, and gives him a hug instead. Vlad hugs her back, his head nestled adorably at her waist.

"Do you get money, Mom?" he asks. "How much did you get? And why did he call you Vivian?"

This garners nervous laughter from the audience.

"Indeed," says Mr. Samaraweera, still looking confused.

Who knows? Clemi wants to say. Maybe someday Sveta *will* get some money. Maybe they will even reimburse her for the plane tickets—somehow—but at the moment, it looks like Vivian Adebayo is the recipient of what is almost certainly another a bad check.

Suddenly Howard is back, out of hiding and standing in front of her, in plain view.

"Immanuel! My little fur ball of love," he says, grabbing the cat out of Clemi's arms and burying his face in his coat. He then devolves into cringy baby talk. "Thank God you are okay. I hope that awful man didn't hurt you!"

"What the hell, Howard? I think the FBI is looking for you. I don't even . . . I can't even . . ."

"I'm going to clear it up right now. I'm done hiding from that swine Herring, now that he's in cuffs and Immanuel is okay."

He then sticks the cat back in Clemi's arms and bolts onto the stage in his torn jeans and scruffy t-shirt. Now that he is out from under the cart and fully visible, she sees that he has several days' worth of stubble and . . . oof . . . who knows when he's last showered. Sveta, Vlad, Akhil, and Mr. Samaraweera step aside to give him a wide berth on the stage.

"Ladies and gentlemen. And Sveta Attais," he says, pressing prayer hands in her direction before continuing. "WLNP owes everyone in this room an apology. Also an explanation."

Does WLNP owe everyone an apology? Clemi wonders. *Or does* Howard?

"The clown may have been at the wrong gala, but his words resonated, nonetheless. This profession is a calling. It is impossible to earn a living wage in our once-dignified, indeed revered profession. And the average number of opportunities has plummeted over the last ten years. I stand here as exhibit A. Here I am, a fine writer. How do we know this? I don't talk about it very much, but I was given a multibook deal by the most prestigious publisher in the Netherlands . . ."

Clemi would theatrically slap a hand to her head, but she needs them both to hold on to Immanuel.

"My first novel, featuring Detective Vinke—he is known by his last name primarily, even though his first name is Henkel—was even almost optioned by a production company in the UK. And yet that was the end of my publishing career, just because my sales were . . . not great."

Now Clemi does put the cat down, holding on to the Hermès leash and putting the free hand over her eyes. It doesn't stop her from hearing what seems poised to be Howard's public meltdown masquerading as a mea culpa, but it at least reduces the sensory assault.

"So here I am, in this literary-adjacent role, which is not all bad, mind you! I love being involved in the business of words in any form, and to meet amazing writers like Sveta Attais. And I'm doing the best job I can—I really am—I'm trying to keep my spirits up, and I may have found an agent interested in reviving Detective Vinke . . . Did I mention that I have already written twelve sequels?"

Clemi looks around the room for Skylar but doesn't see her. She doesn't know what to do. They need to get Howard off the stage.

"Apologies," Howard continues. "I know this might seem like a digression, but it's not entirely. I'm just giving you context. It's all been a lot. You see, what has happened is that our financial advisor, Harry Fishman, known as 'Herring,' has been—"

Clemi feels some responsibility to curtail this train wreck. She tries to intervene. "Howard, let's go to the greenroom," she shouts to him on the stage. "Let's talk about this in private."

He ignores her, or maybe he hasn't heard her. Whatever the

reason, he is still talking. "Extorting WLNP for the last few years. And extorting me as well . . ."

This soliloquy is interrupted by a commotion as a woman rushes into the room and leaps onto the stage. "Excuse me! I hate to crash your party and interrupt this ridiculous speech, but do you happen to have my keys?"

It's Mae Zhang. Even though it is warm outside, and it is night, she is nonetheless wearing a trench coat and sunglasses. Clemi wonders if perhaps in their happier days they dressed up like this and did a little detective novel research role-playing.

"So sorry, Mae. I do have the keys! I know I screwed up big-time, but I can explain everything, and I really didn't mean to take the keys." He reaches into his pocket and tosses a ring of keys to her.

"Thanks," she says, putting the keys in her pocket. "And save the rest of your bullshit for the lawyer."

"Speaking of lawyers, your wife has a point. You might want to stop talking right now," says a voice from the back of the room. "I'm an attorney, and I advise you not to say whatever it is you are about to say. I can give you my card if you'd like."

"Happy to offer my services too!" someone offers. "I'm in Georgetown. Very close to WLNP."

"Thank you for your concern, but I want to come clean, consequences be damned," Howard continues. "I need to salvage my reputation. I may have done bad things, but I was doing them at the command of the board. This man called Herring, he is the villain. Me, I'm just a schmuck."

"Point of order: Herring is not technically on the board," notes Mr. Samaraweera, who is still planted on stage left.

"Okay, fair enough. This so-called financial advisor to

WLNP has been giving me bad counsel for more than two years. It began so casually I didn't even realize what was happening. First, he said something like, 'No one has been monitoring these accounts for decades. We could be earning far better returns. It's my fiduciary duty to put this money to work.' So he told me to take $50K and invest it in a certain fund that was consistently getting better returns than the Schwab fund it was sitting in for years. And then, like a month later, he presented me with a statement that showed we'd doubled our money, which was nuts. So he told me to invest $50k more.

"It went on like this for about a year until I asked him why this money wasn't appearing in the WLNP accounts."

"Why didn't you tell me?" Mr. Samareweera asks. "You kept presenting me with these cheery budget reports as if all was well."

"Because he started to threaten me. He told me to not talk to anyone on the board. Plus, it was my word against his, and he said he would deny having anything to do with the withdrawals. He said there was no paper trail to him and that these funds were . . . well, what I figured out was that there were no funds. The money was going straight to him."

Howard's voice pitches, and he begins to choke up. "He told me that if the board got wind of this, he'd . . . well, he said he'd do unspeakable things to my family. And my cat . . . And once he'd finished ravaging the WLNP accounts, he had me start in on our personal accounts . . ."

"I am seriously suggesting you stop talking right now," says the first lawyer in the audience.

"What was he doing with the money?" asks someone in the back of the room.

"He was using it to fund his lavish lifestyle, of course. He had so-called problems. A whole second family, three kids, private schools, property taxes to pay, and his own money had been frozen by the British government because of his connections to Putin. He was a minor oligarch of some sort. I don't understand how that all works, but he was on an allowance from the Brits that didn't even cover his grocery bills."

"Those must have been some grocery bills," someone shouts.

"All I know is that his mistress was threating to tell his wife."

"This sounds like a good plot for your next novel!" someone shouts encouragingly.

"Not so sure, really. I think this story has probably been done. Especially the whole extortion thing. You'd need to really mix it up somehow," another counters.

"Well, maybe instead of detective fiction, you could try your hand at comedy. But this is such a stupid story, you'd have to cast a moron in the lead role."

Clemi has been standing quietly, taking this in. No one seems to be asking the right question. It does not seem her place to ask, but she finally blurts it out.

"What does this have to do with Sveta Attais?"

"Good question. I know it's on me, but you might want to ask Akhil, here, to explain. He's the one who offered a sack of cash to give his wife the prize. All *I* had to do was convince the board. And now, like these attorneys suggest, I think I've said enough."

Chapter 32

"WHAT THE HELL, Akhil?" Sveta can be heard snapping as she and her family decamp from the stage and rush toward the exit.

Clemi follows them to the hallway, pulling the recalcitrant cat on the leash. After being kidnapped and then racing around the hotel this afternoon, Immanuel would no doubt like to find a cozy spot in which to sleep. Instead, he is being forced to endure more of these human shenanigans, now in the form of Sveta shouting at her husband.

While Clemi was chafing at her nanny duties only moments ago, her protective instincts now kick into high gear: Vlad should not be here, witnessing this parental calamity. She picks up the cat and hands it to Vlad, who enfolds him in his arms.

"Why don't you take Immanuel back to the table," she suggests. "You can hang out with Colman for a bit. I'll be right back."

"Colman left a little while ago," Vlad says, nuzzling the cat.

"He left?"

"Yes. He said to thank you and said maybe he'll see you at yoga, but that he had expected something different."

"Different? How?" Clemi doesn't know why she suddenly feels insulted by this.

"He said something about how the evening had devolved into farce."

"Ah well. This is true. I can't argue with that. I'd leave too, if I could."

"He wasn't unhappy though. He said he wanted to explore the hotel."

"Um, okay. Then go hang out with my friend River and his agent."

"No, thank you."

Clemi can't blame him. It looks like River has his hand on Martha's thigh. What is it with him and these much older women? Surely nothing to do with the literary connections of the two he has, at least most recently, been doing whatever he is doing with, or to, which is something Clemi would prefer to not consider in too much detail.

Okay, so Vlad is not going anywhere, but at least she tried. She supposes she can't blame him for wanting to hear what is transpiring between his parents. Certainly Clemi wants to hear.

"You *bought* the prize?" Sveta cries.

"Yes, and I upgraded your hotel room! Sent you a spread fit for a queen. Which you are. *My* queen."

"Never have I been so humiliated in my life!"

"I just thought . . . I miss you so much, my darling. I thought, well, I thought this might bring us together again. I thought you'd be more appreciative!"

"I don't need you to *buy* me a prize! I'm doing just fine, thank you very much, which is more than I can say for you!"

"Hey, I'm doing okay! Give me a little credit, please. Not everyone has a spare half million lying around for buying their wife a prize!"

"How did you even finagle this?"

"I met the fish man on a flight. We were seated next to one another—"

"Come again? You were seated next to a fish? What, did you fly coach?"

"Don't be silly. Of course not, darling. I was seated next to that man they call Herring. The guy that bonehead on the stage was just talking about. We were on KLM, Zurich to Dubai— first class, of course—and we got to talking. A few drinks in, we discovered we were pretty simpatico. I mentioned that I was married to you . . . I'm so proud of you, Sveta, you have no idea. I talk about you all the time—"

"Oh, please. Also I'm not sure KLM has first-class anything. Only business from what I recall."

"Sure, whatever, you are probably right. So we were in business class then, and a few more drinks in I told him how I had screwed it all up, how I'd been unfaithful. How no woman could ever compete with you. How that whole situation with the Malaysia Airlines stewardess had been a mistake, how I'd do anything to win you back and—"

"The Malaysia Airlines stewardess?"

"That's not the point. But I thought—"

"I thought you'd slept with a journalist. There was also a *flight attendant*?"

"It's over, darling. History."

"Spare me the bull, Akhil."

"Well, it happens to be true. And this guy Herring, he told me he's the financial advisor for a literary nonprofit. I mean, what are the odds? Pure serendipity. By the time we landed—"

"I don't even understand how this could happen. You can't *buy* a literary prize!"

"But darling, you can! You can buy anything. I did! I did a little day trading, moved some crypto around, and I have the money right here! Cash! I was supposed to give it to Herring, but I don't see him here."

"If you were going to buy me a prize, Akhil, you might have at least made it a Pulitzer!"

"Next time, my love. Anything if you give me another chance."

The conversation is interrupted by a cry from Vlad. "That's my cat!"

Howard is now here, trying to pry Immanuel from Vlad's arms.

"No, it's my cat! Give him back!"

A tussle ensues.

"Howard, please, just let him hold the cat," Clemi says. "You should be grateful that they've bonded because you're probably going to jail." She can't believe she just said this. She is bossing around her boss, but under the circumstances, this seems the only reasonable thing to do.

Hyperfocused as she is on Howard, Clemi fails to notice a big man approaching, carrying a tuba. "Excuse me, lady," the tuba-carrying man says, tapping her on the shoulder. "Where do you want us to set up?"

"Us?"

"The band."

"The *band*?"

"Well, we're here to deliver the instruments. I'm with the band, and the rest of us are on the way. They're having trouble parking."

"Hey, Dima," he says, shouting to another man who is emerging from the elevator, pushing a large metal case on a dolly. "This way."

The tuba man presents Clemi with a clipboard and a pen. "I need you to accept delivery."

"Of?"

"The drums and the tuba. Also the keyboard. I think it's on the next elevator."

"I'm sorry," Clemi says. "There must be some mistake. We're winding down here."

The man pulls out his phone and taps at it. "Plotkin bar mitzvah, 9:00 p.m., Friday night. Isn't this the Columbia ballroom?"

"Yes, it is."

"That's all I need to know. Just sign here, for Christ's sake."

"Isn't Friday night at nine an odd time for a bar mitzvah?"

"Listen, lady, I'm just doing what it says here. Are you going to sign or not?"

"I'll sign," Howard says, taking the clipboard.

"Seriously, Howard?"

"We have more important things to discuss. I want to explain."

According to Howard, who is leaning against the wall and looking as depleted as his cat, the selection subcommittee of the board awarding the Chestnut Prize for Prescient Fiction had initially recommended honoring Vivian Adebayo—a highly acclaimed Nigerian-born author whose latest novel, *Awe, High Risk, Patriot*, had received glowing reviews and won last year's Booker Prize.

"The subcommittee's recommendation is rarely contested," he continues. "It seemed a done deal. But then I started getting calls and texts from Herring. Honestly, I didn't know what was happening. I didn't know about the whole Akhil-slash-Herring backstory. All I knew was that I was under tremendous pressure to convince the board to change the decision..."

A woman wearing too much blue eyeshadow and a puffy floral dress appears, holding an enormous wrapped gift. "Excuse me, I don't mean to interrupt," she says, interrupting. "Where should I put the gift?"

"The gift?"

"For Benji."

"Benji?"

"The bar mitzvah boy. Benjamin Plotkin."

"There seems to be some confusion. Maybe you have the wrong ballroom? We're a literary nonprofit."

"Oh, never mind. I see cousin Sharon," she says, ignoring Clemi and waving excitedly to a woman alighting from the escalator, presumably said cousin Sharon.

"Okay, no idea what is happening here. But where were we?" Clemi says. "Oh, right. Getting the board to change the decision."

"Right. I tried to explain to Herring that the decision was out of my control. I don't pick the prize winner; it's a board thing. But he kept turning the screws. He told me I would go to prison if all the missing funds were discovered—which is no doubt true—and that half a million dollars would take care of the problem. He promised this would be the end of the whole situation.

"I was desperate. I mean, I knew that if Mae discovered our missing money, which was likely to happen any minute, she would probably put ethylene glycol in my coffee or something."

"Why ethylene glycol?" asks Vlad. "That's weirdly specific."

"Ethylene glycol is an ingredient in antifreeze. It has a sweet taste, apparently, so I wouldn't even know she'd poisoned me, and by the time you learn you've consumed it, you can't see, your kidney function is kaput, and you are on your way."

"Did you use that in one of the novels you can't sell?"

"I did actually!" Howard's face seems to brighten at the recognition of him as a writer, even though it's from an eight-year-old.

"And I didn't even want to think about what she might do to my cat. Mae is a virulent ailurophobe."

"Mae is a what?" asks Clemi.

"Ailurophobia is like anti-Semitism, except for cats," Vlad explains.

"Yes." Howard nods in Vlad's direction. "I think it really has more to do with a fear of cats, but in Mae's case, it's more of a hate situation."

Immanuel's eyes seem to widen, possibly contemplating the virulence of Mae's condition.

"You're probably wondering why I believed him this time, that he'd hand over the money, but he had a whole story about how he'd received a tip that the Brits were about to look into his mistress's finances and . . . well, he wanted to clean everything up before that happened. It was more complicated than that, but he was pretty convincing."

Now a pretty thirtysomething woman in pursuit of a toddler rushes by, trailed by two older children and a man wearing a yarmulke who is presumably her husband.

"Excuse me," the man says to Clemi. "Are you with the Plotkin bar mitzvah party?"

"No, I am not," says Clemi, sounding more abrupt than she intends. "And we are still using this ballroom."

"Hey, Phil!" cousin Sharon yells to him. "You made it!"

"We did! Traffic was pretty bad along the turnpike, but it eased up just after the Delaware Bridge. What an awkward time for a bar mitzvah!"

"Here's the thing," says cousin Sharon. "I just called Cheri, and she said there's been some mistake. The bar mitzvah is tomorrow. There were a couple of typos on the invitation, and she was all incredulous, like it's my fault I didn't read the emails with the correction. Like I have time to read all these emails!"

From inside the ballroom is the sound of a tuba warming up.

"I hear Benji is going to do a tuba solo. He's quite the prodigy apparently," offers Phil.

"Oh my God," says Clemi. "I can't even . . . Whatever. Back to the prize."

"It was easier than I would have thought," Howard says proudly. "Thank God for the internet. I did a little opposition research on Vivian, inflated it a bit admittedly, and then began a private whisper campaign.

"I brought to the attention of the subcommittee a tweet that Vivian had sent some years ago that read: 'Forgive me, I am having a senior moment.' She went on to apologize for mangling the name of a fellow author in a podcast she had just recorded. It was no big deal. There was some lighthearted back-and-forth on her comment thread about that having been an ageist remark, but to say the least, it wasn't the sort of thing that would rise to the level of PEN America or the ACLU intervening.

"But I convinced them that WLNP couldn't withstand one more scandal, and that they would risk alienating their older donors if they got wind of that tweet."

Cousin Sharon is back. "Phil! Tova! Come on in. They are about to serve dessert, and the waiter has set out some extra chairs for us."

"Be my guest," Clemi says, not that cousin Sharon seems to be asking.

"They agreed to postpone the decision," Howard continues. "And to revisit the issue at the next meeting. They are all too busy to schedule meetings, so that's part of my job—which is a ridiculous thing to ask an executive director to do especially since I haven't had a raise in three years—but in any case, I used this to my advantage and scheduled the meeting for a time when I knew Eric would be giving a book talk in Stockholm and the three remaining members of the subcommittee would be away at writing residencies without reliable internet connections.

"You know how they are—when they are present, they take every little thing so seriously. We once had a board meeting where we spent forty minutes discussing the placement of a comma on the proposed new mission statement, which was then voted down anyway—but the minute they're back on their book deadlines or running around the world on tour, they can't be bothered with WLNP. So, it was pretty easy. I just held the meeting without anyone present and declared Sveta the winner."

"But then . . . You're not a board member, right? I assume that technically you don't get to vote. What do the bylaws say?"

"Excuse me," says an older gentleman wearing a striped bow tie and leaning on a cane. "Is this the Plotkin bar mitzvah?"

"You're early," Clemi says, motioning toward the ballroom. "But come on in and have dessert. Cousin Sharon is inside."

"The bylaws! That's hilarious," Howard continues. "No one has consulted the bylaws since who knows when, probably 1959. The bylaws still refer to communication via telegraph messages.

"I mean, maybe technically you are correct, but I just went ahead and did it. That's all it took. Vivian hadn't been notified yet, and only a few people on the board had heard about the initial decision. The only unfortunate thing is that someone had already told Sam that Vivian was the winner, and I guess we forgot to update him. That guy, I love him, but he's a little too efficient. I can't believe he went ahead and wrote the check.

"The only other real problem was Didi. She was the programs director before you took over, Clemi."

"Yes, I'm aware. Didi Feldman."

"She was outraged. She quit on the spot. She put a curse on me, even."

"A *curse?*"

"Yes. She said, 'My grandmother had a wish for someone like you,' and then she said a lot of gobbledygook that sounded kind of like, 'Ale tseyn zoln *something* nor eyner zol *something* oyf tsonveytuna.'"

"Come again?"

"Apparently that's Yiddish for 'May all of the teeth fall out of your head except for one, so that you can still get a toothache.'"

"*Oh* . . ." Clemi says. "Is that why . . . ?"

Howard nods and puts his hand to his right cheek. "Actually, I think it might be infected.

"Anyway, I'm so sorry, everyone. Really, I was just trying to do the right thing."

Now Joe, the FBI agent, is back.

"We're going to need to bring you in, my friend," he says.

"I'm aware," says Howard.

Sveta has been leaning against the wall, taking this all in. At last she speaks.

"Goodbye, Howard," she says. "Thanks for your help, such as it was."

"Listen, Sveta. If I can say one thing: Had it been up to me to begin with, I would have hands-down given you the prize anyway. And technically you are the winner! I mean, I'm no longer in charge, obviously, but we can change the name on the check."

Sveta smiles weakly. As if the prize money is the point.

"For what it's worth, I wholeheartedly agree," Clemi says. "You are truly my favorite writer in the world. Getting the chance to meet you is why I even took this job in the first place."

"My darling Clementine," Sveta says, wrapping Clemi in her arms.

As Howard walks away, he turns to Vlad.

"Hey, kid, I don't know what's going to happen to me, but while I'm away, will you please take good care of my cat?"

Chapter 33

DESSERT IS SET out—plates of chocolate, platters of mini cheesecakes, trays of truffles, macarons, and berries. The phantasmagoria of sugary confections even includes enormous glass bowls filled with gummy worms. And on each dessert plate is a small filigree of spun brown sugar in the shape of a book. Mr. Samaraweera returns to the podium.

"And now," he says, clearing his throat nervously, apparently no longer so enthusiastic about resuming his board duties after this evening's Vivian Abedeyo debacle. "It is my honor, as board treasurer, to announce the winners of the silent auction."

The silent auction! Clemi had almost forgotten about the silent auction.

He begins to read from the piece of paper in his hand.

"I know we've been thrown a few curveballs tonight, but do not fear, we are going to end on a high note. I have some very good news."

Good news! Clemi is all in favor of some good news.

"Our silent auction has been quite the success." He stops speaking for a moment and looks again at the piece of paper in his hand. "Well, maybe not an across-the-board success, but some of it has been a great success!"

There is a round of perfunctory applause. It seems most of the guests have had enough. They just want to be left in peace to eat dessert and mingle and network and flirt.

He presses on. "Running down the list: For the private lunch at the Tabard Inn with Ellie Grossman, author of *The Snowbirds*, we listed the starting bid at $800 and we have . . . Oh, okay. I see. The starting bid is a little below target, but that's okay! Our board member Percy Garfinkle will be joining Ellie Grossman for lunch at the Tabard Inn for $100. Thank you very much, Percy!

"Moving on, dinner for four at Masseria with editor Renata Chakrabarti. The starting bid was $2,000 and . . . again to our generous donor Percy Garfinkle, who has offered . . . ah, $50. It's your lucky night, Percy! You will be dining with some lovely ladies and doing a lot of delicious eating!"

Clemi adores Mr. Samaraweera, but it's a good thing he's a math teacher and not a professional emcee. His attempt at sounding cheery right now is completely unconvincing. Clearly he, too, is ready to call it a night.

"Is Percy buying everything?" Vlad asks. "I think if he could, he would buy my mom."

Your dad is trying to buy your mom too, Clemi thinks but does not say.

Speaking of Percy, where *is* Percy? He is no longer at the table. Clemi looks around the room and sees that he is now in the back of the room, where Sveta is still having words with Akhil. Percy has just put his hand on Sveta's back, and Sveta bats it not-so-gently away. This can't be good.

"Alas, no current bids for the weekend in the Vail condo or the dinner party with Booker Prize-winning author Francis Ruben," Mr. Samaraweera continues, speaking to pretty much no one.

"Now the private lunch with superagent Lilian Getter. Starting bid: $5,000. And again to our friend Percy for . . . the amount of the final bid is not important. What's important is the enthusiasm we see on display here tonight!"

Clemi keeps her eyes trained on the Sveta, Akhil, and Percy situation. It's a little hard to tell what is happening from this distance, and she might be projecting, but things look tense.

"Wait, ladies and gentlemen. You are not going to believe this, but unless there has been some mistake . . . or maybe a typo . . . we have a bid for lunch with the public intellectual set at . . . Hold on, I'm going to pull out my glasses to be sure I am reading this correctly. I can see quite well without them, in case you are wondering how I managed to read the previous results, but there are a lot of zeros here and I want to count them correctly. Yes, indeed. We have a bid of $200,000. Amazing! Thank you, Ambassador Zamora!"

Clemi turns back to the stage. Is this for real? Someone bid two hundred grand for a TBD public intellectual? How crazy is this world? This could certainly take care of some of WLNP's financial problems, the only issue being that they need to find a respiring public intellectual for the ambassador to dine with. But that's not Clemi's problem. As soon as she calls a car to take Sveta and Vlad to the airport in the morning . . . well, she doesn't know what she plans to do, but it does not involve staying here and cleaning up this mess.

"Ambassador, why don't you come to the stage and shake hands with . . . where is he?"

Mr. Samaraweera looks around the room anxiously.

Clemi looks around too, unsure of who she is supposed to be looking for.

"Mr. Gladwell, are you here? Perhaps he has stepped out to use the restroom."

"Mr. Gladwell? Do you mean Malcolm Gladwell is here?" asks cousin Sharon. "Funny story. I thought I saw him in a diner in Schenectady a couple of years ago, and I went up and asked for his autograph. But it wasn't him! I was so embarrassed!"

Oh, dear God, they haven't auctioned off Colman, have they? Her mind is racing. She supposes she can give Colman a few talking points, teach him some Gladwellisms like "the law of the few"—something she recently learned from Google—and then send him off to lunch and say a little prayer.

Mr. Samaraweera is sputtering, stalling for time, not sure what to say or do, but he makes an impressive recovery.

"Before we move on with our program, ladies and gentlemen, let's all take a moment to remember our friend Javier Jiménez-Jiménez, who so tragically passed away last week."

There is a collective bowing of heads for what nearly passes as a moment of silence but for the continued sound of clanking silverware and someone asking a waiter for some noncaloric coffee sweetener.

And then there is a crashing sound from the back of the room, where it appears that Akhil has just slammed Percy into the wall. Clemi turns just in time to see Percy accidentally knock into Vlad, who is tossed against a ginormous Baccarat opaline vase.

The vase falls to the floor and breaks into many, many shards.

Clemi rushes over to be sure Vlad is okay, which he is. She helps him stand and brushes off the bits of ceramic. Somehow he is still clutching Immanuel in his arms.

She recalls the gossip item about the $52,000 worth of destruction at the Hôtel du Cap. She hopes this will turn out to be at least a little less.

Chapter 34

PERCY IS FLAT out, surrounded by shards of opaline and a spray of mostly beheaded flowers. He looks peaceful, like he's doing savasana at the end of yoga, except for the blood gushing from his forehead where it collided with the wall.

Sveta is huddled over Percy trying to staunch the bleeding with her scarf. "These are not the Dark Ages, Akhil. I don't need you to fight a duel for me. I'm able to manage my affairs on my own, thank you very much."

"I'm sorry, Sveta. I just could not abide the way that man was groping you. His hand was practically on your ass. I'm not a fool. I know something was going on between the two of you. But I forgive you.

"Not only do I forgive you, but I love you I love you I love you. I would do anything to win you back. I'll buy you a diamond as big as the Saint Moritz."

"As big as the Ritz, you idiot."

"That too! And we can jump on a plane and go anywhere you like. Don't forget, I have $500,000 in cash!"

"You're giving that cash to WLNP," Sveta says. "It's the right thing to do. Clementine, my darling, come here!"

Clemi is now kneeling over Percy with her hand on his wrist. She is checking his pulse, not that she knows how to check anyone's pulse, but he has one, and she can confirm that he is alive.

"Are there any doctors here?" she yells.

The man with the bow tie rushes toward the back of the room. "I'm a retired pathologist," he says, taking Percy's pulse. "He's still alive!"

"My husband, Akhil, would like to make a cash donation to WLNP," Sveta announces, trying to distance herself from the Percy situation. "Five hundred thousand dollars."

"What? Um, wow! But again . . . help! This man needs assistance urgently!" Clemi shouts.

She does a quick mental tally. Math may not be her best skill, but this one is easy. They've made more than $700K tonight, factoring in the silent auction plus this "donation," and not counting whatever they may have made, or lost, on the dinner itself.

Clemi wonders about the tax implications. What happens when a person tries to purchase a literary prize, and then instead decides to gift the money? Is there a particular designation on the 1099?

Percy has just made a sputtering sound.

"Is there a currently practicing doctor in the house?" Clemi asks more urgently.

No currently practicing doctor materializes, but she glimpses, from the corner of her eye, a clown. Of course there's a clown.

"Would you like me to call hotel security? Also 911?"

"Please!"

"Here, let's prop his head up a bit," says the Russian gentleman who had earlier crashed the bar. He drops to his knee and lifts Percy's head.

"Give him some water," someone suggests.

The Russian gentleman pours into Percy's mouth something from the glass he is holding. "Vodka is always better than water. There is nothing it can't fix."

The liquid does seem to revive Percy, who then opens his eyes and tries to sit up.

"See! It works! Here, have some more!" The Russian gentleman helps Percy up and then pours the liquid down his throat.

Now Percy is waving his arms, trying to speak.

Clemi's eyes widen when she realizes what is happening.

"Wait! No ice!" she says.

"Well, you're right. Usually, I'm a purist. But on an evening like this, I take my vodka on the rocks. It maintains the flow while lowering the dose. I don't want to be too entertaining, if you know what I mean."

"No, I mean *don't give him ice*! He's allergic to ice!"

There is some collective laughter from the crowd of gawkers.

"I'm not joking! He has a condition! It's a real thing!"

It's too late. It seems Percy's throat is already swelling up. He can't speak. Fortunately, within a few minutes, hotel security appears, followed by an EMT. They lift him onto a stretcher and roll him away.

There is a hand on her shoulder, and she turns to see an unfathomably handsome man with bright white teeth and skin so smooth you could write a song about it.

"Hi there! So sorry I'm late! The traffic, unbelievable! There was a crash on the Dulles Access Road, and don't even get me started on the Beltway."

Clemi stares at the man blankly. She is on overload. Her hard drive is crashing. She is trying her best, but she cannot process this greeting and has no idea who this man is.

"Dr. Jolly, MD. The board president," he says. "You must be Clemi! It looks like everything went quite well!"

Sunday

Chapter 35

HERE'S A TELLING detail about Clemi's mother. She is oblivious to the fact that, at least in May, the time in London is four hours ahead of the time in Washington, DC. Then again, chances are she knows but doesn't care. When Clemi's phone rings at 5:00 a.m., she is not entirely surprised to find Elena on the line.

It is darker than a bat cave in the bedroom, where the windows are covered by blackout shades. Clemi had been in an especially deep sleep, so it takes a moment for her to orient.

"Martha just called me. I heard."

"Hi, Mom. How are you? You heard what?"

"Hi, darling. You with all the formalities. I'm just fine, thank you. A little too busy, with two books at auction right now. Thanks for asking. So, Martha told me you met."

"Yes. She was at the gala on Friday." Clemi is not ready for this conversation, or for any conversation really. She was up late last night texting with Vlad, who shares with Elena an almost enviable lack of awareness about time, which is to say that when it is 10:00 p.m. in Los Angeles, it is 1:00 a.m. in DC.

Then again, perhaps the most telling detail of all is that Clemi does not think to silence her phone.

"What did you hear?"

Clemi rises and pulls open the shade. She sees neighbors outside walking dogs, a few people already streaming into the gym, also a delivery truck idling in front of the coffee shop.

"I heard she offered to represent you."

This is something of a relief, given the many things Martha might have communicated to her mother about the chaos that was Friday night.

"She did," Clemi says. She loves that this news, which she had not thought much about because it seemed to her nothing more than polite dinner table banter, has already made its way to the UK.

"I didn't know you were looking for an agent, darling. You never tell me anything."

"I'm not withholding information, Mom. It was just kind of serendipitous. She was sitting at my table. She's representing my friend."

Clemi looks at her messages while talking to Elena and sees that she has slept through a string of texts from Dr. Jolly, asking her to meet him for breakfast at the Four Seasons at eight o'clock. She should say that's way too early, especially for a Sunday morning, but she is already up. That said, she's not sure why she would meet with him in person—on her to-do list today is to compose a resignation email—but she supposes that quitting in person is the more respectful thing to do. Plus, free breakfast at the Four Seasons! It seems a fitting way to round out Friday's grand celebration of literature, such as it was.

"It's a little hurtful is all, darling. I'm surprised you didn't consult me about agents. I suppose I can understand why you might not want *me* to represent you, if you're looking for representation, but I don't see why you haven't spoken to me about this. I didn't even know you were working on anything. Are you? Plus, wouldn't you have wanted my professional opinion about Martha? I wish we could be closer, darling! I wish we could be *friends*!"

"You're making too much of this, Mom."

"Well, before you commit, you should know that Martha is a snake. I'm sure she only offered to represent you in order to get her venom under my skin."

"Of course, Mom. It's always about you."

"I'm glad you recognize that, darling. And listen, Martha also mentioned that your executive director was taken into custody?"

"Oh boy, she did?"

"You need to get out of there. That place is star-crossed. If it's not one thing, it's another."

"That's my plan."

"Good thing you were able to keep your name out of the press."

"What press?"

"There's an item in *The Sun*. Something about a Mr. Herring. Or maybe it was Herring Something? A gossip item. Apparently, his children from one marriage are at the same school as the children from his mistress, and they only just learned they are related on account of all six of them not being able to cover tuition for the spring term! The article went on to talk about how his assets were frozen in the UK on account of his being a

Putin-adjacent oligarch. A rather *minor* oligarch—but still. It's entertaining. A comedy of manners, or lack thereof, wouldn't you say? Seems he was siphoning money out of your little nonprofit to support his secret family. Which is so cute. He should really meet your father, darling."

"Yes, he was extorting our executive director. Who was also draining his own family's accounts."

"Well, this is doing wonders for your reputation. And mine. Ezra Pound, a man named Herring, Putin, a false Jew, FBI, handcuffs. I've been thinking more about it, darling, and really, you should get out of there and come work for me ASAP. I could really use an agent in New York."

"I live in Washington, Mom."

"Well, you don't actually *live* in Washington, as we both know. You are currently plant-sitting in Washington."

"Yes, but . . ."

"I can help you move. I'm not sure I can help you *physically*—it's a busy summer for me, and I'll be in Tuscany for all of June and July, but I can help find you another living arrangement. I have a client in Chelsea who has a huge loft and might need some help with her kids after school, so you could be an agent in the morning and Mary Poppins in the afternoon. That would work out well for me."

"I don't want to move. And I don't want to be Mary Poppins. I hate Mary Poppins. Well, maybe I don't, but I don't want to be her."

"Okay fine, you can work from DC. I suppose you can take the train back and forth when you need to take meetings. My friend Gail does that."

"Mom, it's too early in the morning for this! I haven't had

The Literati

any coffee! I have to get ready for a breakfast meeting! And no! I don't think I want to be an agent any more than I want to be Mary Poppins! I might want to go to law school! Or not! I don't really know what I want to do, but can we talk about this later?"

"Sure, if you feel that way. I'm leaving for Paris this evening because your father needs a hand. He's gotten himself in a little bit of a situation, but you know you can always reach me."

"A situation?"

"Not a big thing. He just went on a bit too long at a reading. It's not entirely clear what happened, but maybe he threw something at someone. One of the booksellers, I think. It's all a little convoluted, something about threatening to drown him in the Seine. I need to go sort it out."

"He threw something at a bookseller?"

"A book, I think."

"But . . . who was threatening to drown who? The bookseller was threatening to drown him, or he was threatening to drown the bookseller?"

"It's not clear. But it doesn't matter, darling. It's all hearsay. Cut your poor father some slack. Plus, the Seine is clean now, which should make it less problematic, I would think. And also, please, please, please stay away from Martha."

"Whatever you say, Mom."

"Good girl."

Clemi considers squeezing in another hour of sleep, but this time even the blackout shades and exquisite bedding cannot counter the jangly effect on the nervous system produced by her mother.

She picks her phone back up and reviews her texts with Vlad last night.

The first is a picture of Immanuel floating on a pink raft in the middle of a gleaming swimming pool, a row of palm trees in the middle distance. She looks hard at the picture, trying to intuit Immanuel's state of mind. Aren't cats supposed to be afraid of water? But Immanuel doesn't look scared. He looks nonplussed. In fact, his expression is more or less the same as it was when he was planted on Howard's desk. He looks like he's just taking it all in. Synthesizing. Philosophizing. She misses this cat—and this kid!—more than she might have expected.

Immanuel says hi. Come visit!

Vlad has typed this beneath the photo, sent from Sveta's phone. The image looks like it could have been issued by the Los Angeles board of tourism.

Tempting! Clemi replies.

My mom says you can stay here anytime!

This *is* somewhat tempting, really. The surreal blue of the water, the palm trees, the pink raft. Maybe someone could bring her a fruity drink in a coconut shell.

She also says you should take the job. But if you don't, you can come be my nanny again.

What job?

Vlad replies with a shrugging shoulders emoji.

Also good news. My mom got me a new chicken!

The next text is a picture of the pollo diablo. And the text after that is a voice message from the chicken in what is clearly Vlad's voice, converted into a high-pitched cartoonish screech: *"Also good news. My mom got me a new chicken!"*

Note to self: She is not moving to Los Angeles to become Vlad's nanny. Nor is she going to work for her mother. Nor will she seek representation from Martha Thomas should she ever finish a project. As for WLNP, well, no question there. She is as done as done can be.

She has no idea what she actually *will* do with the rest of her life, but she has at least successfully eliminated a few options.

Dr. Eric Jolly, dressed in head-to-toe blue and taupe Vuori running clothes, pops up from the table where he is already seated in the far back of the restaurant.

He takes Clemi's hand and pumps it eagerly. "Thank you for meeting me here. I don't know where you live, but I appreciate you coming from wherever, so early in the morning on such short notice."

"No problem. I was up early anyway."

Clemi looks around the room, soaking in the Washington-ness

of the place. The interior design reminds her a bit of the Hilton. Or maybe it's just the mid-century vibes: the atomic light fixtures, the industrial carpeting. Or the whiff of money, which might actually be the smell of expensive perfume wafting over from the next table where a young couple is possibly on their honeymoon. At the table next to that is a well-appointed older woman being attended to by two waiters—one pouring coffee, the other refilling her juice glass—as she turns the pages of her print copy of *The New York Times*. Clemi looks more closely; she thinks she is supposed to know her, like maybe she is a news anchor, or a senator, or the head of some important federal agency.

Dr. Jolly motions toward the seat across from him, indicating she should sit, which she does. The man is so conventionally, plastically, Syntaxically™ handsome that he looks like the handiwork of the Mattel corporation, or perhaps of AI.

"I wasn't sure what you wanted to eat, but I went ahead and ordered a couple of things since I must run to catch a flight. I hope you don't mind. Of course you can supplement with whatever you want."

"Oh sure," Clemi says. "That's fine." This seems to her both presumptuous and a little weird—she has studied the menu online and was fantasizing on her way over about what to have for breakfast—but she's not sure what choice she has.

"Not to worry. I ordered a wide range of things. But really, it's mostly for you. I'm on a liquid diet at the moment."

Three waiters appear and begin to set out so many dishes of food—eggs, bacon, chicken and waffles, and an order of shakshuka—that Clemi is confused. This is all for *her*? One of the waiters catches her eye, as if to share his amusement either at the very existence of Dr. Eric Jolly or at this orgy of food.

"Thank you again for your hard work, Clemi," says Dr. Jolly. "Here, have some juice. It's full of antioxidants. Beets, ginger, not sure what else. It will make you feel ten years younger."

Clemi smiles politely and takes a sip of the juice, although she is not sure that she wants to feel ten years younger. Sixteen was not her best age. Pimples. Awkward hair. Her braces had not yet come off.

"You did a spectacular job Friday night, despite a few hiccups," he continues.

Hiccups. Clemi smiles politely and nods, marveling at his word choice. Explosions. Cataclysms. Fireworks, but not in a good way. Those seem the more appropriate descriptors. She wonders if Dr. Jolly is one of those preternaturally calm beings who thinks having the executive director taken into custody by the FBI, a board member with a life-threatening allergic reaction removed on a stretcher, and the board treasurer present the award to the wrong writer—or to the right writer, as the case may be—count as *hiccups*. Maybe he is taking horse tranquilizers. Or perhaps his brain has been so Syntaxitized™ that, like his face, it is no longer capable of expressing emotion.

She takes a sip of the red juice, which is surprisingly tasty, and suddenly she hiccups. Okay, that's weird. It's surely just the power of suggestion.

"In addition to wanting to thank you," he continues, "I want to discuss your future."

Clemi looks at him and hiccups again. Loudly, this time. She doesn't get the hiccups often. In fact, she can't think of the last time this happened to her, but here she is and there they are, these annoying little spasms of air that seem to be erupting from her diaphragm.

"My future?" is all Clemi can manage to say before hiccupping again.

Dr. Jolly looks at her with concern while pausing to sip from one of the three beverages that have been set in front of him. This makes sense, his liquid diet, because she suspects he might be unable to chew. His mouth does not appear to move as he speaks. It looks like his jaw has been either recently broken or, more likely, frozen.

"Ah, my future," she says again, stuffing a piece of waffle into her mouth. She chews slowly, trying to think how to continue the sentence without hiccupping. Or choking. Or sounding too abrupt.

I'll take my first and my final paycheck in cash, right now, is the gist of what she would like to say.

"More specifically, I mean your future at WLNP."

"My future at WLNP," she echoes, and there it is. Another hiccup. "Sorry. Excuse me?"

"Here, drink something," he suggests, handing her water glass to her. Clemi takes a sip.

"No, not like that. Drink the whole thing quickly."

She picks up the glass again and drains what is there. Then she hiccups again.

Dr. Jolly flags the waiter, who rushes over. He is cute, this waiter who fills her glass. He has curly dark hair and big brown eyes that are somehow familiar. She thanks him and then hiccups again so loudly that she sounds a bit like a bleating goat. The woman at the next table turns and stares.

"Swallow a teaspoon of sugar," the waiter suggests as he refills her water glass.

Clemi nods, opens a sugar packet, and empties it into a teaspoon, which she then dutifully consumes, wincing at the taste.

The waiter nods and then walks away, leaving her once again alone with Dr. Jolly.

"Okay, so where were we?" he asks.

"My future..."

"Ah yes. Your future."

Clemi's future, insofar as she has plotted anything out, involves an afternoon of LSAT prep, followed by a yoga class and take-in Thai food. Rounding out this meant-to-be restorative, future-forward day, she has plans this evening to look at a too-good-to-be-true apartment-share that will become available mid-August, which is nearly perfect timing. One of her former bookstore colleagues had messaged her about it last night. The rent is affordable, and she already knows, and likes, the other two occupants. It sounds ideal, even if what she would prefer is for Fiona to decide to live permanently at writing residencies, leaving Clemi reclining in a Ludwig Mies van der Rohe MR Adjustable Chaise Longue, drinking free coffee, and attempting to keep the plants alive for another year or two or three.

But one thing she is sure of: Her work at WLNP is done. She feels another hiccup coming on and braces herself, but this one fails to materialize.

Dr. Jolly is about to say something when his phone beeps. He pauses to look at the screen. "Oh geez, look at the time. Sorry, I don't mean to be rude, but it's my car service. I have a hard 'out' here at eight thirty, which I should have told you at the outset. I'm going straight to the airport for a dermatology conference in Antwerp."

"Well, I don't want to keep you," says Clemi, relieved. Email now seems the preferred method of resigning from the job.

"It's okay. I still have a few minutes, and I can be brief: Clemi, we want you to step in as executive director."

She doesn't know whether to begin laughing, crying, or hiccupping again, so instead she repeats the question. "You want me to step in as executive director? Also, I don't mean to be impolite, but who is *we*?"

"Fair question. I guess there's no real *we* at the moment. But that's sort of the point. What I mean is that *I* want you to stay on. And Sveta wants you to stay on."

"*Sveta?* Why does Sveta care what I do?"

"Sveta is now our biggest donor. She made a deal with Akhil, her husband, to give the money to WLNP, with one condition."

"What money?"

"The money he used to buy the prize—or rather, to *try* to buy the prize, since of course one cannot *buy* a WLNP prize. That would imply we have no integrity!"

"What is the condition?"

"I suppose I am failing to make myself clear. The condition is that you are made executive director."

Having just taken a poorly timed bite of waffle, Clemi does her best to stifle a laugh, thereby causing a piece of waffle to lodge in her throat, temporarily blocking her windpipe and triggering a massive, liberating cough. Dr. Jolly hands her the glass of water again, and the cute waiter looks worriedly in her direction. She drains another glass of water and manages to pull herself together.

"I mean, that's flattering, but—"

"Think about it, Clemi. Between this new infusion of money and the results of the silent auction, WLNP is in the best financial shape it's been since Arthur founded the place. Possibly even better because no one kept great records back then. We can pay you properly." He mentions a number, and Clemi begins to laugh/choke/cough again.

"This is not what I expected. But me? I mean, I'm . . ." She stops herself mid-sentence. Maybe it's time to stop running herself down. Her mother does a good enough job of that for her. Maybe it's time to Stand Up Straight! Instead of saying she's too young, or too inexperienced, she says, instead, "I'm thinking of going to law school."

"That's not disqualifying, Clemi. You have your whole life ahead of you. Do the job for a year, at least. You can still go to law school. I didn't write my book until I was twenty-seven."

He wrote his book when he was *twenty-seven*? This is very young to have written a book. This is the opposite of comforting. It is also a bit of a shock, given that this must mean he has been out there promoting this same book, which is still on the bestseller list, for at least twenty years.

"But there are so many problems."

"No, not at all. I update it frequently. Also, the properties of Syntax ™ have not changed in the last two decades. It was a perfect product from the get-go. But rest assured that the book has the most up-to-date science in all other respects."

"No, I'm sure the book is . . . the best. I'm talking about the problems with WLNP."

"Oh sure. But everything is fine now."

"Everything? The problems were kind of extensive."

"I've taken care of Penelope, if that's your concern."

"That was one of the concerns. But what about Vivian? That was all pretty shocking and awful."

"Nothing to worry about. I called Vivian to clear up any possible misunderstandings in case she heard about Sam's faux pas. I told her it was an administrative error and explained that our programs director had recently left and that we had new staff."

"You blamed it on *me?*"

"Not you explicitly. No names came up. It was just an inconsequential little fib. She'll never know who we were referring to. Besides, she didn't seem too upset. She said she'd never heard of our prize anyway."

"And what about . . . well, there are so many layers of dysfunction. I mean we . . . you . . . WLNP . . . The nonprofit doesn't even have a name."

"You're not wrong. But that's why we need you. You can get us pointed in the right direction. No question, we need to reboot."

His phone is dinging again.

"Sorry, my driver is being harassed out there for blocking traffic. I had better run. But I hope you'll seriously consider the offer. You can settle in pronto. Move over to Howard's desk while you are thinking, if you want."

Clemi wonders if Dr. Eric Jolly has ever actually seen the WLNP office. Who could possibly want Howard's desk?

"Have you even seen that desk? It's so old the wood is starting to splinter. And my chair is literally falling apart. It looks like it was pulled out of a dumpster."

"Go to IKEA and buy a new desk then. And buy new chairs. Get whatever you need. Pens, notepads, desk lamps, computers, a fish tank."

A fish tank? Clemi does not want to admit, even to herself, how tempting this is beginning to sound—the shopping part anyway, if not the job.

"Also, I just remembered another thing," she says. "What about the silent auction?"

"That's what I'm saying, Clemi. It brought in so much money we are basically set."

"Yes, but under false pretenses. Ambassador Zamora seems to think she is having lunch with Malcolm Gladwell."

"Oh, she is! I called Malcolm yesterday. He's good with lunch."

"Seriously?"

"He thought it was hilarious. He wants to meet your friend, the look-alike. Anyway, I've known Malcolm for years. He went to school with my former brother-in-law."

Dr. Jolly's phone dings again.

"Okay, look, I'd really better go. Please think on it."

Clemi rolls her head noncommittally.

"Sleep on it if you must. I'll text you when I get to Antwerp, and you can let me know if you have any questions. And stay here and enjoy the rest of your breakfast."

Clemi stands and shakes his hand, then returns to her chair. She plans to take his advice. Now that he is gone, she can concentrate more fully on this obscenity of food. She eats more waffle, then has some eggs, a croissant, and most of the shakshuka. She gulps down the juice, then eats some chicken, a piece of which drops into her lap. As she plucks it from the napkin, she notices a small rectangular plaque affixed to the edge of the table.

"In loving memory of loyal guest and longtime friend Mike Berman. This is 'his table.'"

Hmm . . . She wonders who this Mike Berman is. She has been here so long, it seems, that it now feels like it ought to be *her* table.

The cute and somehow familiar waiter comes by and asks if she would like more coffee. She says no. She has consumed so much liquid that her bladder is about to burst. She can't eat or drink another thing, but she doesn't want to leave. She is enjoying this nice piece of real estate here in this sunny power-breakfast spot. She could sit here and people-watch all day.

"Who was Mike Berman?" she asks.

"I've only been working here a couple of months, so I never knew him, but he was a regular, obviously. This was his table, like the sign says. I think he was a lobbyist and a political strategist. He'd been an aide to Walter Mondale. A real Washington guy, big man on campus. Ate a lot, too, judging by the photos I saw when I googled him on a slow day."

Clemi imagines what that would be like, to be so rooted to a place, not just a city but to a table in a restaurant, that you become memorialized. She finds this surprisingly endearing. Also, the more this waiter talks, the more familiar he seems. But Clemi is tired of this game after the whole not-Malcolm situation. There are only so many variations on the human form—ears, noses, sizes, shapes—that invariably, the older she gets and the more people she meets, it probably makes sense that the distinguishing features will begin to merge.

He is still standing there holding the coffeepot, and it occurs to her that perhaps she has overstayed her welcome here at the Four Seasons, at Mike Berman's table.

"I'll get out of your way now. But thanks! This was great."

"No worries. I'll just leave this with you," he says, setting down a little tray with the bill.

Clemi looks at the bill, looks at the cute waiter, then back at the bill. "He . . . left this?" she asks. "For *me*?"

"I mean, I guess he did. He didn't pay it, so I assume that means I'm supposed to give it to you."

Clemi picks up the bill, sees the number $221.93, and makes an involuntary gasping noise that is hopefully not the precursor to another bout of hiccups.

The waiter, who is still standing nearby, senses her concern. "Was your friend a guest at the hotel?"

"I don't know. He's not really my friend. He's technically my boss. My boss's boss anyway. My former boss's boss—*former*. I guess he could have been staying here? But I just assumed he lives in DC. I have no idea, really . . ."

"And he stuck you with the bill?"

"Well, I don't know if he meant to. He is likely one of those people who has so much money he fails to think about it. He ordered more for breakfast than I spend on food in a week. But whatever. I'll pay it, and I'm sure he'll Venmo me when I ask him."

She rummages through her bag and pulls out her wallet, then produces a card.

"Would it be okay to put half on this card, and the other half on my Apple Pay? I'm close to the limit on each, but I'll get paid—I hope!—next week, so this should work."

"Hmm. I'm not supposed to do this, but I do have certain superpowers."

"What do you mean?"

"I can make things disappear."

"Oh, I'm not asking you to do that. I'll deal with it."

"Well, we'll just disappear it anyway."

"What, are you a magician?"

"Ha ha, no. But you may recall that I'm magician-adjacent. Watch this." He picks up the bill and tears it in half, then stuffs the pieces in the pocket of his apron. "Poof! It's gone!"

"It is, indeed," she agrees, confused. This is definitely more than another doppelgänger situation; clearly she is supposed to know him somehow. "So . . . remind me, when you are not a waiter, you do something magician-adjacent? What does that even mean? Please don't tell me you're a clown."

"I am a clown."

"Ha ha, very funny."

"Not trying to be funny. I'm a clown. But I do a lot of other things too."

Clemi looks up at the cute waiter, mortified. "Oh my God! Oh no . . . no, no, no way. I knew you were familiar. Your voice. Your eyes. You're Zeke, the studying-for-the-LSAT clown!"

"The very same."

"Right! I remember, you said you work in a restaurant."

"Yup. I work part-time in a law firm, part-time waiting tables, part-time clowning, although that's mostly volunteer. I was thinking about you all weekend . . ."

He was thinking about her all weekend?

"What happened to that guy? Did the EMTs come? Is he okay?"

Clemi now remembers that as she was standing over Percy on Friday night, a clown had appeared and asked if she needed help.

"That was *you*?"

"That was me."

"I didn't realize . . . I'm so sorry I didn't recognize you. I mean on Friday. Also now."

"So is he okay?"

"He is. It was touch-and-go, apparently. His esophagus swelled from the cold urticaria—he is allergic to ice—but they were able to get it under control, thank goodness. And how was your clown conference?"

"It went quite well, thank you very much, although there was some confusion in the beginning. Our board president got lost, so we waited, like, half an hour for him show up. But our VP stepped in, and it worked out in the end."

"Nice," Clemi says, and leaves it at that. She does not wish to admit her culpability in The Case of the AWOL Board President.

"This is a kind of crazy coincidence" is all she can think to say.

"In the realm of crazy coincidence—both of us taking the LSAT, I mean—I picked up the study guide you were telling me about. The one with the clowns."

"Ugh. The clowns. I don't know why that first exercise got under my skin. I could probably figure it out if I tried. It just seems so irrelevant . . ."

"You will definitely figure it out. It looks more difficult than it is."

"Maybe."

"You just have to stick to the rules that apply to the situation and start eliminating possible other scenarios. Just don't get distracted. Stick to the need-to-know."

"I get it, but my problem is that I'm more interested in the nice-to-knows. The possible extenuating circumstances."

"Maybe because you're more of a storyteller than a litigator."

"Well, they might be the same thing, right?"

"That's true."

A family has just settled in to the next table, and already they are trying to get Zeke the waiter/clown/future-esquire's attention.

"I'd better get going. But . . . would you maybe want to study together sometime?"

"Sure. Maybe."

"This afternoon, even? Unless that's too . . . whatever."

"No, that's good. I was actually planning to study today, so that works."

"I get off here at two, and then I have a gig over at George Washington University at four. But maybe around five? Want to meet me outside the hospital? There are a bunch of coffee shops nearby."

"The hospital? Are you okay?"

"Oh, totally. We entertain patients. Mostly kids."

"Oh! Nice! Does that mean you'll be in costume?"

"I usually bring a change of clothes."

"Oh, that's disappointing. I was hoping you'd have those big clown hands."

"I mean . . . sure, I could leave those on."

"And maybe you'll wear your clown nose?"

"I suppose I could."

"What about the shoes?"

"When we spoke the other day, I didn't mean to go overboard on the whole people-hating-on-clowns situation. You don't have to overcompensate."

"What if I'm not? What if I'm developing a thing for clowns?"

"Like now you're a clown obsessive? That sounds possibly worse than if you were hating on us."

"Well, now that I think about it, I guess I began as a clown agnostic, but I'm becoming more and more intrigued."

THE END

Acknowledgments

I AM once again incredibly grateful to the DC Commission on the Arts and Humanities for their support of my work—and of this very DC-centric book in particular.

A note on geography and on the layout of the Hilton Hotel: liberties were taken, balconies were added, the imagination may have, in some cases, overtaken brutalist reality. Ditto for some of the Ezra Pound and Robert Lowell material.

Thank you again to everyone on the amazing Harper Muse team, especially my lovely, whip-smart editor Kimberly Carlton. And Jocelyn Bailey, thank you once again for helping to untangle more than a few narrative glitches. Thank you to everyone on the HM team, including Amanda Bostic, Savannah Breedlove, Nekasha Pratt, Margaret Kercher, Colleen Lacey, Kerri Potts, Taylor Ward, and many, many others. Thank you to Sandra Chiu for yet another excellent cover. Thanks also to Suzanne Williams and everyone at Shreve Williams. And enormous thanks to Josh Getzler for always having my back, and also for the dog photos.

Ally Coll, Molly McCloskey, and Paul Goldberg were all invaluable early readers. And Ally, Bruce, Emma, Dave,

Acknowledgments

Charlie, Max, Katie, Ricky, Sarah, and Daniel—all the heart emojis.

Most of all, thank you to my husband, Paul Goldberg, the best editor a person could ask for, my partner in all things sweet and funny.

Discussion Questions

1. Have you ever been thrown headfirst into an absurd or complicated work situation, the likes of which made you question your professional choices or your sanity?

2. What are the risks involved with meeting your heroes? In Clemi's case, how does her romanticized idea of Sveta Attias compare to the reality of Sveta Attias?

3. Between working at a bookstore and being raised by a literary agent, Clemi has amassed a lifetime of experience among literary circles. Why do you think she keeps choosing to work among the literati? What unique perspective does she have on their quirks and tendencies, and does she consider herself an insider or an outsider to their world?

4. What is the purpose of WLNP in theory and in practice? By the end of the novel, has the organization justified its existence?

5. A *comedy of manners* is a work of fiction that depicts the values, behaviors, customs, and complicated social world

Discussion Questions

of a specific community of people. With this definition in mind, how might you talk about *The Literati* as a contemporary comedy of manners?

6. Of all the adults, kids, and creatures Clemi meets over the course of this story, who surprised you the most? Which characters are the most memorable?

7. Should you, like Clemi, find yourself in need of a public intellectual, how might you go about finding one? Name a few dream candidates who could fill the role.

8. What qualities does Clemi possess that help her survive her first week at WLNP? What does she learn about herself as she is put through the proverbial wringer?

9. Discuss the presence of clowns in this novel. Why do they seem to be following Clemi? What might they represent?

10. As the novel ends, what choices do you envision Clemi making for herself? What future do you imagine for her?

11. Who is the worst person in this book, and why is it River?

About the Author

Photo by Marvin Joseph

SUSAN COLL is the author of eight novels, including *Bookish People* and *Real Life and Other Fictions*, a *USA TODAY* bestseller. Her third novel, *Acceptance*, was made into a television movie starring the hilarious Joan Cusack. Susan's work has appeared in publications including the *New York Times Book Review*, the *Washington Post*, *Washingtonian* magazine, *Moment Magazine*, NPR.org, and Atlantic.com. She is the events advisor at Politics and Prose Bookstore in Washington, DC, and was the president of the PEN/Faulkner Foundation for five years.

Visit Susan online at susancoll.com
Instagram: @susan_keselenko_coll